Note from Author

Readers,

 Drawn to the Sea was my first attempt at writing a novel and along the way I've learned it takes more than a great story to make a good novel. Some of those lessons came easier than others.

 I owe so much to my family, friends, loyal readers and critics who've taken the time and with great care and gentle persuasion offered constructive suggestions to improve.

 Drawn to the Sea (First Revision) has incorporated these recommendations. Those of you who've read the original version, it's the same story – just reformatted.

 To all, thank you for your patience and support.

Rex Inverness
June 2018

Drawn to the Sea

Book One
The van der Waterlaan Dynasty

First Revision
Republished June 30 2018

Rex Inverness

Praise for Rex Inverness and
Drawn to the Sea
(First Revision)

"Like Melville and Conrad, Inverness can graphically capture the passion and danger of the sea and bring the heart pounding experience to his readers in the safety of their living rooms."

J.P.

Novato, Ca

***

"Inverness is a remarkable writer and story teller. His knowledge and firsthand experience at sea pours out in every word."

S.P.

Glen Cove, NY

***

"The first time in years the reader can experience life at sea without the fear of getting sick and drowning."

M.S.

Middletown, RI

***

"Drawn to the Sea crosses generations, cultures and oceans as the story unfolds."

D.K.

Vero, FL

***

"The first of three entwined stories of the van der Waterlaan family and the shipping dynasty they control. *Drawn to the Sea* is rich with intrigue, romance and twists. Readers will find they can't put the book down."

T.V.

Amsterdam, Netherlands

***

"*Drawn to the Sea, Torn Between Destiny and Desire* and *The Gentleman Pirate* … read all three. You'll be glad you did."

J.F.
Newport Beach, Ca
***

Other Books by Rex Inverness:

Torn Between Destiny and Desire
The Gentleman Pirate
Two Warriors Collide
Bonnie Mae
The Cursed Seven
Leviathan/Death of a Liberian Seaman

MV2

Maritime Fiction Novels
Bristol, Rhode Island
02809
www.rex-inverness.com

DRAWN TO THE SEA
(First Revision)

The cover is a copy of an original painting by the maritime artist Bradley Van Vleck

(First Revision)
Copyright 2017 Rex Inverness
MV2 Maritime Fiction Novels
All rights reserved.
www.rex-inverness.com
ISBN -13: 978-0692833599
ISBN-10: 0692833595
CreateSpace Independent Publishing Platform
North Charleston, South Carolina

Drawn to the Sea

One day Ian is an average New England kid destined to live an average life while visiting the Port of Rotterdam, he and his girlfriend, Hanna, make a bizarre discovery. From that instant forward his life begins to move at warp speed.

Fate continues to influence his future when the next day, in front of the Lutz Theater, he is approached by an elegant woman flanked with bodyguards and handlers. She swears he looks exactly like her dead son and nearly faints. Ian almost does too, when he learns she's his grandmother and he is the only heir to a massive fortune.

It isn't long before he realizes this could be better than winning the lottery but … there must be a catch.

Rex Inverness

Dedication

To my wife … with all my love. Her incredible patience and understanding helped me to write this story and pursue my dreams.

Acknowledgements

Thanks to Bradley Van Vleck for the cover picture and to John and Judy Sewell for reading the original version manuscripts when no one else would.

DRAWN TO THE SEA
(First Revision)

Chapter One
One Life Ends ... Another Begins

Months after a forgotten ship and its crew had
perished in a Pacific storm, Susan Blokker ran a hand over
her swollen belly, still awed by it. The doctor smiled as he
reviewed the sonogram. He looked up from the screen.
"My dear you're going to have a son."

Her mind flashed to ten years before -- the year
she moved to Tampa on a dare right out of high school.
She and her boyfriend, Matt, on a wild impulse, left New
England and drove to Florida. Shortly after the young
couple arrived in Tampa, she became ill and her body
began to protest in ways she'd never experienced. After a
quick examination, the doctor at the clinic announced she
was pregnant and Matt ran away, never to be heard from
again.

She remembered how it felt to be eighteen, alone,
pregnant, broke, and too ashamed to ask her parents for
help. With few options, she became easy prey for the local
pimps and soon became part of the skin trade in the port
district, aptly known as Hooker's Point.

After her initial pangs of guilt and self-disgust had
subsided, she found it was simple and dependable
employment. Mariners and stevedores were always willing

to pay for easy and uncomplicated affection. Most of her clients over the years were so 'driven' their passion was measured in minutes not hours and the going price was the same regardless of the time the girls invested. Now ten years later, she found herself pregnant and alone again.

It was while she worked in a local bar called Charlie's that she met Ian. He started coming to Tampa in nineteen-seventy-five. Shortly after they met, she'd become his steady. Fortunately for them, he was there three or four times a month. Though they kept their arrangement uncomplicated, there had always been a connection they'd felt, but both seemed reluctant to acknowledge. It remained intimacy for money, but without trying very hard it became so much more. It was companionship, emotional security, and yes … love!

She'd made a point of knowing when the *Amore Islander* would be in town and would shed a tear when Ian set out to sea two days later. Susan knew he liked coming to Tampa and it was because of her.

Alas, their love was never openly expressed and acknowledged. But in Ian's death, love was cemented and a child conceived of that love.

Chapter Two
Susan's Decision to Start Over

With the doctor's news still ringing in her ears, she strode out of the office feeling like she was on an emotional roller coaster. She didn't need another child or a disruption in her earning potential. "Hell," she said under her breath. She was already getting old for this line of work and had few other options. Yet on the other hand, she did the math and knew the father was van der Waterlaan. After all, he was the only one she allowed in her bed without a condom. She could never understand why, but she loved him and wanted to carry his child someday.

She knew she wouldn't be able to continue to work with a baby on the way and the cold reality also stared her in the face. She couldn't compete with the younger girls and their fresh faces and tight bodies. *Let's face it, after I realized I was in love with Ian, I really didn't want to be with other men any longer.*

Her daughter, Sarah, was almost ten and beginning to notice her mother was not like other mothers. She was beginning to ask hard questions about the endless cycle of men who would come to the apartment, disappear into mom's bedroom, and then leave an hour later without a word.

11

"Mom, who was he?"

"Never mind, he's a friend of mine."

"Why can't I meet your friends? You meet all of mine?"

"Honey, they're not that kind of friends."

"What kind are they?"

"Never mind …"

The frequent conversations between Susan and Sarah had gotten more and more embarrassing and uncomfortable and Susan knew she couldn't avoid the truth for much longer.

She had only one close friend in Tampa and that was Candy. Candy was about ten years older and got caught up in Tampa's skin business around a decade before Susan. Candy, however, came to Tampa with dreams of making a fortune in peddling flesh. A dream she'd since realized.

Candy had grown up on a small ranch outside of Odessa, Texas. Her mother had remarried a struggling rancher who kept a small herd of cattle and a handful of horses on a small patch of land. The meager ranch had been in his family for three generations.

Candy grew up to be a stunning young lady. She was street smart and learned how to make good money without working too hard for it. She lived fast and hard and easily found men who would fund her extravagant lifestyle. As soon as she finished high school, she left for Tampa and never looked back.

She started working for a pimp but quickly moved on to become a madam in her own right. She selectively brought a better quality of girl like Susan into her employment and took care of her girls. Candy was a good employer and was genuinely concerned about her girls and their welfare. In addition, she kept a stable full of strong and ruthless body guards to watch out for her investment. If there was an incident, the customer was quickly and severely dealt with. For Susan and the others, it was relatively safe and secure work.

With a shaky finger, Susan dialed Candy's number and asked her to meet for coffee. As usual, Candy was there for her. They hugged and sat down.

Susan got right to the point, "Candy, I'm not getting any younger and I know the younger talent is where the money is." Candy just listened. Susan continued, "I never thought it would happen but I fell in love with one of my clients. He was a mate on one of the regular ships which called here at Hooker's Point."

Candy asked, "Which one?"

Susan knew Candy knew exactly which one. She was too smart not to. She stirred her untouched coffee and said, "The *Amore Islander,* his name is Ian van der Waterlaan. I mean, was," and her voice fell off. "I had a dream he drowned and I haven't heard from him in two months. The ship was reported missing in the Pacific a month ago."

"I'm sorry to hear that. Don't give up hope just yet," Candy offered.

When Susan saw the sympathy on Candy's face, her eyes filled with tears. She didn't want pity. Reaching for a tissue, she blew her nose and said, "There's more …"

"Okay"

"I'm pregnant with his baby," Susan blurted, covering her eyes with both hands.

"Oh, we can take care of that anyway you'd like, Susan. Let me know and I can make arrangements at the clinic. Or, Candy arched an eyebrow, "are you thinking about keeping the baby?"

"Yes."

"Have you considered this carefully? You already have a ten year old daughter. Can you handle a second child? Regardless, Susan, I'll support your decision."

"Candy, I think I need to move back to New England and raise my children and provide them a normal life. Candy, you have been my best and dearest friend these last ten years," Susan said with tears running down her cheeks. "I will miss you so very much."

They hugged and cried, and then between sobs tried to enjoy their coffees.

Candy reached into her purse and slipped Susan an envelope with ten thousand dollars and said, "This was last night's earnings. Take it as your severance package. Let me know if you need more. I'm always here for you."

"Thank you," Susan said.

"Keep in touch. I'll visit you in New England." Candy forced a smile and then began to tear up. They stood up and hugged and kissed. Candy turned and walked out the door. She made her way to her Mercedes convertible.

Susan watched her go. Even though her vision was blurry from crying, she could read Candy's lips as she said, "Damn it."

Susan sat back down for a few minutes and thought, *would my parents even want me to come back to Bristol, Rhode Island? Will I be welcome in her hometown?*

DRAWN TO THE SEA
(First Revision)

She thought, *I must try and start anew and live a respectable life for my children.*

Chapter Three
The Man in a Black Suit

The day Susan had conceived, the father, Ian, left the office while Captain Strauss of the *Amore Islander* watched him leave then returned to his paperwork. Moments later, the captain's mind wandered far away. He leaned back in his chair, removed his reading glasses, closed his eyes, and drifted into memories of the tortured youth which led him to the miserable life that consumed him like cancer.

***

The owner's representative stood on the dirty pier next to the large ship and he looked out of place. The temperature was nearly ninety degrees and there he was in a black suit, starched white shirt and dark glasses. He looked back at his black limo then he straightened his bright red tie and came up the brow, taking the steps two at a time. He knew the sooner he finished, the sooner he'd get off the miserable ship. As he boarded, the mate on watch met him, and with barely a word exchanged, he escorted him to the captain's office.

The captain expected the visitor and Strauss was convinced he would be fired for incompetence. *So this is how it will end,* the drunkard thought as he heard the stride of a confident man echo through the passageway. The sound got louder as the stranger approached.

***

Out on deck, cargo operations were underway and the Aragonite, white sand from the Bahamas, poured into the discharge hopper at two-thousand tons an hour. In another six hours the ship would be empty. Neil, the chief mate, had finished up his watch and was satisfied with the progress. He smiled and jotted a couple of comments into his pocket sized notebook, then leaned against the rail in his stained overalls and closed his eyes for a moment, facing into the hot Tampa sun.

***

Strauss wiped his sweaty palms on his grungy pant legs. When the visitor appeared in the doorway, Strauss tried not to grimace at the expensive briefcase and Italian shoes which must have cost a fortune. The man's silk tie was just an added insult. Strauss knew if the ship owner had paid for this metro-sexual to fly halfway around the world for a private meeting, he was in deep trouble.

Still wearing his Armani sunglasses, the visitor struck an imposing figure. He was tall, handsome yet rugged, and extremely fit. Strauss blanched and glanced down at his bulging stomach and rubbed the stubble on his chin.

The man removed his dark glasses and looked into the captain's averted eyes.

"I'd like a drink," he said with an efficiency that cut like a knife. Strauss scurried around the desk to a cabinet and produced a bottle of Scotch in his shaking hands.

"Will this do?" he asked, wishing it was a better brand and his desk wasn't sticky.

The man nodded. "Two fingers straight up."

Strauss poured two glasses and asked, "Why did you come out here in person?" He still couldn't look into the man's eyes. "You could have fired me over the phone."

The man leaned back in his chair and laughed. Then leaned in close to the captain, stared through his skull and said, "Is that what you think I am here to do? You think I'm here to fire you? If I was going to do that, wouldn't there be another captain here with me?" He chuckled. "Don't worry, old man, sit down and relax. I came to this filthy ship with instructions. That's all."

He held his glass up and scowled. Taking a handkerchief from his lapel, he wiped the rim of the glass. He still didn't look happy when he held the glass up again and took a drink and said, "The owner has a proposition for you and no one, and I mean no one, can know of it. If you play your cards right, you'll be well-compensated and have the ship of your choice in the Y.G. Yang fleet." The tendons in his jaw line tighten. "Do we understand each other?"

Strauss thought for a moment. He knew he wasn't one of the better captains. What he lacked in competence, he tried to make up for with blind loyalty. But he knew from the look of the man that whatever it was … it was illegal, likely immoral, and most certainly criminal. He also knew if he declined, he'd be unemployed and destitute. With his reputation on the waterfront, there was no future for him except suicide and he wasn't quite ready for that yet.

Strauss looked up and nodded. "I understand and I am ready to listen. Let me close the office door and freshen up our drinks." Strauss shook himself and tried to muster confidence as he stood up.

After locking the door, he refreshed their drinks and this time he poured heavily. The two men moved over to the couch, sipped their drinks, and after what seemed like an eternity, the owner's representative began to lay out the plan.

While the two discussed opportunities and the future in hushed and conspiratorial tones, the engineers were doing what they could to maintain the machinery with the few spares parts and limited tools on hand. The mates and deck gang were discharging the ship and doing what they could with limited stores, and the stewards were staring into a boiling cauldron conjuring up spells to make their meager food taste like something edible.

Several hours later the two men came out of the office. The visitor wore his sunglasses as they walked together to the brow. Strauss thanked him for the visit. The visitor turned, shook the old man's hand and told him he'd see him again soon.

Strauss watched as the nameless man in an expensive dark suit, sunglasses, and a designer briefcase left his ship, climbed into the limo and seconds later headed to his awaiting plane. Strauss replayed their conversation and realized, *he didn't even open his briefcase.*

The limo rolled up to a black corporate jet with no identification markings, the pilot threw some switches and the jet roared to life. As the plane climbed into the bright blue sky an encrypted call was made to Hong Kong.

"Yes …"

"He agreed … the plan is a go."

"Good"… and the phone call ended.

"Bring me a martini, straight-up with a twist," said the only passenger on the luxury jet. He removed his sunglasses and watched the flight attendant with unconcealed lust. The pretty Asian woman smiled, and a moment later she delivered him the drink. At thirty-thousand feet he winked at the young lady who was there for one reason … to tend to him on the long flight back to the Far East. He smiled, sipped his drink, and loosened his tie.

She steeled herself and thought, *a few more rich men with nasty fetishes like this one and I'll be able to move my family out of the Kowloon projects into a small home outside of the city.*

She slid onto the couch next to him and waited for his groping hands and probing tongue to assault her.

Chapter Four
Bristol

Susan decided to leave Tampa and raise her kids in New England. Her childhood friend was the first one she called. They had been best friends even after Susan headed to Florida after graduation. Her fingers shook with excitement as she punched in Maria's number.

There was a fluttering in her stomach when Maria answered on the second ring. "Maria, it's me. Sorry it's been a while. There's been a lot going on."

"Susan? Geez, it's so good to hear your voice. I've been worried."

"I know and I apologize. You may not be only hearing my voice soon, but seeing my face too. I've decided I'm coming home."

"What?" Maria shrieked. "You're kidding me. That's the best news I've heard in a long time. When? What are your plans?"

"Soon," Susan said, switching the phone to her other ear. "That's about the only concrete detail I've worked out so far, but it's a start."

"You're staying with me." Maria said, "And I don't want any argument about it. I have a big house and it's just me. There's plenty of room for you and Sarah. Oh,

I can't wait for the company. I want you to stay as long as you want."

Susan smiled, picturing Maria with her hand on her hip. Maria had always come up with all the exciting things for the two of them to do, and she wouldn't let Susan back out of any of them. They even lost their virginity on the same night during a double date after a high school dance. Maria taught Susan how to get away with things like weed, vodka, and boys even while under the diligent supervision of their parents. "You're the best, Maria," Susan murmured, feeling a bit nostalgic. "It's not going to be just Sarah and me, though," she said rubbing her stomach. "We're going to have someone else with us too."

When Maria learned the news of the baby, she sounded ecstatic, even calling herself 'Auntie Maria' already. Then Susan had to tell her about Ian and she could hear the sympathy in Maria's voice.

Now, a week later, Susan and Sarah were headed north. Although Sarah had met Maria several times, Susan felt compelled to tell her how much Maria meant to her over the years. "She came from a strict Portuguese family, and they were very nice. Her mother was quiet and reserved when they were out in public but at home she ran her house with an iron fist. Maria used to call her 'The Iron Maiden'."

Sarah giggled, "What was her dad like?"

Susan tilted her head and thought about it. "He was hard-working and honest. Sometimes he worked two or three jobs to support the family. He was a proud man, and stubborn. He wasn't the kind to take hand-outs from anyone. Back then, not everyone had the chance to graduate from high school. A lot of boys quit school to go to work. He was one of them. He always dreamed of Maria going to Brown University to become a doctor."

"She didn't though, did she? She's not a doctor," Sarah said, wrinkling her forehead.

"Nope, but she went to Brown and became a pharmacist instead. That made her father very happy."

Sarah grinned, and took a bite of her licorice. "Yea, Auntie Maria!"

Susan giggled, "Right, Auntie Maria did 'good'."

"Why isn't she married?"

Susan gripped the steering wheel. "She was married once but you probably don't remember him. It didn't work out and they went their separate ways." She wasn't about to tell her little girl Maria's husband had been caught cheating. Susan cleared her throat. "Anyway, Maria's father passed away in his sleep a few years back and her mother had dementia. You know what that is, don't you? When people get older and don't remember stuff so good. Well, Maria took care of her and made sure her mother lived out the rest of her life in the best possible way. Maria is a good person, Sarah. I'm lucky to have her in my life." Her throat tightened and she stopped talking.

Sarah sat up and grinned. "Now we're both going to have her in our lives!"

"Yep," Susan said, smiling. "Things are looking up."

It was late by the time Susan drove her Sirocco into Bristol. Sarah was excited but exhausted. She woke up at the city limits and nodded off again. Susan had called ahead at the Connecticut/Rhode Island border. Maria picked up on the first ring. "I'll be waiting for you. The address is 12 Gibson Terrace."

"I see Gibson on the map and it looks like we should be there in about an hour. See you then."

It was fifty-six minutes later when Susan pulled up to a large brick home on a large piece of semi-wooded property. Every light in the house was on. Maria and her Black Labrador, Thor, were waiting in front. Susan turned off the road into the circular driveway and parked in front of the door where Maria and Thor stood. Thor barked and spun in dizzying circles as the car came to a stop. Sarah, startled by the dog's bark, wiped her eyes and smiled at the big dog. "Look, Mommy a dog!"

"Yes, honey, we're here. Say hello to Auntie Maria."

Maria and Thor approached the car and Susan jumped out. The two ladies hugged each other and cried while Thor was busy smelling and wagging his tail with such excitement that his rear-end was thrown from side to side by the movement. Sarah came around to the other side where all the commotion was. "Hi, doggy, my name is Sarah. What's yours?"

The women turned to Sarah and Susan said, "Sarah, you remember Auntie Maria."

"My, you've grown. I see you've met Thor. He's a good boy and loves to go for walks. I hope you'll help me take care of him. He's a big teddy bear." Maria said, "I bet he'd even sleep in your room if you'd like."

"Oh, could he, mommy? Please!" Sarah's eye danced with excitement

"If it's okay with Auntie Maria."

"Welcome to your home, Susan and Sarah. Come in." Maria said, her smile revealing all thirty-two of her perfect teeth.

Inside, they walked around as Maria showed them her home. It was large and everything was immaculate and cared for. The tour started in the family room, next to the kitchen and the bathrooms. On the second level, Maria opened the first door on the right and turned to Sarah, "Honey, this is your room."

Sarah ran in and smiled, twirled around a few times, and fell on the bed. The room was set up with furniture and pictures perfect for a ten-year-old girl. "Nice, you didn't do this special for Sarah I hope?" Susan said as she looked at the room.

"Of course not … well maybe a little." Maria shot Susan a guilty smile.

Susan laughed and shook her head.

Sarah was left in her new room for a few minutes and Susan was introduced to her room. It was a spacious room with a private bath and a king-sized bed. "Perfect." Susan said and Maria smiled.

"Welcome home."

The ladies got Sarah settled and in her new bed after she washed her face and hands, brushed her teeth and said her prayers. In addition to thanking God for her baby brother, she added Auntie Maria and her new best friend, Thor, to her list of thank you(s). Susan and Maria kissed her good night, and as promised, Thor jumped on the bed and found a comfortable place for the night at Sarah's feet. She'd never owned a dog, but they looked like old friends when he snuggled against her legs. She smiled as she nodded off for the first time in her new room.

"Welcome home ..." she could hear her mother's voice in her ears.

Before they went to bed, Maria squeezed Susan's arm. I am so happy the two of you are here. This house finally feels like a home again. Susan gave her a tight hug before settling into her room. She lay in bed thinking, *what's my next step? Thank God for Maria.*

Susan drifted off to sleep thinking about how to reconnect with her mother and father, if that was even possible.

Chapter Five
The Cycle Continues

Two months after the *Amore Islander* had sunk, Y.G. Yang Shipping Company headquarters in Hong Kong, received notice their agreed value rider to the insurance policy would be honored by the underwriter. The authorities determined the ship was properly manned and properly loaded with seventy-six thousand tons of iron ore at San Metalous. The ship was kept within classification and Liberian Maritime standards. The official report called the loss an "unfortunate accident."

The protection and indemnity insurance covered compensation for the families and any liability to creditors. The North Korean transaction remained invisible and carefully concealed by its government.

Records of the overage had long since been covered up in San Metalous. So to the world, and any prying eyes, Typhoon Diana was blamed for the accident.

Y.G. Yang was a clever man who had all the angles covered. He sat behind his large desk with a glass of expensive Bourbon in his hand. He looked out the fifty-sixth story window down onto the Hong Kong Harbor. His slender young female assistant stood behind him, caressing his shoulders and nibbling on his ear. He chuckled at how well everything had worked out. He was just about to invite his assistant to lock the door when his receptionist rang, "Mr. Yang, you have a visitor." He looked into the eyes of the pretty woman next to him. *She'll have to wait.* He waved his hand and dismissed her and she slipped out the side door, smiling seductively, as she pulled it closed behind her.

"Send him in," Yang spoke into the intercom.

In walked the Man in the Black Suit. He sat down in front of the desk and his calculating eyes assessed the owner.

Yang was a heavy Asian man with skin pulled so tightly over his excessively round body that he looked like a balloon. The phone rang again. He lifted the phone and listened intently. A smile came over his fat face. *I'm one-hundred million dollars richer today. Not a bad trade for a rusty old ship and forty-four seamen that no one is going to miss anyway.*

He placed the phone back on the receiver and rubbed his belly as if he had just finished a delicious meal.

He looked across the desk and said, "Well the *Amore Islander* case is closed. Your timing is perfect. Your share will be wired to any account you choose. Let me know by tomorrow and I'll transfer the money myself."

The Man in the Black Suit nodded and half smiled. He got up and without a word headed to the door. Before he reached the exit, the sound of gunfire echoed through the room as bullets tore a fist sized piece of flesh from his back. He spun around and faced Yang. Yang smiled, his pistol dangling from his finger.

DRAWN TO THE SEA
(First Revision)

"Nothing personal, its only business," was the last thing the fat man ever said. The Man in the Black Suit drew his pistol with lightning speed and fired three rounds, removing Yang's nose, eyes and forehead so Yang entered 'Hell' fifteen seconds ahead of the assassin.

Chapter Six
First Day of a New Life

Maria had prepared breakfast before Sarah and Susan came downstairs. Susan stared at her in her black pants, violet cashmere cardigan, and ponytail. "Wow, you're ready for work already? You make me feel like a slob. I love the diamond stud earrings. They're gorgeous."

"Thanks," Maria said, flipping the bacon, "and you're not a slob. You had a long drive yesterday and needed the rest. Anyhow, you know how I love taking care of people. I was happy I woke up before the alarm. "Now," she said, "how do you two like your eggs?"

After they finished eating, Sarah petted Thor under the table while the women talked. Maria said, "I hope I haven't overstepped my bounds, but I took the liberty of letting the admissions department at school know that Sarah was coming."

"Oh, great," Susan said, "That's one less thing for me to think about."

"And," Marie continued with a wink, "I found out the local paper is looking for dependable people, so I mentioned you may be interested."

Susan laughed. "Is there anything you haven't thought of?"

"If there is, I'll try to remember it on the way to work," Maria said, giggling. She stood up and put her plate in the sink.

"Don't worry about the dishes," Susan said. "I'll take care of them."

"Great," Maria said glancing at the clock. "I should probably take off then. Sarah, do you mind taking Thor for a walk today?"

"Sure!" Sarah gave Thor a scratch on the head. "That'll be fun!"

Maria left the kitchen with her coat, pocketbook, and keys in hand. Susan watched from the window as Maria climbed into her Cadillac. She looked like she was whistling. Susan smiled and looked at Sarah hugging Thor around the neck. *I'm glad we're not going to be a burden,* she thought.

Susan and Sarah worked together and cleaned the table, washed the dishes, and readied Sarah for her first day of school in Bristol. "Mommy, will the girls like me here in Bristol?"

"Yes, sweetheart."

Maria had done all the preliminaries with the school administrator and Sarah was in the classroom in under a half-hour. Susan returned to her car and drove slowly by her parent's home but didn't stop. It looked the same as she remembered. The color was a little different and the yard matured but it was the home she had grown up in. *Would I ever be welcome there again?*

She found a small coffee shop on Hope Street and was keenly aware of the local's curious stares at a stranger with out-of-state plates. She didn't let it bother her as she ordered a coffee. The old man behind the counter finally recognized her and then he warmed up. After a half a dozen questions were asked and answered, she took her coffee, found a seat, and opened the paper to the 'Help Wanted' section, along with the list of potential employers Maria prepared.

Susan thought about Candy and her old life in Tampa. She was nearly thirty years old and had never had a "normal" job. How would she explain that to these employers? *Would their wives let me work with their husbands if they knew what I did? How do I explain my life in Tampa? Though I'd never been arrested,* Susan felt a pang of guilt or remorse, then steadied herself.

I made a commitment to start over and work a real job. I must for the sake of Sarah and my new son. She looked to the sky. *Where are you, Ian? It would be so much easier with you here with us. I love you.* She sipped her coffee and mustered the courage to call the names on the list.

Across town, Maria hummed to herself as she filled prescriptions. Her cheeks had a rosy blush to them and her eyes seemed to sparkle more than usual. Several of her customers asked her if she had just had a facial or met a man.

Susan finished her coffee and bid the man behind the counter goodbye. His mind was still rolling over her answers. She drove her Volkswagen thru town to Colt State Park. The locals took notice of the pretty woman who drove a car registered in Florida. *I have to go to the DMV*, she thought.

In the park, she found a quiet bench overlooking Narragansett Bay and began to scrutinize the list. She mumbled, "An opening at the local deli on Wood Street and another as a bookkeeper at a family gravel and rock company." She shook her head. *What do I know about bookkeeping?*

Then there was the Prestige Rug and Carpet Company. *That place has been in business as long as I can remember. Located in a large brick building on the harbor, it's a thriving business. That sounds like back-breaking work. I'll leave that one for later.*

She got back into her Sirocco and went back to the house. She dialed the human resources office of Converse Industries, the shoe manufacturer, and was easily given an interview for shift work.

The woman on the other end of the phone, in a heavy Rhode Island accent said, "Hon, be here at nine o'clock tomorrow morning for an interview with the foreman. If he likes you, you'll start tomorrow evening."

"Thank you." Susan replied and hung up.

She thought *that's a success or sort-of success* and gathered up the courage to make another call. This time she called Kaiser Aluminum and was granted an interview at eleven o'clock the next morning, but they were hiring for third shift work.

A few more dead ends and she came back to the rug manufacturer. She dialed the number and an older gentleman answered. Susan introduced herself and asked if she could be considered for a job there. For some reason she was at ease with the voice on the other end of the line, Susan told him she was raised in town and left after she finished school. She had a ten-year-old child and another on the way. She also said she recently lost the child's father in the Pacific. The story came so naturally it was believable. In fact, it was more true than not. The man on

33

the end of the line asked her, "What kind of work are you looking for? There are several openings. There is line work, manufacturing work, and office work. I would think that you would prefer office work to be there in the evenings for your family."

"Yes, that would be better."

"Can you type and file?"

"A little, but I am willing to learn and work hard."

"Would you be willing to work a forty-hour week? There is a profit sharing package and medical and pension benefits too."

"Oh my, that sounds wonderful. May I ask the salary, sir?"

"Seven fifty an hour to start. When can you start?"

"As soon as you'd like, sir."

"How about tomorrow morning, about eight o'clock?"

"Thank you and I'll be there. Thank you!"

"Oh, by the way my name is John Gates. I'll look for you after you check in with our human resources department. I'll let them know you're coming."

"Thank you again," and the phone went dead. She leaned back in her chair, tilted her head and yelled, "Hell, yeah!"

Thor jumped up, startled by her sudden outburst. "It's alright. I'm just happy, that's all," Susan said, scratching his head. "You're a spoiled dog, aren't ya?" when he rolled over on his back for a belly rub. "I think you're going to like having us here!" Thor licked her wrist.

When Susan pulled up to the school, Sarah ran to the car and jumped in with a grin. "I have made so many new friends. I really like my teacher too. She is so nice. How was your day mommy?"

"Fine, honey, I found a job and start tomorrow morning."

"Cool! Where?"

"The Prestige Rug and Carpet Company near the harbor. Let's drive by and you can see the building."

"Cool!"

They drove down Hope Street and merged onto Thames and followed it past a large brick building on the right side of the street. Susan's heart beat a little faster and Sarah was awe struck by the size of the building. They turned up Constitution Street heading north back to Maria's home. Maria was already preparing dinner when they walked in the door.

"Hi girls, how was your day?"

"Hi Auntie Maria. I love my new school and I have a bunch of new friends."

"How was your day?" asked Maria as she handed Susan a glass of red wine.

"It was fine. I found a job at the rug factory."

"Congratulations! Mr. Gates is a wonderful gentleman. I'm sure you will like him."

"Do you know him?" Susan asked.

"Of course I do. I'm the pharmacist in a small town. I know everybody. At least everybody that takes medication," and they both chuckled.

They ate a pasta dinner with tangy red sauce. Each in turn shared their day's events at the table, enjoying the food, company, and the conversation.

Sarah leaned over and put her head down on the table after dinner. She yawned. "Is it okay if I go to bed early tonight?"

"Of course dear, get ready and we'll tuck you into bed in a few minutes," her mother said.

Sarah smiled, rubbed her eyes, and in a flash was up the stairs. Thor was half a step behind her.

The ladies looked at each other and smiled. After a few minutes, they hugged and walked up the stairs to check on Sarah.

By the time they knocked on the bedroom door, Sarah was in bed and Thor curled up by her feet. Sarah was nearly asleep and reciting her prayers as she lay with her eyes closed.

"Thank you for Mommy, Auntie Maria, my little brother, and Thor ..." and she was asleep. Thor was half a second behind her as he began to gently snore. Susan and Maria kissed the girl and left the room leaving the door slightly open. The night light burned softly in the corner near the closet.

The ladies returned to the family room and poured another glass of wine. After they talked for a few minutes Susan asked, "Do you think people here know what I did in Tampa?"

"First of all, who cares? And secondly, no, only you and I know and I'm not talking. Don't worry," and Maria patted her hand.

They enjoyed their wine and barely spoke a word between them. They sat side by side on the couch, their heads leaning towards one another as they gently propped each other up. Susan marveled at how their friendship, distant for ten years, could still be so strong. It was like they had only been apart for a few hours, not a decade.

It was getting late. They took their wine glasses into the kitchen turned off the lights and walked up the stairs. At the head of the stairs, they kissed each other on the cheek and wished the other a good night, then went to their separate rooms. It had been a good day but Susan was glad it was over.

Susan dreamed of her first day at Prestige and hoped it would work out. What would it be like to be a normal mother with a normal job? She hoped Sarah was dreaming of school and the children in her class, and Thor was dreaming about a juicy bone. It was a quiet night in the Highlands.

Sarah and Susan were off to a good start in their new life.

Chapter Seven
Ian Jr. Arrives

Susan's due date was fast approaching as she settled into her new job and new life. Her boss had turned out to be one of the most generous and supportive men she had ever known. In fact, she'd never met a man before, except her father, who hadn't, soon after they were introduced, expected sex from her. Not Mr. Gates, he was an absolute gentleman.

Susan re-established herself in town and was relieved that no prying questions were asked of her long time in Tampa and the two kids. Susan's story was simple, "I worked a few part-time jobs and my husband/boyfriend had died at sea when his ship sank." No one cared much beyond that and she had no designs for political office so she hoped no one would dig further.

Her original plan was to find a place of her own as soon as possible but Maria had put an end to that. Maria, in a nice but pushy way, insisted she, Sarah, and the baby live in her home, and convinced Susan it was the perfect arrangement for everyone.

Once Susan was making money, she insisted on paying rent and helping with some of the bills. This arrangement afforded Susan the support and help of her best friend with the children and Maria was no longer alone.

Maria attended every doctor's appointment and Lamaze classes with Susan, even exchanging notes with the other partners in class. As Sarah watched her mother's belly grow, she asked millions of questions and never forgot to pray for her yet unborn brother each night. She squealed with joy when the baby kicked and moved in her mommy's belly and she'd cry out, "Cool … Way Cool!"

Things for Susan were almost too good to be true. She and her mother had reconciled and met regularly at the coffee shop. Her father wasn't so forgiving, but he was smitten with Sarah. Susan's mother kept saying, "Just be patient, he'll come around." She'd give Susan a smile and a gentle squeeze with her arthritic hands.

Over the months, several men had expressed interest in dating Susan and two nice men were rather insistent, but she wasn't ready on so many levels. "How can I do that? I'm a mother of two." She discussed the offers with Maria and could sense coolness in her reaction and Susan began to sense jealousy.

At first Susan was confused and denied her instinct. But it was true that Maria had, little by little, asserted herself more and more as a partner as much as her best friend. Albeit discreet, all the signs told Susan the same thing and it was something Susan would have to gently manage. Not that she was repulsed by it. It was nineteen-seventy-nine and the people in Bristol would have little tolerance for a professional, the town pharmacist, to be openly lesbian and Susan's family and her children would be victimized in scandal.

It was fine that Maria was helping her friend overcome the tragedy of Susan's husband's death at sea. That was their story and it played well in town for all parties. In just a short nine months, Susan and Maria had grown as close as any couple without the intimacy and it wouldn't be an issue for the New England townsfolk.

***

On a wonderful spring morning the temperature was in the mid-seventies, humidity low, and the air crisp and clean. Susan was at full-term but insisted on working. She sat at her desk, clearly uncomfortable and, *very pregnant,* as Sarah would tell her.

Susan completed reconciling Mr. Gate's travel account. It was a rather complicated one which included a number of stops throughout the southern states and she'd paid the week's invoices. Satisfied with her accomplishments, she sat back with a cup of tea and tried to find a comfortable position.

Suddenly she felt a tear internally, her seat got wet and the pressure in her mid-section lessened. It had been ten years since she had gone into labor with Sarah but she immediately knew, the baby is on his way.

Susan became bright red with embarrassment. Gates and her co-worker Shirley noticed the change and rushed over. "Are you okay, Honey?" said Shirley, her face etched with worry and concern. Gates looked down at Susan and asked, "Do you need an ambulance?"

"No, I think my water just broke. Could I please get a ride to the hospital?"

"Of course, I'll get my keys and bring the car around front."

DRAWN TO THE SEA
(First Revision)

Susan asked, "Shirley, would you please call Maria at the pharmacy and tell her I'm heading to the hospital? Please call my mother and ask her to pick up Sarah at school too. Ummm ... I think I'm starting contractions!"

Susan began to perspire and her belly periodically contracted without warning. Then, just as abruptly as they'd spasm, the contractions would stop.

Shirley and Gates gently placed Susan in the car and closed the door. Gates was around to the driver's side in a flash. As he climbed in, he turned to Shirley and said, "Please call my wife and tell her I'll call her from the hospital. Cancel all my appointments for the rest of the day. I'll keep you posted."

He drove fast, but responsibly, to the hospital in Providence and Susan felt safe. Twenty minutes later, they pulled up to the emergency room entrance where they were met by orderlies and a wheelchair. As she was being administered by a number of nurses and their aides from local nursing schools, Gates took care of the paperwork with the admissions staff.

Shirley contacted Maria and she was on the road and in the waiting room thirty minutes later. Maria met Gates in the waiting room and they shared a private glance which only people with a secret history together would recognize. They were still close friends and comfortable together. They exchanged a sterile hug and together asked the passing nurse if they could see Susan. The nurse smiled, and with the grace of a professional acknowledged their concern and asked for a moment to check on the patient.

The nurse, who was overweight and whose uniform was uncomfortably tight, waddled down the hall with her clipboard pressed closely to her breast. Minutes later she returned, "Please follow me," and they followed her to Susan's room. They looked in, thanked the nurse and the focus was now on Susan. She had several machines connected to her, monitoring her heart beat, blood pressure, contractions and oxygen in her blood. She was semi-reclined in the bed and already in a hospital gown. They moved into her room and Susan smiled and greeted her friends. Her face was pale and her eyelids looked heavy.

"How are you doing Susan?" Gates asked. He sounded more like her father than her boss.

"Okay, I guess."

Maria stood near the door, then ran to Susan with tears in her eyes and hugged her. "I love you Susan. We are going to have a baby."

"I love you too," Susan responded without thinking about how that might sound. Gates appeared oblivious, his senses overwhelmed by the sights, sounds, smells, and emotions surrounding him.

Then, Susan's mother and Sarah arrived. Sarah rushed up to the bed and clutched her mother's hand, smiling with a grin that took up most of her face.

"Mommy, today my brother is coming out, right?"

Gates cleared his throat and announced he would be in the waiting room. As he walked toward the door, he turned and said, "Susan, if you need anything please just let me know. Good luck. I'll say goodbye for now."

"Thank you for everything, Mr. Gates."

"Thank you," Maria said as she nodded to Gates and he nodded back with a smile.

Maria and John again shared a private look and their hearts began to pound in their chests. They shared a secret together. A secret that had been only theirs for the last three years and it would remain that way. He gave a casual salute and left, the focus in the room was on Susan.

"Oh, I think I'm starting labor. Mom, please call the nurse."

Her mother was already out the door and down the hall before telling Susan her father was in the waiting room. From Susan's perspective, it seemed like an eternity but the doctor arrived in a matter of minutes. He looked at Susan and said, "It's time for your family to move to the waiting room while I examine you."

Susan nodded, Sarah and Maria each kissed her and they left the room together holding hands.

The doctor reached under the sheet and began the examination. She thought, *It's the same sensation I'd felt many times in my life by clients with a hand fetish. This time, at least, it's professional and clinical.* She sighed with relief.

When Maria, Susan's mother and Sarah entered the waiting room, Susan's father was hunched over and wiping his eyes. Sarah ran into his arms and said, "My little brother is coming today."

She jumped onto his lap and kissed him on the cheek. His face lit up and he gave her a tight squeeze. "You remind me of your mother when she was your age," he whispered in her ear. He looked into his granddaughter's eyes with tears streaming down his cheeks and said, "Thank you, princess. You have made me finally understand what a fool I've been for the past eleven years. I love you, peanut," and he squeezed her.

"Grandpa, I love you too! And you're no fool!" You're the best grandpa ever!" His wife and Maria watched without a word as they watched his shoulders quake with emotion. Sarah patted her grandfather's forearm and looked into his troubled eyes, "Grandpa … it's okay … Grandpa, it's okay!"

Meanwhile, in a room down the hall, Susan was in the full throes of labor. She'd dilated and was wheeled into the birthing room. The nurse came to the waiting room to fetch Maria. "It's time, hon." Maria was on her feet in a flash and followed the lady in white to the dressing room where she was prepped, scrubbed and told what to expect. Maria arrived just as Ian was entering the birthing canal and made it there in time for the delivery. She performed her role of support and encouragement flawlessly. Her face glowed as if the baby being born was her own.

The boy was born a healthy eight pound, ten ounces and measured twenty-one inches long. His eyes were piercing blue just like his father's. The doctor looked the baby over and announced, "Ms. Blooker, you have a healthy baby boy. We'll do a few more tests in the next few days. Don't worry this is routine", he said as he handed the baby to a nurse so she could clean him and wrap him in a light blue blanket.

Susan felt more alone than any time in her life until the baby was put back in her arms. In the meantime Maria combed Susan's hair and gently washed her face and arms.

Susan looked into the baby's face and knew she'd chosen his name after the two men she loved and respected. Tears filled her eyes and she quietly said, "Ian Stanley Blooker welcome to this life. I am your mother," and she pulled him into her bosom.

The new mother, her baby, and Maria were moved to a recovery room by two student nurses who had just experienced a birth for the first time. The room was identical to the room they'd occupied hours before. The mother was gently placed into a clean bed while Maria held the baby. Soon the warm baby was placed back in his mother's arms. Maria asked, "Are you ready for me to get your family? I know they're anxious to see young Ian and you."

"Yes," Susan whispered.

Maria still wore her surgical gown and sported a huge grin across her face as she floated into the waiting room. When Susan's parents saw her joyful face, they clasped hands and put their heads together and closed their eyes. It appeared they were giving thanks. Sarah raced to Maria. "Auntie Maria, where is my brother? I want to see him."

"Your mother and Ian would like you to come and introduce yourselves." Maria said.

Sarah turned to her grandfather and held out her hand and said, "Grandpa, let's go!"

Maria led the way. Sarah was right behind dragging her grandfather and skipping with excitement. Susan's mother followed a few steps behind. She smiled at her husband and said, "I love you, Stanley."

Stanley looked over his shoulder and said, "I love you too, Ellen. I'm so sorry about the way I've been." His eyes were still teary. "Will Susan ever forgive me for being such a fool?"

"Time will tell." She smiled and then in a cheerful voice said, "Congratulations, Grandpa! You have a boy to teach how to be a good man." She smiled again.

The introductions were, of course, one sided. Everyone in the room was excited except for Ian who just wanted to sleep.

Susan was choked up when she saw her father doting over Ian. She didn't even know if he'd come to the hospital. A quick glance between them was enough to know he was over his grudge and wanted to re-establish their relationship. With tears in Susan's eyes she said, "Dad, I missed you so much."

His eyes grew watery and he said, "Me too, sweetheart."

The family sat around the bed and talked for twenty minutes or so until the nurse came in and announced, "The mother and baby need to rest and visiting time is over for now." Sarah's bottom lip jutted out and she started whimpering. Her grandmother took her hand and prodded her away from Ian. Sarah sighed. "Good night, mommy. Good night, Ian"

"Good night, Sarah. Mommy loves you." Susan smiled and waved.

As the others left, Susan's father remained.

"Susan, I'm so sorry for being such a pig-headed idiot," he gushed. "I can never expect you to forgive me for shutting you out of our lives. I was angry, bitter and felt betrayed. I know I was the fool. You had every right to do what you wanted to do. I hope you will let me back into your life and your heart."

DRAWN TO THE SEA
(First Revision)

Susan was exhausted and emotionally spent. Still, she had tears in her eyes as she listened to her father. Looking into his eyes she knew he meant every word.

"It's okay, dad, I love you."

He smiled, his eyes welled up and he said, "We have so much catching up to do. I love you, sweetheart. See you soon."

He kissed her cheek, lightly brushed her forehead with his thumb, and ran out the door. His face was flushed and beads of perspiration dotted his temples. He stopped at a drinking fountain in the hallway and doused his face with the cool water and wiped it off with his handkerchief. When he caught up with the others, he gave his wife a bashful grin and she smiled as she stood on her tip-toes and gave him a kiss on the cheek.

Up on the tenth floor, Susan and Ian were sound asleep before the cars left the parking lot. Without knowing it, Ian had a busy first day. He reunited his mother and her father, helped Maria release her repressed feelings, and made his big sister very happy. Oh, and he was born that seventeenth day of May nineteen-seventy nine.

In time, he would come to understand his family responsibility had only just begun.

Chapter Eight
Growing Up

Susan flipped through a stack of photo albums as Maria inserted pictures in the most recent one. "I can't believe they are all grown up," Susan moaned. "Where did the time go?"

"I'm not sure." Maria said, rubbing Susan's back. "At least you know you did a damn good job raising them."

"I hope so," Susan said, biting her lip. "If it wasn't for you and my parents, who knows how it would have all turned out?" She leaned in and gave Maria a feathery kiss on the cheek. "You're an angel," she whispered

"I love you, too," Maria said, grinning then she turned serious. "Don't forget Sarah had a big part of raising Ian too. She thinks of herself as his third parent."

Susan laughed. "You're right, she does, and it's true. She was a huge help. It's hard to remember anything she did wrong growing up. She was such a good natured, obedient little girl. It was a cinch to raise her." She wiped her eyes. "And now, she is a mother herself, raising two little girls. It's just unbelievable to me. I can't believe I am getting so old."

Maria put a picture down and grabbed her hand. "You're still gorgeous and you always will be."

"When I moved here," Susan said, playing with Maria's fingers, "I was scared to death. I could never have predicted how it would all play out. Sarah getting married and Ian graduating high school." She gazed into Maria's eyes and kissed the back of her hand. "You and me, I never saw it coming. If I did, I probably would have packed up and run like hell." She threw her head back and laughed. "I would have thought for sure the good citizens of Bristol would have burned our house down!

"They're not so bad," Maria said, going back to the photo album. "They're good people and they've never caused us any problems."

"Only because they turn a blind eye to our living situation," Susan pointed out. "What women in their early forties would have been living together eighteen years just as friends unless they were ugly, fat, or socially inept?"

Maria smiled. "Thank God we're none of those things. Times have changed and while Bristol may not be the most forward-thinking town in the world, it has come a long way since we grew up here."

"Oooooh, look at this picture of my dad and Ian in his garage. The hammer in Ian's hand is almost as big as he is!"

Maria glanced over and laughed. "That must have been one of your father's famous 'teaching moments'. I swear, every time your parents babysat, your dad would teach the kids a new 'life lesson'." She peered closer at the picture. "Oh my God, do you see Sarah in the background? I think that's a first aid kit on her lap."

Susan's mouth dropped and let out a raucous laugh. "It is! Geez, that little one was always on the look out to protect Ian from any emergencies. She must have thought the tools in the garage were a potential hazard!" Her smile faded and her forehead wrinkled. "I hate that she lives in California. I want to see her and my grandchildren every day! It doesn't matter that she writes and sends pictures all the time. It's not the same as having her here." She peered out the window at the sound of a car door closing. "Oh good, Ian is home!"

He walked in and tossed his baseball glove in the doorway of the foyer and kicked off his cleats. His practice jersey was soaked with sweat. "What's up?" he said, walking into the living room.

Susan was speechless for a moment. He resembled Ian, Sr. so much it was almost heartbreaking. His eyes were the same piercing blue and his hair was the color of wheat before harvest. She looked at his muscular and athletic body and shook her head. *No wonder the girls fall at his feet.* Thankfully, he was too involved in academics and sports to notice. He treated girls and women with respect, but acted oblivious to their obvious swooning. Her father had taught him well. "How was practice?" she managed.

"Not bad. Coach worked us hard, though, in order to prepare us for the state championship, but I expected that. We need the extra conditioning."

Susan's chest swelled with pride. "Maria has a roast in the crock pot. Why don't you take a shower before dinner?" She wrinkled up her nose at his dirty baseball pants.

"Don't worry, mom, I'll toss my clothes in the washer right now."

Susan sat up, "Hey Ian, take a look at this picture of you and your sister at her wedding. I love this one." She eased the picture out of the protective covering and handed it to him.

Ian grinned, "Yeah that's one of my favorites." Under his breath, he muttered, "It's one of the few that doesn't have Jeff in it."

"What did you say? Susan asked.

"Nothing," Ian said, combing his messy hair with his fingers. "You know I don't like that guy."

"I don't know why not," Maria said. "He has a great job and gives Sarah and the girls everything they could dream of."

"Yeah, right," Ian said, scowling. "That's why her arms were loaded with bruises when I visited her on spring break. Even the most expensive make-up can't mask a swollen black eye."

"She fell down the stairs carrying a laundry basket and tripped on one of the girl's toys. You can't blame Jeff for that," Maria said, her face adamant.

"Huh, it's amazing how steps can bruise like fingers and fists." Ian sighed, "Whatever …" He walked towards the bathroom and said, "And it's awful funny how many business trips he takes with his hot secretary. How much business is conducted on private beaches?"

Susan and Maria's eyes met and Susan's shoulders slumped. The suspicions she had of Sarah's marriage were confirmed.

***

During much of his junior and senior years Ian, his

mother and Auntie Maria drove up and down New England visiting a number of colleges. They were all good, but Ian wasn't sold on any of them. Then, during one of those conversations where he asked his mother to tell him about his dad, he began to mull around an idea. *My father had been a mariner. Maybe the best way to understand him is to become a mariner too.*

One afternoon, while sitting together at the kitchen table Susan told Ian about his father as they each held their cups of hot tea in their hands. Ian looked seriously at his mother and said, "Mom, I have been thinking about college and I know where I want to go and why."

"Where is that my dear?" she said, looking at him over the top of her piping hot cup.

"The merchant marine academy. I want to go to sea like my father. Maybe I'll be able to understand more about him if I do. The school is close, so I can get home to visit you and Maria," he gushed. "It's the best maritime school and I submitted my application this morning."

Susan sat back in her chair and the room began to spin. She felt like the wind was knocked out of her. She had lost her lover to the sea and she wasn't ready to risk her only son to a similar fate. She focused on Ian's cheek and fought to compose herself before she spoke, slowly putting herself back together.

Ian watched with curiosity as his mother transformed before his eyes. She cleared her throat and said, "Ian, this is a surprise." She chose her words carefully. "I think we should see the merchant marine academy. Where is it, again?"

"New York," he responded puffing out his chest

"I will make arrangements for us to go down next week," she said

Ian glanced at his watch and said, "Mom, I need to be on my way to practice now. See you for dinner."

"Okay," she said, drifting off into another dimension. She could see her lover, the father of her son as vividly as if he sat in the chair across from her.

Ian, she cried to her vision *...What should I do? I can't lose him to the sea too. Damn you, I love you so much. Why did you have to die?* She was in tears as the door closed behind her son. He was late to baseball practice.

Susan looked at the vision she had conjured in her mind and saw her handsome lover. "Don't worry, Susan, I'll always be with you and I'm looking after our son," the image spoke to her, "I'll protect him," he said softly, the way he always did when he was with her. Susan cried and reached out for his hand, but he faded away as her hand probed for his. She shook her head and realized what had just happened.

Oh my God! She jumped up from the table and went out onto the patio to get some fresh air and question herself and her sanity.

Later that evening, after Ian retired and Maria and Susan were alone on the couch sipping wine, Susan began to explain, or at least tried to explain, the afternoon's events. She started with the conversation she and her son had shared and his desire to attend the academy. Maria had heard of the school and its superb reputation.

"Susan, remember Joe Balzano from school? He went there and is now a ship's captain somewhere on the West Coast."

53

"Wow, yeah I remember him." She paused, knowing how bad Maria wanted Ian to go to Brown. Maria never said it, but Susan knew she was jealous of Ian's father. She took a large swallow of wine and tried to steel her nerves. "He wants to get to know his father better, to be like his father." She could barely breathe as she waited for a response. Even though Ian, Sr. was dead, they both knew if he was alive, Susan would have chosen him over Maria.

"If that's what your boy wants, he should pursue it with all his heart and he'll be safe at the academy." Susan decided not to tell Maria about her vision as they sat across the kitchen table.

The next morning Susan sat at her desk and hurried to finish her paperwork. She stepped into Mr. Gate's office and asked if she could make a long distance call to Long Island and the reason why. He smiled and said, "Of course. My, how time flies, I remember the day Ian was born."

"Me too, thank you, Mr. Gates." She returned to her desk and dialed the academy admissions office. A helpful woman answered and the ladies spoke for nearly an hour. By the end of the conversation, Susan had arranged for Ian, Maria, and herself to visit the school the following week. She was feeling better and anxious to share the information she'd gathered. That evening Susan said, "Then there is the congressional appointment …"

Maria broke in, "Congressman Manny Almeida is one of my customers and a good friend. I'll talk to him about how to get a congressional appointment." The hairs on the back of Susan's neck prickled at the name Manny Almeida, but she didn't know why. She knew he and

Maria were old friends, but it was something about the way Maria said his name and the way her eyes glossed over when she spoke of him.

Susan tried to shake off the feeling because it wasn't like her to be envious or possessive. She pasted on a smile and said, "That'd be lovely if he'd help!"

***

The next day Maria called Congressman Almeida's office and was passed straight through. "Manny?"

"Hi Maria, what a surprise. What can I do for you?"

"How do I go about getting Ian Blooker a congressional appointment to the merchant marine academy?"

"Are his grades good enough?"

"Yes, and he is Bristol's darling, an athlete, and all around good kid."

"Have him contact my office and we'll make an appointment to interview him, all nice and proper. If the academy screens him as minimally qualified, I'll take care of the rest."

"Thanks, Manny."

"It was nice talking to you again, Maria."

"Thanks." And the phone went dead. Maria pushed the memories of her forbidden evening with Manny back into the recesses of her mind and returned to filling prescriptions at the pharmacy.

A week later, they headed to Long Island and the academy. Four hours later, Maria pulled up to the security guard standing next to the massive iron gates at the entrance. He came to the window and asked for their names, checked his list, and smiled. "We have been expecting you. Please pull your car into the parking lot over there," he pointed with his gloved hand, "and an academy representative will be with you shortly. Welcome to the merchant marine academy, ladies, young man."

Before Maria had put the car in park and stopped the engine, they were met by an academy recruiter. His grooming was immaculate. He was polished and was good at his job. He escorted them around the grounds and provided his pitch and endless interesting facts and information about the school, its history, and the dynamics of the academics and the year, he called 'sea year'. He continued, "'Sea year' is the time cadets are paired up and sent to commercial ships. They'll sail on working ships and travel to many foreign and domestic ports for six months during their third and second class year. It's really a great experience."

It sounded like a good fit to Ian who grew more enthusiastic as the visit progressed. Maria and Susan walked a few feet behind and glanced back and forth. Susan knew Maria was still wishing he could go to Brown, because this wasn't a 'normal' college, and Susan couldn't get past the fact her son wanted to do something dangerous like go to sea.

The ladies surveyed the surroundings, the campus was beautiful, the grounds were perfectly manicured and the buildings impressive and massive in their construction. The academy overlooked Long Island Sound with water to the north and wooded forest to the south. The midshipmen were on leave so the campus was nearly deserted which added an unrealistic sense of serenity and calm. The birds chirped happily in the trees as the warm sun shone down on the guests. Susan turned to Maria and said, "It really is a beautiful place." Maria nodded.

All-in-all the visit was an overwhelming success. Ian was hooked. Next, the guide walked them by the admissions office. An older gentleman in a maritime uniform invited them into his office. He had been expecting Ian and had reviewed his folder. He looked over the folder again and cleared his throat, "Ian, it appears your SAT scores, grades, classes, and athletic achievements have been reviewed by our admissions board and you are considered highly qualified. All you need now is a congressional appointment."

"I am working on that now, sir."

"Good. I'll look forward to seeing you class-up next summer." The older man closed the file and stood behind his desk indicating the meeting was over. The three visitors rose and exchanged farewells and the escort met them in the outer office and guided them back to their car.

Slowly they drove to the gate and absorbed the sights to preserve lasting memories. They waved to the security guard and Maria took control and maneuvered her car through the New York traffic and back up to Rhode Island. The trip back to Rhode Island was a short one and Ian spoke the whole way home. Maria and Susan were lost in their own thoughts.

Ian's congressional interview happened three weeks later. His appointment letter came in the mail in October of his senior year. Congressman Almeida had come through and Ian was headed to the merchant marine academy and a future at sea. The time would fly and it would soon be time for him to report for Indoctrination, a process that consumed his summer until his academic year started, and after his first year he was off to sea for his practical education.

Chapter Nine
Sea Year

Ian came home to Bristol and was relieved his first year at the academy was behind him. He felt stronger and more confident than a year ago when he'd left for Long Island. The new stripe on his uniform sleeve was a constant reminder he'd survived plebe year and was now a third classman. He smiled. *Off to sea and then just three more years and I'm done with school.*

He strolled into the coffee shop and ordered hot chocolate and an omelet. "Anything you want, Ian," the waitress told him with a wave and she sashayed to the order window. She turned back to him, but he wasn't looking.

There were two older gentlemen shaking his hand and slapping his back. Ian's laughter rang through the small room. When his breakfast was served, there were three girls standing at his booth, one draped over the bench. "It was great seeing you all again," Ian said, "but I don't want to be rude and eat in front of you." They wandered off with pouty lips and disappointed faces.

The two weeks at home were relaxing and the weather warm and pleasant. Ian found time to sail each day with his grandfather in the sloop they'd built together ten years before. It was as beautiful as it was on its maiden voyage and something they'd shared together for many years. Ian learned much from his grandfather during those sailing excursions. He learned how to be a man of honor and dignity. He learned about respect and how it is earned and easily lost. Ian learned about respect for women, animals and people in general. He also learned to sail well and respect the ocean. The later lesson, coupled with his father's genes, helped frame his drive to explore the world by sea.

Susan was both proud and terrified by his passion for the sea. After all, it was the sea that had stolen Ian's father from her. She'd spent many sleepless nights lying in bed worried about her son and wishing he would pursue another profession.

Susan restlessly tossed and turned in her room. Down the hall, Ian dreamt of the adventure, traveling the world, and experiencing things most people never imagined. Stories at the academy, told by upper classmen and faculty, about the life of a mariner fueled Ian's fascination.

During the third week, the phone rang at ten o'clock Tuesday morning. Susan answered the phone and was greeted by an older gentleman who introduced himself. "Hello, Mrs. Blooker. My name is Captain Earl Mann, East Coast, Academy Training Representative. May I speak with Midshipmen Blooker?"

"Just a moment please," her heart dropped through her feet knowing her son would soon be on a ship. She took a deep breath, set down the phone and went straight to the garage. She opened the door and Ian looked up from the project he was working on with his grandfather.

"Ian, Captain Mann, is on the phone for you. He wants to speak with you." She was in a mild state of shock.

Ian ran to the phone while Susan ran to her father and fell into his arms. "Dad, I'm scared"

"I can only imagine, my dear."

"My Ian died at sea. I can't lose my son too."

"I know dear. He'll be alright," he said as he embraced her hard and his eyes began to tear.

"I know, dad."

As Susan and her father shared a private moment, Ian raised the phone to his ear with excitement. "Midshipmen Ian Blooker fourth class. I mean third class, sir." His knees quivered.

"Ian, this is Captain Mann, from school."

"Yes sir!"

"I have your first ship assignment. Are you ready?"

"Yes sir!"

"Good. Do you have a pencil and paper to write with?"

"Yes, sir!"

By this time Susan and her father had come in from the garage. Susan was under her father's strong and supportive arm. They stood side by side in front of Ian and listened to the conversation.

"Ian, you're to report to the *American Spirit*. It's a containership running between New Jersey and Rotterdam. You're to contact the operations office and get the details, when and where to report to the ship. Do you understand?"

Ian jotted down the information, "Yes, sir!"

61

"A copy of your orders will be sent to you by email. Any questions young man?"

"No sir, and thank you, sir."

Very well, and have a good day."

"Good bye, sir." The phone went dead.

"Well?" his grandfather asked, his mother still securely held under his arm.

"The *American Spirit,*" Ian excitedly replied, his face aglow. "A containership that runs from New Jersey to Rotterdam,"

Susan said, "Rotterdam, the Netherlands?"

"Yes mom, why?"

"Your father was a Dutchman," and she began to cry. Was there a horrible circle threatening to stab her in the heart once again? She knew she couldn't survive it. Not again. Her father looked at her and said," That's the first time you have told me anything about Ian's father. Is there anything else?"

She reeled back from her father and said, "Yes, he was the most handsome man I have ever known and Ian is the spitting image of him." She went on, "He was kind and good but haunted by the sea and I'm afraid your grandson will be too." Her voice fell silent. Then she continued, "Dad, I still love Ian to this very day." She began to cry like a little girl with heavy uncontrolled sobs and tears. Her body heaved as she cried into her father's shoulder. Stanley held her tight and gently rubbed her back.

That evening the family had grilled steaks, and Ian's grandmother made salad and lemon pie for dessert. Sarah called from California to congratulate Ian and wished him well. She, too, had known Ian's father, albeit for a short time.

DRAWN TO THE SEA
(First Revision)

At nine o'clock the next morning Ian called the operations officer for the details and the timeline for the *American Spirit.* He took careful notes as the man spoke. Susan hovered over Ian, smiling through watery eyes. The young midshipman conducted himself professionally, with confidence and maturity. Ian concluded, "Thank you, sir. I'll report as ordered. Thank you."

He hung up the phone and looked at his mother.

"Mom, I need to be at Port Elizabeth, New Jersey at terminal six the morning of June fifteenth, the day after tomorrow. Can you drive me or should I ask grandpa?"

"Of course, I can and I bet your grandparents will want to make the trip too. Call and tell them the news." She excused herself and slipped off unnoticed to her room to wipe the tears from her eyes.

Ten minutes later his grandparents were knocking on the door for the details and making plans for the trip to New Jersey.

The next evening there was an impromptu Bon Voyage party where Maria, Susan, Stanley, Ellen and a few of Ian friends gathered together. Stanley and Ellen helped Maria put out a New England Clam Boil with sweet clams, hotdogs, chorizo, buckwurst, potatoes and onions steamed together for hours. It was simple to prepare and the meal savory.

The evening was warm with a gentle breeze from the south. The mosquitoes were kind that evening and allowed the party to proceed without molesting the guests. All evening there were embarrassing stories of Ian's childhood. The stories kept the atmosphere light and happy. All of them were exaggerated but told in loving perspective and everyone within ear shot laughed with each memory.

Initially, Susan busied herself with helping prepare the food and setting up the party. As the evening progressed, she found herself drifting into the shadows watching her son. She needed to absorb every detail. Maria saw Susan withdraw and made her way over to her friend and as she approached her presence was enough. Susan needed the support and she knew Maria cared. Susan said, "This is not about me, it is about Ian."

"What?"

"Nothing, Maria."

Maria looked into Susan' eyes and smiled, "Do you know I love you, Susan?"

"Yes, Maria. I love you, too."

Little by little, the party goers said goodbye to Ian and slipped away. By ten o'clock the last of the guests had left, the dishes washed, the garbage consolidated and put in the trash barrel. Ian was already in his room resting. Susan and Maria looked at each other, smiled and made their way up the stairs, and for the first time crossed the bedroom threshold together, undressed each other and fell passionately onto the bed, crossing the Rubicon as they wildly explored each other's bodies in frenzied desire, heightened by years of restraint.

Later that evening, Susan's mind was still spinning. She looked over at Maria who was in the soundest and most peaceful slumber. Clearly she had considered this evening and come to peace with the consequences years ago. It was not so easy for Susan. She listened to Maria as she slept. *Was this right or was it a mistake?* She needed space to figure it out.

DRAWN TO THE SEA
(First Revision)

Quietly, Susan crossed the hall and entered her room. She placed her clothes in a pile on a chair next to her desk and crawled into bed. Lying in the freshly made bed, with its cool sheets, she longed to return to the warmth and coziness of the bed across the hall. She didn't dare. Instead she looked at the ceiling, her eyes had long since acclimated to the dark and spoke in hushed words, *Ian my love, what have I done? I still love you. I will never feel you beside me again. Is it wrong for me to find love in the arms of another after nineteen years? Is it wrong for me to love?*

She lay there for a few minutes like she expected an answer. As the sheets warmed from her body, she began to relax and soon was asleep. Though she slept, it was anything but restful.

The morning came early for the Blooker family. Across town, Susan's parents were up at four o'clock. They had coffee and breakfast and were driving the rented town car over to Maria's home by six-fifteen. Stanley had always been a punctual man and he wouldn't be late today. Ellen had long ago become accustomed to his obsession for punctuality and it was now second nature to her too.

The streets were empty except for the occasional delivery truck and a car or two that brought someone home from a place they shouldn't have been the night before.

In Maria's home Susan was up, showered and dressed. She looked into the mirror across her room. *Don't think about last night. Not yet. Get Ian off to his ship and then you and Maria will work things out.*

Maria was already in the kitchen making coffee, scrambling eggs and toast. She still wore her silk robe and expensive embroidered silk slippers which added to her

65

well-dressed look. Her hair was pulled back and her complexion was rosy and flush. She had never looked like that in all the years Susan had known her. Maria's appearance slapped Susan in the face as she came down the stairs. She looked beautiful. Ian was still in his room getting ready and the women were alone for a moment.

"Thank you for last night, Susan"

"Thank you, too, Maria"

And they kissed each other on the cheeks like they had so many times in their lives. Friends, very close friends.

Ian came down the stairs a moment later in his starched white uniform. His hat neatly tucked under his arm, he strolled into the kitchen right out of a movie scene.

He inhaled deeply and said, "Auntie Maria, breakfast smells great. I'm really hungry." The women looked at each other and laughed.

Maria said, "Sit down and I'll bring you some eggs and toast. Would you like bacon too?"

"Oh yes! Thank you."

Maria served Ian and Susan poured coffee for herself and refilled Maria's mug. The ladies joined him at the table as he devoured his meal. Neither woman had an appetite but the coffee really hit the spot.

Ian did a double-take at Maria. "Auntie, you look a little different today. You look exceptionally beautiful." Catching what he said, "I mean you always look beautiful." Maria blushed, smiled at Susan and as Maria was about to respond, Susan's heart jumped into her throat.

"Ian, you are such a charmer."

Susan relaxed and started to breathe again. Maria hadn't dropped a bomb shell about her and his mom just as he was leaving for the ship. *Thank God!*

As Susan resumed breathing, her parents knocked and Maria was up in a flash to answer the door. For a moment, Susan was alone with her son. She smiled as she thought, *Ian, you're so handsome, just like your father in his uniform. Will you understand my relationship with Maria?* Maria led Stanley and Ellen into the kitchen and offered them coffee and breakfast.

Stanley replied, "We've had breakfast but the coffee sounds good."

"How about you Ellen?"

"No thank you, dear," Ellen said. Maria poured coffee for Stanley and they all gathered around the kitchen table and admired how handsome Ian was in his uniform. He finished the last few bites of his breakfast as four pairs of eyes watched. He blushed and brought his dishes to the sink.

Almost as if on cue, they all got up from the table. Ian and Stanley left to put the luggage into the rental. The ladies cleared the table and put the dishes in the dishwasher, then sat for a moment at the table again. Susan and Maria held their cups of coffee in their palms as Ellen said, "Is everything okay? You two are acting funny."

Sweat pooled under Susan's arms. Maria saved her when she shrugged her shoulders. "Just an emotional day, that's all. It's exciting, happy and sad all at the same time." Ellen nodded, but didn't look convinced.

Stanley stuck his head in, "Time to go ladies."

Their private moment abruptly ended and the ladies rose from the table without a word and followed Stanley as he marched out the front door to the circular driveway where the white Lincoln was running. Ian was standing by the passenger door.

Maria still held her coffee mug between her hands as Susan turned and kissed her on the cheek and whispered in her ear, "Thank you. This is all possible because of you."

Ian helped Susan into the large road car. Ellen was already seated in the front seat with her seatbelt on. The Map Quest directions Stanley had printed the night before were open on her lap. Stanley was in the driver's seat, the defroster blasting.

Ian walked over to Maria and kissed her goodbye. "I love you Auntie Maria. You are the kindest woman I've ever known. Please continue to take care of my mother. She really loves you more than you might imagine."

Maria flinched and her face turned crimson. "Thank you, Ian. I love you very much. Come home to us safe and sound."

Ian flashed his bright white teeth in a full smile, saluted her and then jumped into the car next to his mother and slammed the door.

Stanley maneuvered the Lincoln down the driveway and turned onto the road. Maria stood there at the front door in her robe and waved until all that was left were the red tail lights. It was just about sunrise and the colors of New England were coming into focus.

They headed out of Bristol and started the long trip down the I-95. There was a frenetic static in the air, one mixed with anxiety and excitement as the car continued along the interstate to Port Elizabeth.

Four and a half hours later, Stanley maneuvered the vehicle into the visitor parking lot at the shipping terminal. Everyone gasped at the enormity of the terminal and the thousands of containers stacked four-high. Large tractors placed and retrieved containers from chassis behind trucks. There were trucks as far as the eye could see as they waited for a chassis with a container. It was amazingly well-choreographed symphony of coordinated movement. Far off in the distance behind the large field of containers was the *American Spirit*.

"There it is," said Ian, his eyes wide and dancing. They parked and waited as the ship's agent was contacted to escort Ian to the ship. After a few minutes the agent, a young man with a heavy Newark accent, walked in and introduced himself to the family. A few more minutes of friendly conversation and he looked at Ian, "It's time to get you aboard the ship. Are you ready?"

"Yes, sir!" Ian turned to his mom and kissed her, "Mom, I love you. I'll email or write you often."

"Be careful, Ian"

Ian turned to his grandparents who stood side by side, Stanley held his wife close. Ian said, "I love you two. Please take care of my mother. I'll write, I promise" With that he shook Stanley's hand and kissed Ellen's cheek.

"Bye," and Ellen started to cry

"Bye," Ian murmured.

"Take care, son," his grandfather said in a deep and distant voice.

Ian picked up his gear and boarded a shuttle bus with the agent. The door closed and the shuttle began the short trip. Susan and her parents watched as the bus disappeared into the maze of containers pointed in the general direction of the ship. The three of them held each other and sobbed.

After several minutes the family climbed back into the Lincoln and headed back to Rhode Island. The trip back home was the longest five hours of the Blooker's lives. Not a word was exchanged as Stanley skillfully piloted them up the I-95 corridor. All three were too deeply immersed in their own thoughts for words.

Chapter Ten
American Spirit

Before his family started their trip home, Ian was aboard. Several members of the crew met him at the gangway, took his bags, and brought them aboard. "Welcome aboard midshipmen. What's your name?"

"Ian Blooker,"

"Welcome aboard Mister Blooker,"

At the head of the brow was an older man in khakis. "Mister Blooker?"

"Yes sir."

"I'm the third mate, Joe Kelly, I attended the academy, class of ninety. Follow me to the chief mate's office. He is expecting you."

"Yes sir."

"Cut the 'sir' crap with me. I'm only the third mate." Joe smiled, *that's the way I felt years ago when I was boarding my first ship and the third mate told me the same thing*.

Joe took Ian up two flights of stairs and into the house. A quick walk forward and Joe knocked on the chief mate's door frame and entered. "Mate, here's the deck cadet, Mister Ian Blooker"

71

"Well, Mister Blooker, welcome aboard." The mate screwed his eyes up tight as if trying to look into Ian's soul. Ian stiffened. He knew it was all a game to intimidate and belittle the new academy midshipman assigned to his ship, but it was still unnerving. Ian resolved to prove he was serious about the seafaring profession and he wanted it to be his life. "Cadet, I'm busy now. When we get to sea tomorrow, we'll have a chance to chat." He glared at Joe, "I'll let the captain know the deck cadet is aboard and call you when he wants him to come up to his office to sign articles."

"Yes, mate."

"Anything else?" He glared then said, "I'm busy!"

"No, mate." Joe said with an ever so slight sarcastic spin lost on the chief mate.

"See you later, cadet."

"Yes, sir!"

Joe and Ian walked out of the mate's office. "That went well." Joe smiled as he remarked, "Let me show you your stateroom. Your gear should be there waiting for you. Stow your stuff and get into khakis and wait there. I'll come get you in twenty minutes or so."

"Yes, sir."

"Cut the 'sir' crap … remember?" Joe turned the corner and opened the door. "There you are. See you in a few."

"Yes sir." Joe just rolled his eyes and walked away shaking his head.

Ian entered the room, closed the door, and leaned against the bulkhead as he surveyed the room. The room was small yet there was room for a bed, desk, closet and a settee. There was a door to the right of where he stood which lead to a toilet and shower. This space would be his sanctuary, his prison, and his purgatory for the duration of his time onboard. The room was efficiently laid out, with only the essentials and nothing more.

Ian remembered the mate was coming for him in a few minutes so he rushed to stow his gear and changed into his khakis. He was ready to get to work.

As he pulled up his trousers, there was a knock on the door. Ian opened it somewhat bewildered. There was a young woman he vaguely recognized from the academy. "Hi, Ian. I'm Hanna Thorton. I'm a second class engineer midshipman and the other cadet aboard. Put your shirt on, silly!"

"Yes, ma'am"

"My name is Hanna and don't call me ma'am."

Ian fumbled for his shirt and let her in. The door to the passageway was secured open just as they were taught at school when male and female midshipmen were together. *You MUST have the door completely open at all times!* An un-named and faceless voice bellowed from their academy training.

Hanna asked all the important questions, "Is this your first ship? Where are you from? Do you have a girlfriend? What does your father do for a living?"

She spoke like a machine gun, firing one question after another, without waiting for an answer. Ian finally interrupted, "My father died at sea before I was born."

"Oh, I'm sorry to hear that," she said.

Joe came around the corner and Ian blew out a sigh of relief, grateful for an excuse to break away from this aggressive woman. Joe smirked as Hanna continued grilling Ian, who was inching his way into the corner.

"Come on, Ian. I see you've met the engine cadet, Hanna." Joe nodded.

Ian nodded and bolted to Joe's side.

"Uruugh," she said, glaring at Joe. She put her nose in the air, turned on her heels, and with arms crossed, marched out of the room. Over her shoulder, she said, "Ian, see you around."

Joe led Ian aft and out on the deck, down the ladder, to the main deck, and walked to the stern. Ian was overwhelmed with new smells, sights, and his senses were alive as he tried to absorb everything he could. He could smell grease, rust, paint and a number of other odors from the cargo containers as they moved to and from the ship. He was careful to stay right behind Joe.

The mate said, "During cargo operations, always walk on the off-shore side of the ship unless there is a good reason to be pier-side. If you do, never walk under a container or men aloft, understand?"

"Yes, sir,"

Joe cuffed Ian gently on the head. "Kid cut the 'sir' crap already." Joe and Ian shared a smile and Ian knew he had a good mentor and a friend in Joe.

"Kid, let's check the mooring lines. We need to do this every hour to compensate for tide and draft changes."

Joe stood next to a mooring line between the opening in the rail and the drum on the mooring winch fastened on deck. The line was stretched tight and horizontal to the deck about knee high. "Watch me." Joe put his foot on the line and gently felt the tension by bouncing the line up and down. "That's about right. Here, you try it."

Ian did as he was told and copied Joe's technique.

"See how that feels?"

"Yes, sir. I mean, yes!" Ian's cheeks turned pink and Joe just laughed.

Joe took Ian forward to the bow and they repeated the procedure to check the mooring line tension and adjusted several of the lines. Some of the lines were adjusted in and some out to balance the strain. Next, Joe took Ian up to the bridge.

They walked through the door onto the bridge and Ian couldn't contain himself. He looked forward and imagined what it would be like to command this ship at sea. It would only be a few more hours and cargo operations would be complete and the ship headed to Europe.

As Joe filled out the log book, the chief mate called on the walkie talkie. "Joe, bring the cadet to my office."

"Aye, mate." Joe responded and turned to Ian. "Ian, it didn't take long for you to fuck up! The mate wants to see you!"

Ian broke out in a cold sweat. "What did I do?"

Joe laughed again and winked. "Nothing kid, I expect you'll get to meet the old man." Joe escorted Ian down to the mate's office, "Call me and I'll come get the cadet when you're finished, mate."

Even though the mate summoned Ian, he grunted and tossed down his pen. "Follow me, cadet," as he led the way to the captain's office. The mate knocked on the office door frame and waited until he and the cadet were invited in.

The captain came around the corner from his stateroom drying his hands with a towel. He was an older gentleman in a heavy knit sweater, and from the weathered lines on his face, and the thickness of his hands, he had spent a great many years at sea. He said with a genuine smile, "Hello, young man, please have a seat."

The captain nodded to a seat in front of his desk. The mate sat on the settee behind Ian. The captain took a long look at Ian as if to size him up. "Tell me about yourself, young man."

"My name is Ian Blooker. I am from Bristol, Rhode Island. This is my first ship. Thank you for having me assigned to your ship, sir." The last comment made no sense except he was nervous.

The introduction took all of ten minutes and the captain smiled the whole time as he asked several questions. As Ian came to the end of his short introduction, the captain produced an official looking journal and explained the shipping articles. "Each member of the crew signs before the ship can sail off-shore." Ian had already been told about shipping articles and was prepared.

The captain opened the journal and turned it around and pushed it in front of Ian, handed him a pen, and pointed on the ledger where he would sign. His information was already neatly filled in, an indication they expected him. *Good!*

Ian signed as he was told. The captain smiled as he closed the book and placed it back in the top desk drawer. He looked at Ian, "You'll work for the chief mate. He'll assign you to your daily tasks. You'll be expected to work on deck for part of the day and stand watch the other part of your day. He'll provide you the details. You'll work on your sea project," he said, with a serious note in his voice.

"And I'll review your progress weekly. Bring it to me on Saturday morning by ten."

Captain Horne leaned back in his chair and became conversational. "We expect you to take full advantage of this opportunity to become a competent and capable mate. Do you understand?" Horne smiled. This was the same first meeting speech he'd given a hundred times before.

"Yes, sir!"

"Good, then that is all."

Ian stood at attention and saluted. Why, he didn't know, it just felt right. Captain Horne smiled, "Son, this is a merchant ship, we don't salute onboard. Welcome, Ian, and good luck."

The mate slapped Ian on the back of the head gently. "Come on, cadet, follow me." In the meantime the mate and Ian returned to the mate's office and the officer called Joe on the radio. "Joe, where are you?"

"Mate, I'm near hold four starboard side."

"Standby"

"Cadet, can you find hold four starboard side main deck?"

"Yes, sir, I think so."

"Good."

"Joe, the cadet is on his way to your location."

"Standing by"

The mate looked at Ian. "Okay, cadet be on your way. Careful."

"Yes sir, mister mate."

"Mate is fine, cadet"

"Yes, mate."

Ian found the stairs and went down, then walked to the starboard side and out on deck. He missed by one level and ended up standing on the deck above his destination. He found an external stairway to the main deck and hoped no one saw his error. Ian moved forward and found Joe several hundred feet ahead, and with unbridled enthusiasm nearly broke out in a run. Joe pushed his ball cap back and smiled. "Well, kid, how did it go?"

"Very well, I think. The captain seems like a good man."

"He is. He's an academy grad too. Class of eighty-one I think."

Ian looked at Joe. "Why does the mate seem to be put out with me? I haven't done anything to upset him have I?"

"Naw, kid. He's just prickly about cadets. See, he's a hawse-piper and thinks all of us academy guys were born with silver spoons in our mouths. He'll warm up to you. He'll see you really want to sail and not just graduate and go ashore. Give it time, kid. You'll be okay. Stick with me. I'll show you the ropes."

"Yes, sir."

Joe took a good natured swipe at Ian with his ball cap. "Cut the 'sir' crap."

Ian followed his mentor around and listened to every word as he explained the ship, cargo operations, safety and the "do's and don'ts" on a ship. The lessons were conducted as they watched sea containers come over hold four. "Stay out of the crew spaces unless you have official business there. Be polite to the stewards. Never be late to your watch or any function. Always keep one hand on something to support yourself in case the ship rolls.

Ask questions. Work on your sea project. Have fun. This is a great life, kid! Let's get some supper."

They walked aft to the house and the officer's mess. The third assistant engineer smiled and greeted Joe. "Who's your side kick, Joe?"

"Cadet Ian Blooker"

"Hey, kid, my name is Larry."

Just then Hanna walked into the mess. She wore blue overalls stained with soot, oil, and grease from top to bottom. Her nose had a black smudge of grease on the bridge and her hands were dirty from handling machinery and tools.

"Hey, Ian, how are you settling in?"

"Just fine, Hanna. Looks like you've been busy fixing something in the engine room."

"Yes, Larry and I rebuilt an auxiliary pump. It's great! How about you?"

"I'm assigned to follow Joe around and learn the ropes." They shared a smile.

The stewards took meal orders and had the food on the table in a matter of moments. Ian ate slowly as he was still getting used to shipboard life. The other three inhaled their meals and were ready to return to work before Ian had eaten four bites. The engineers stood up, and together looked at Ian and said, "Later, slow poke."

Joe lingered as Ian set down his fork and knifeid, "I'm finished, sir."

Joe smiled. "You'll be hungry later. I'll show you where the stewards put out the night lunch after watch," then they left the mess and returned to the bridge where Joe made a number of entries in the log book.

At twenty-hundred ship's time, the third mate walked onto the bridge. He and Joe chatted for a moment and Joe said, "This is Cadet Ian Blooker."

"Hello, Ian, mein nama ist Fritz," he said with a heavy German accent. Then he turned to Joe and they proceeded with the watch turn-over.

Joe stated, "We should finish cargo operations on your watch tonight. The sailing board is set for zero eight hundred in the morning. Please remind the watch to call out the deck cadet, okay?"

"Ja, okay. Herr Cadet … Velcome aboard."

"Thank you, sir."

Fritz smiled and looked at Joe. "Polite junger, Joe. I have the watch." Fritz said.

Joe turned to Ian. "Follow me, Ian, I'll show you where the night lunch is stored."

Once Ian made a plate, Joe said, "Okay, kid, you're on your own. Good night."

"Good night."

Ian found his stateroom without too much difficulty, opened the door, and sat on his bunk. His mind was racing as he thought about the day. *This morning I was in Bristol and now I'm on a ship with new people and really don't have a clue.* He heard a knock in the bathroom. He walked over and looked in.

He realized there was a door on the other side of the head. Ian reached for the lock on the door and twisted it. He carefully opened the door. Hanna grinned at him. "Hey, silly, you need to keep the door unlocked when you're not in the head. We share the head and shower. I lock your door when I'm in the room and I keep my door locked when I'm not in the head. You may want to do the

80

same. No visits, understood?" She had her hands on her hips.

"Yes, of course," he replied completely surprised at her forwardness.

"Okay, good night."

"Good night," Ian said as she closed the door in his face. He heard the lock click from the other side.

Hanna's a strange woman. In every way she was an independent person who stood on her own, yet she was a woman and an attractive woman at that. She was quite overpowering. *She must be tough on her boyfriends,* he thought.

He backed out of the head, closed the door on his side and locked it from his stateroom. He was ready to lie down and rest. He carefully hung his clothes in the closest and lay down on the bed and his eyes closed before his head hit the pillow.

Ian awoke with a start to knocking on his stateroom door.

"Cadet, it's seven in the morning, we are sailing in an hour and a half. The mate wants you on the bridge in thirty minutes."

"Yes, thirty minutes on the bridge." Ian turned on the lights and looked at his surroundings. This would be his home for a few months. He quickly went to the head and the door was locked from the other side. Hanna was in the shower. He started to dress and listened for the inside lock to be opened. *Click!*

He passed through the door, washed, shaved, dressed and out in fifteen minutes. He found the officer's mess and ordered breakfast. He sat next to Joe.

Joe looked over the top of his newspaper and said, "Good morning, kid. How did you sleep?"

Ian in an overly enthusiast voice said, "Well, thank you, Joe. How did you sleep?"

"Fine"

As the men spoke, Hanna walked into the mess wearing the same dirty overalls she had worn the day before. Ian was in clean and pressed khakis.

As she slid into her seat she said, "Good morning, Ian."

"Morning, Hanna"

Joe and Ian spoke briefly while they ate. Ian was hungry and not bashful about eating a large meal with the speed of an Indy driver.

After they finished, they headed to the bridge and prepared the ship for sea. Ian watched and listened to Joe as he tested gear and prepared the bridge for departure. Ian wondered, *had my dad done the same thing years ago*?

Ian was overwhelmed to see what was involved. Joe did it all with experienced ease and explained each step with clarity and precision. It took twenty minutes, and the bridge was ready. Joe could see the ship's pilot as he arrived by taxi.

"Ian, it's time to get the pilot. This is one of your jobs. Follow me."

They were down the stairs in a flash and stood on the main deck at the brow. As the pilot came up the gangway. By the time he made it to the top of the ninety foot ladder, his cheeks were red and his shoulders heaved as he struggled for breath. Joe thought, *the aging man needed to retire soon or he'd die on the job.*

"Good morning. I'm the third mate and this is our deck cadet. We'll escort you to the bridge. I'm sorry we don't have an elevator on this ship."

The pilot growled something under his breath.

Joe led the pilot and Ian followed a few feet behind. With a minimum of effort they got the pilot to the bridge and offered him coffee. The winded pilot sat in the captain's chair and caught his breath. Joe called the captain.

"Sir, the pilot is in the wheelhouse. Ship is ready for sea."

"Thank you, I'll be right up." Horne said.

"Yes, sir."

"Ian, I'll show you how to hoist the 'hotel' flag," Joe said and grabbed a signal flag that was half red and half white in two vertical panels. Joe, with Ian in tow, left the wheelhouse and went up a ladder to the flag bridge.

"The signal flag tells other ships in the area the ship has a pilot aboard," Joe instructed.

By the time they returned to the bridge, the captain was talking with the pilot. The familiarity of their conversation made it clear to anyone within ear shot they'd known each other for years.

Joe made the final preparations, called the engine room, and informed them to expect engine orders in a few minutes. The chief engineer answered the phone from the control room and confirmed they were ready.

Joe leaned over and whispered to Ian, "Follow me, but be quiet and stay out of the way. It will get busy here in a few minutes. Trust me, you'll feel like a cat on a hot tin roof." Joe moved to the offshore bridge wing and saw two tugs coming fast. The pilot noticed Joe's attention was drawn to the tugs and he said, "*Sarah Jane* forward and the *Laura M* will be aft, mate."

"Thank you, pilot."

Moments later, the tugs were tied to the ship. "*STAND BY ENGINE,*" the captain ordered. Joe moved the engine telegraph and a bell rang until the engineers acknowledged it. Joe looked at the seaman standing behind the helm, "Are you ready, Doug?"

"Yeah, mate." Doug said in a raspy, hushed voice and winked at Ian. Joe kept track of everything and recorded it in the bell book and deck log. Ian watched and thought it was a beautiful chaotic symphony of activity as the ship came to life. Each man, a professional, knew his job. He wanted to be one of them. In fact, with a sudden surge of confidence he thought, *I'll be the best of them one day!*

The pilot and the captain, like they had done hundreds of times before, skillfully positioned the ship into the channel and then, with a burst of power from the propeller, maneuvered the ship away from Port Elizabeth, under the Verrazano Bridge and past Sandy Hook.

As the lighthouse fell behind the ship, the gentlemen bid each other adieu and the pilot headed down on deck to the ladder which had been prepared for him. Ian and Joe escorted him, while the captain stopped the ship and turned it broadside to the wind and created a sheltered lee for the pilot to disembark. The pilot looked over the side next to the ladder prepared for him. The pilot boat was in position below. He looked up to the captain on the bridge wing some sixty feet above him, clasped his hands together and shook them over his head and Captain Horne returned the gesture.

DRAWN TO THE SEA
(First Revision)

The pilot climbed over the rail, balanced himself there for a second, and descended to the boat positioned under the ladder. Once he was safely on the boat deck, he waved as the pilot boat increased speed and pointed away from the ship. The captain saw the boat clear, put the engine telegraph to *HALF AHEAD,* and gave the helmsman a new course of zero seven eight. The pilot boat headed off to deliver the pilot to his next assignment.

The captain looked at his watch, noting the time, reached forward, and pushed the engine telegraph all the way forward to *FULL AHEAD.*

Joe instructed the seaman on deck to secure the ladder for sea and he and Ian climbed the stairs back up to the bridge. By the time they were back in the wheelhouse, the ship was making ten knots on its way to a sea speed of twenty knots.

The helmsman steadied the ship on the course directed and Joe resumed the watch. Captain Horne looked at Ian and with a grin said, "Well, young man, what do you think?"

"It's great, sir. I'm learning a lot. Thank you."

"Remember your sea project. I'll be looking for it on Saturday," then Horne turned and left the bridge.

The *American Spirit* gathered speed and headed off to Rotterdam, the Netherlands.

Eleven
Crossing the Atlantic

The ship was headed towards Ambrose Light, south of Nantucket, cruising at sea speed. Each member of the crew had settled into a routine. The bosun and his deck gang ensured any loose gear had been stowed below deck and each man had tended to his personal belongings long before. Anything not safely secured would move or break as the ship began its constant rolling from side to side in a long, steady pendulum motion. At times, the ship rolled up to twenty-five degrees.

Ian was busy on the bridge with Joe while they plotted the ship's position on the chart and kept a vigilant lookout for ships and other vessels. Ambrose Light was a few miles ahead and marked the point of convergence for ships as they approached or departed New York and New Jersey. Ships of all sizes, configuration and speed approached Ambrose from the north, south, east, and the outbound traffic like the *American Spirit*, used it as a departure point.

Joe was an experienced mate and made the outbound maneuver seem second nature. He was professional, alert and confident. Doug, the able seaman, was a rough, middle-aged man. His rugged face had a Brooklyn meanness etched into its texture, and he enhanced his persona with a godfather-like raspy whisper. His clothes were clean, but the color combinations left no doubt the concept of clashing color combinations and gaudy dress were lost on him.

Doug stood behind the ship's helm keeping the ship on the course Joe had directed. He drove the ship with experienced ease and kept his eyes moving between the gyrocompass, the magnetic compass, the rudder indicator and forward, using the mast sticking up from the deck like a lone tree some seven hundred feet ahead to judge the swinging of the ship in the mounting seas.

"Hey, Mister Blooker," he whispered in his Brooklyn accent. "Wherez youz from?"

Joe broke in, "Doug, not now, steer the ship. There will be time to chat when we're on auto pilot."

"Ya, mate." Doug replied and returned to looking at the compasses.

Joe left the bridge and moved to the chart room where the large table held a number of charts. He looked at the chart on top, did some calculations, put a position on the chart and then moved over to the log book and wrote his summary comments for the four hour watch. He looked into the grey haze for a moment and thought. Then he said,

"Ian."

"Yes, sir." Joe didn't correct him about the 'sir' crap in front of Doug.

"I'll be concentrating on charts for the next five minutes. Keep a good eye out and let me know if you see anything of concern."

"Yes, sir!" Ian felt ten feet tall. In effect, Joe had given him the watch. He really didn't know what to do, but the sense of power and responsibility was awesome. Doug watched and chuckled under his breath. Joe, too, was watching through a crack in the heavy curtain separating the chartroom and the bridge and smiled.

Ian put his hands behind his back and slowly paced back and forth along the forward rail intently looking out over the bow and the port and starboard sides of the vessel. Occasionally, he looked behind, to something driven home by his academy navigation instructor.

"Don't forget to look behind you, too." The voice of Professor Johnson rang in his ear. Meanwhile, Joe finished up his log entries and used the electronic navigation equipment to fix a twelve hundred position on the chart.

"Hummm ... twenty-one point six knots." He commented to himself. "That's fast for the *American Spirit*."

The final thing he needed to do before Fritz relieved him was the weather observation. Joe grabbed his jacket, threw it over his shoulders, and walked onto the port side bridge wing. He stood next to the compass binnacle and sighted over the compass in the direction the sea, swell, and winds were coming from. He noted on a piece of paper, *Swells are eight feet from the north, northeast. Seas are two feet from the north. Winds from the north force two (eight to ten knots).* He looked to the skies. The clouds were scattered and scribbled, *low scattered alto cumulus.* He mumbled as his pencil traveled over the paper.

Joe walked back to the bridge and near the door was a wooden box mounted on the bulkhead. He opened the door and two thermometers were inside. One standard and the other had a moist wick over the sensor. He noticed the dry and wet temperatures. With that, he could determine the dew point. He wrote, *Wet temperature, seventy on the nose and dry temp seventy-six.*

Joe looked over at Ian, "How's it going?"

"Just fine, sir!"

"Good. I'm almost done in the chartroom."

Joe returned to the chartroom and the log book, made the final calculations and entered the wind direction and speed, the sea and swell direction and height, and the wet and dry temperatures, dew point and a weather observation. All that was left now was to wait for Fritz. Joe came out of the chartroom and rejoined Doug and Ian.

"Doug, it's time to put the ship on the 'Iron Mike'. Set your course for zero-seven-nine true."

"Zero-seven-nine mate."

For the next five minutes, they looked out the bridge windows and each thought about something or someone. The long monotonous transit to Europe officially started with the engagement of the auto steering system the ship crew affectionately referred to as 'Iron Mike'.

Fritz and his able seaman Mario "Mugsy" walked through the door right on time.

Mugsy and Doug chatted about nothing in particular. Then Ian heard Doug say, "She's on the 'Iron Mike' zero-seven-nine true; zero six-eight magnetic. Okay?"

"Okay you rat fucker," Mugsy smiled and winked at his friend.

"Fuck you, too, Mugsy," Doug said as he returned the smile and walked by Joe and told him he'd been relieved. Doug turned to Ian, "Seez youz later, kid."

Ian walked over to listen to the officers turn over. Joe explained where they had been and what happened during his watch. He showed Fritz on the chart the projected course and where the ship was at twelve hundred local on the chart. They talked about the weather and the forecast over the next eight hours. Next, they walked out onto the bridge and Joe addressed each ship on the horizon, their course and speed. Finally, he told Fritz they were on course zero-seven-nine true and zero-six-eight magnetic. A black board on the bulkhead in front of the helm had the courses written in chalk as a reminder.

With that Fritz said, "Ja, I have tis vatch."

"Okay. She's all yours," Joe said, and he turned to Ian. "Let's get some chow."

Ian was all too aware Fritz was staring at him. Fritz was trying to recall someone from his past that Ian reminded him of. He couldn't remember but he knew it would be a painful memory when it came back to him.

Ian left the bridge and followed Joe to the mess where they joined Larry and Hanna. Their faces were drawn out and worn as if they hadn't slept in months. While they ate, it was quiet and Ian noticed how attractive Hanna was when she wasn't being haughty and snippy. She was tall for a woman with an athletic figure and her long slender fingers seemed graceful, even though there was grease under her fingernails. Then, there was her skin. It was smooth.

"What're you looking at?" Hanna snapped

"Nothing, sorry," Ian hung his head, feeling heat on his cheeks.

"Keep your eyes to yourself, mister," she said, glaring.

"It won't happen again," he mumbled and kept his eyes looking down at his lap.

Joe and Larry looked at each other, hid their faces, and smirked. Ian caught their expressions and hung his head again. He'd made a newbie mistake. Hanna wasn't a fun-loving college coed looking for romance. She was a career woman, on a ship and had to keep men at arm's length for survival. She was determined to excel in this career without the drama or disasters which had done-in many women before her.

The four finished their meals. Joe and Larry filled their coffee mugs and moved to the adjacent lounge and talked about their car hobbies. Ian stared at his plate and didn't dare look elsewhere lest he get another ass chewing.

His appetite was gone and he asked permission from Hanna, reverting to his academy training, to leave and didn't waste time disappearing. Hanna stirred her food without lifting her fork and then left thirty seconds after Ian. Joe and Larry gave each other a knowing look and grinned.

Ian entered his stateroom and closed the door behind him. His heart raced as he fell onto his rack. *How could I be so stupid? Was it obvious? Have I ruined my chance to make a good impression? Would this get back to the academy?*

He was so preoccupied he didn't notice the heavy rolling had cleared off the papers and books he'd neatly placed on the desk hours before.

In the cabin next door, Hanna paced in her room like a condemned prisoner then grabbed her pillow, pulled it tightly over her face and screamed. *Why did I embarrass him like that? That was mean. Why did I do it? He's a nice guy and wickedly handsome and he doesn't even know it. He wasn't being a pig like most men looking at women. He'll probably never talk to me again.* "Shit! You screwed up, Hanna" she told herself.

In two rooms separated by a bathroom door, two young people, already attracted to one another, struggled in their own drama until they fell asleep exhausted from the activity of the morning and the emotionally draining noon meal. As each slipped off to sleep, their hearts ached knowing there was little possibility they'd ever be together.

At thirteen-fifteen the chief mate pounded on Ian's door with a thundering force and threw it open so hard it shook on its hinges. Startled and confused, Ian was instantly awake.

"You fucking lazy cadet! You're supposed to report to my office at thirteen hundred. You're late. Get your ass out of the rack and get to my office in five minutes."

The chief mate slammed the door and stormed off, hiding the sadistic grin on his face.

Ian rushed to put himself together and ran to the mate's office. Hanna heard the commotion next door and sat straight up in bed with widened eyes. She put her ear to the wall then walked to the door to the head between them. Stopping, she swore under her breath and started pacing the small room like a trapped cat. Ian ran down the hall and knocked on the mate's door frame and waited to be invited in.

"Get in here cadet. Let's get something straight. You'll stand the eight to twelve with Mr. Kelly and at thirteen hundred, Monday thru Friday, you'll report to my office for assignments that'll complete your day. You'll be a day worker from thirteen hundred to sixteen thirty."

Ian tried to nod, but was too flustered.

"Got it, cadet?" The mate growled.

Ian flinched, thinking he saw a hint of amusement in the mate's eyes. Then he caught himself and said, "Sir, yes, sir!!!"

"Good, now what size overall do you wear?

"Medium, sir."

"Okay, follow me."

The mate came around his desk at full speed and with his long legs was down the passageway in a flash and Ian had to trot to keep up. They stopped at the stores locker and the mate fiddled with a key ring until he located the proper key and opened the door. Ian looked inside and saw a large inventory of work clothes, boots, gloves and hard hats. The mate turned to Ian and threw him two pairs of blue overalls, size medium, a pair of gloves, and a white hard hat. "What size are your feet?"

"Sir, size ten please."

"Okay, here you go." The mate threw Ian a pair of black work boots.   He took another quick look around the locker and then closed the door and snapped the lock. "Cadet, you have five minutes. Get changed and report back to my office."

Ian ran down the passageway to his room, yanked off his uniform, and threw on the overalls, hard hat, and boots. *This seems like plebe summer all over again,* he thought. He got back to the mate's office in the allotted time but the mate didn't give him as much as a nod of approval.

"Follow me," the mate growled, and then bolted out from behind his desk. Ian rushed to keep up. The mate was out the door heading aft. Through another door he moved across the outside deck near the lifeboats and down two flights of stairs, and barely touched a step on the way down to the main deck. Still with incredible speed, he turned and headed forward, Ian, two steps behind, running every few steps to keep up.

Ian could see a group of men forward where the mate was headed. An older man in the group saw the mate coming and walked over to greet him. "Hello, mate."

"Yeah, bosun. I'd like to introduce Cadet Blooker, our deck cadet" The mate looked over at Ian.

"Hello, Mister Blooker. I'm the ship's bosun. You can call me 'boats'"

"Yes, sir"

"Call me boats, not 'sir'. Save the 'sir crap' for the officers. I work for a living!" He smiled at the mate.

"Boats, I'd like you to take the cadet under your wing and have him work with the deck gang in the afternoons, Monday thru Friday."

"That's fine, mate."

The mate turned and left, headed back to his office. The bosun said to Ian, "Let me introduce you to the deck gang." Ian found he was easily accepted by the deck gang and enjoyed the physical labor he did in the afternoons.

So Ian's routine was established. He stood watch from eight in the morning until twelve and turned-to with the deck gang under the supervision of the bosun from thirteen hundred to sixteen thirty. Before the evening watch, he worked diligently on his sea project to present to

DRAWN TO THE SEA
(First Revision)

Captain Horne on Saturday morning before ten and he stood the evening eight to twelve bridge watch.

He saw Hanna in the mess for breakfast and lunch and from time to time would hear her in the head but not a word was shared between them. Ian didn't want it that way, but the circumstances left him with few other options.

Ian busied himself with watch standing, working with the deck gang and his sea project. He learned the skills needed to become a competent mate from his friend and mentor, Joe, and learned about ship maintenance and leadership from the bosun. He worked hard to keep on top of his sea project and had little time to do much else. Ian ate, worked, slept, and the days flew by.

It seemed it was only the day before they had left New Jersey, but seven days had passed as Ian traced his finger over the chart which showed the European continent at the far right side of the large paper. He thought with excitement, *Tomorrow we'll arrive in Europe.*

His first time overseas ... he could hardly wait.

Chapter Twelve
Rotterdam

The night before the *American Spirit* was scheduled to arrive at Rotterdam, Ian was too excited to sleep. His mind raced ... his first foreign port, what would it be like? He lay awake and thought of all the beauty and mystery waiting for him there.

He wondered if his father had grown up in Rotterdam or if he'd ever been there. Ian knew his father was a Dutchman and his family name was van der Waterlaan but that was about all his mother had told him. Ian thought back to the picture taken twenty years ago of his mother and father which she kept in her bedroom. *It's true, I do look like my father.*

His focus shifted to Hanna for the first time since she had embarrassed him in front of Joe and Larry. He wondered if she was still mad. He wanted someone to explore Rotterdam with tomorrow and he wanted that person to be her.

He got out of bed and moved to the head and looked at the door to Hanna's room. Motionless, he tried to hear Hanna behind the door. Scared, excited, and embarrassed he felt an undeniable sense of desire which spurred him on. Then as if a bolt of lightning rushed through him, he realized what he was doing, spun away from the door, and returned to his bed.

He looked at the overhead as he lay awake. *Why is this so hard?* And he tried in vain to sleep – he'd be on watch in a few more hours.

Hanna flipped her pillow over and curled up on her side. She stared at the door to Ian. Their physical separation was only ten feet and a door but it may as well have been a thousand miles.

On the deck above, the captain sat at his desk and read a message the radio operator had just delivered.

> *From: Berkman Shipping Agents, Rotterdam*
> *To: Captain Horne, Master 'American Spirit'*
>
> *I regret to inform you there is a pending labor strike throughout the Netherlands. It will most certainly affect stevedores and longshoreman. Negotiations between labor and management are ongoing but appear unproductive. Strike is set for midnight tomorrow.*
> *We have contacted your home office and been advised to have you arrive and commence cargo operations. Any delays will be handled as they occur. I regret this late breaking news. I'll meet the ship on arrival with any additional information.*
> *Best,*
> *Joop Sweers, Agent*

Captain Horne read the message for a second time. It was Saturday and no one would be in the New York office. Horne had the operations officer's home number and considered calling him to confirm he didn't want the ship rerouted. It was unusual for a containership company to allow a ship to potentially be mired down by a labor strike. Hell, the *American Spirit* was carrying four hundred and thirty-seven refrigerated containers full of food and other perishables.

Horne reached for his personal phone book and opened it to "Z", found the number next to Zucker, Hiram - Ops Boss, American Shipping Corp. The connection by satellite was as clear as if they sat next to each other. After the third ring New York answered, "Zucker."

"Hiram, this is John Horne on the *American Spirit*. Look, I'm sorry to bother you on the weekend, but I need to confirm a message I received from the Rotterdam agent."

"Okay."

"The message indicated there may be a country-wide labor strike in Holland. It'll start tomorrow at midnight. We're scheduled to arrive in the morning and will most likely get tied up in any delays or work stoppages. The message leads me to believe you're aware of this and directed me to proceed to port as scheduled. Is that correct? We have 437 refrigerated containers aboard with perishable cargo. Any delays and we may lose the cargo."

Zucker looked at the lush garden through the window of his massive Long Island home and said, "John, we're aware and tried to reroute you to Antwerp and even Bremerhaven, but the terminals were backed up. I ran it by the company president this morning and he understands the risk and directed we stick to the original schedule. We'll hope for the best."

"Hiram, thank you for your time. I'm sorry for bothering you. We'll arrive at the sea buoy at zero nine hundred local tomorrow. I'll communicate with you from port as the story unfolds."

"Thanks … do that, John. Good night."Zucker watched his wife climb into the hot tub.

"Good night" and the phone went dead.

The captain shook his head. "Maybe it's time for me to retire. This decision makes no sense," he muttered to himself. Sighing, he said, "Oh well, that's why I go to sea and the sand crabs stay ashore." Horne smirked and hung up the phone.

He reached for the ship's phone again and dialed the chief mate. The phone rang once and the mate answered, "mate."

"Mate, captain here, sorry it's so late, but please come to my office, I need to talk to you."

"Yes sir."

Horne hung up and dialed the man in the office next door, the chief engineer. "Skip, can you step into my office."

"Be right there, John."

Captain Horne walked around his desk and stood in front of his Keurig coffeemaker and made himself a strong cup. He checked to see if the water reservoir was full for his guests. A few minutes later, the mate was standing in the doorway. "Boss, may I come in?"

Horne looked over and said, "Yes, of course. Would you like coffee?"

"Yes, please, black." The mate fell into a chair.

"Very well" The captain inserted a coffee pod and pushed the button. "Damn machine makes a perfect cup of coffee on demand. Even my wife can't do that!" Horne smiled.

Just then, the chief engineer rolled in the door and grabbed a seat next to the mate. The familiarity between the captain and chief was common on merchant ships. The fact that John Horne and Skip Prosser were friends and had sailed together since they were midshipmen twenty-three years ago was clear. "Skip … coffee?"

"Nay, Captain. I've had enough for the day! What brings the three of us together at one o'clock in the morning?" Prosser addressed the eight-hundred pound elephant in the room. "God, I hope it's not one of your Italian jokes!" He said as he leaned way back in the chair.

The captain brought the freshly brewed coffee to the mate and sat down at his desk. "Gentlemen, I received this message a few minutes ago." He passed it to the chief who read it and passed it to the mate. When they had both read the message, and the mate returned it to the captain, the room was silent.

Captain Horne said, "I called Zucker in New York to confirm the company wants us to continue into Rotterdam and he confirmed it."

The mate alarmed said, "Captain, we have four hundred and thirty-seven reefer boxes which must get to market or they'll spoil."

"I know, mate, and so does the home office."

The chief piped in, "I have some major engine work scheduled and have contractors flying in from Zurich. They may not cross the picket line."

Horne leaned back in his chair and tried not to be annoyed with his friend and said, "Skip, this isn't Chicago, the Dutch don't have picket lines. They'll just stay home."

The captain gave his friend a gentle smile and continued, "But I understand we may get part way through a job and lose your help. Chief, can you postpone the work or ensure your engineers can put us back together if the contractors walk?"

"Yes, I can."

"Mate, how about on deck? Any major work planned?"

"No, sir."

"Is the steward expecting critical provisions? Can we make it back to New Jersey with the food we have?"

The mate responded, "We took on a full load of provisions in New Jersey last week, we should be fine for another couple of weeks."

"Good. Anything else, gentlemen?"

"Nope," said the mate.

"Nope," replied the chief.

"We'll pick up the pilot at nine this morning. Let's hope for the best. Good night."

"Good night," and the mate stood up handed the captain the empty coffee cup and left the office.

The chief lingered for a moment. "John, remember when we were cadets and the same thing happened to us in Rotterdam? We were stuck here for two weeks."

"Yea, Skip. I remember. It was great for us as cadets. I can't but wonder if the sand crabs running the company know what they're doing. Do you and Dottie ever talk about retiring?"

"Yep, all the time. How about you and Jeanne?"

"Yes, and I think we will very soon," Horne said to his friend.

They smiled at each other and Prosser returned to his office. Horne stood alone and said in a whisper, "Yes, I think it's time for me to retire."

At seven thirty, a deck below, starboard side, aft, there was a knock on the door. "Cadet, it's seven thirty. Your watch is in thirty minutes."

Ian spoke back to the door. "Okay, I'm up." Twenty seconds later he heard a muffled knocking on the door to the room next door. "Cadet, it's seven thirty. Your watch is in thirty minutes, ma'am." Ian heard Hanna as she acknowledged the wake-up call through the wall. Both cadets hadn't slept, and now they faced a busy day with tired eyes and weary minds.

Ian, as usual, let Hanna use the bathroom first. He continued to give her a wide berth and patiently listened as the water ran in the head and then the telltale unlocking of the door from the inside of the bathroom indicating she was finished and had returned behind the door to her stateroom.

Ian rushed into the head and looked at himself in the mirror. He noticed the short time at sea had already etched his face. His eyes were a little puffy and red and his young face had changed into that of a man. His hair was longer than he'd worn it since plebe summer. It felt shaggy, but in a way made him 'a man of the sea'. Ian spoke to the face in the mirror, "Dad, did you watch the same transformation?"

Ian washed, shaved, and brushed his teeth. He heard Hanna open and close the door as she headed down to breakfast. Minutes later, Ian was dressed in a crisp uniform and in his seat at the table.

Breakfast was a blur as the four ate with nothing but a minimum of conversation. Hanna looked at Ian and gave a brief smile. Too discreet for Larry or Joe to notice, but Ian did and his heart jumped with excitement. *Maybe she likes me after all.* As if in unison, all four stood up. Joe and Larry said, "Good luck."

Hanna looked at Ian and said, "See you later."

Okay, see you later," Ian responded.

With that the engineer and mate headed to their watch stations with their respective cadet in tow, Ian was floating in air … *Hanna is talking to me again.* He walked onto the bridge and ran into the captain. "Oh, excuse me, captain, I'm so sorry."

"Damn it, watch where you're going, cadet!" Horne growled.

Joe whispered into Ian's ear, "Stay clear of the old man. Something's eating him this morning."

The ship approached the sea buoy, at nine 'local time', and the captain slowed it to a crawl to allow the Rotterdam pilot to board. The pilot wore a bright orange heavy foul weather jacket and climbed the pilot ladder with experienced ease. *The boat is rather large for a pilot boat,* Ian thought.

Ian was waiting for him at the rail and escorted him from the main deck to the bridge. Then without being reminded, hoisted the "H" flag and returned to his station on the bridge where his job was to observe and assist as directed.

The captain and pilot spoke, orders were given, and the ship began to gain speed and point towards the inner harbor. Large tugs met the ship as it entered the harbor and escorted it to half a mile of the berth before presenting themselves to the crew on deck to tie-up. Again, a well-orchestrated series of tasks ensured the ship was safely and efficiently tied up to the dock under the awaiting gantry cranes. By ten forty-five local time, the captain called from the wing of the bridge, "ALL FAST." "*FINISHED WITH ENGINES.*"

Horne and the pilot came into the wheelhouse and proceeded down to the captain's office. Horne turned to Ian, "Ian, I'll call you on the radio when the pilot is ready to depart. He'll be in my office." The two seasoned gentlemen left the bridge and went down a flight of stairs to the office.

Ian heard the captain as the bridge door closed behind him say, "What about the strike?" and they disappeared from view.

Ian and Joe were left on the bridge where they hurried to secure the equipment prior to cargo operations. Carlos was down with the deck gang preparing the gangway and the hatches for cargo operations.

Chapter Thirteen
A Ritual

No sooner had the ship tied up, stevedores came aboard in buckets slung under the gantry cranes. They were lifted from the dock below and lowered on deck, a dozen at a time. The giant cranes hovered overhead and dwarfed the otherwise large ship. Four cranes were dedicated to the *American Spirit*.

Down on the dock, men, trucks and machines were scurrying around like ants as a line of trucks pulled empty chassis and neatly lined up parallel to the ship ready to be positioned one at a time under a suspended sea container as it hung under the gantry. No sooner was the container on the chassis, the crane released the box and the cycle continued in a pre-determined sequence. This process was repeated over and over by each of the gantry operators as they plucked containers from the ship.

Later the process would be reversed and containers destined for America would be delivered under the crane by the same trucks and the gantry operator would capture and lift the container and place it in a pre-determined location on the ship. And so the cycles would continue until each container intended for off-load in Rotterdam was off and every container destined for the *American Spirit* was properly stowed. Normally, the

American Spirit would be in Rotterdam thirty six to forty hours, then head west back to Port Elizabeth, New Jersey.

Twenty minutes later, the deck gang had the gangway lowered and in place. The customs and immigration agents boarded and cleared the ship in under an hour and by then the pilot had been escorted down to the gangway and whisked away by a waiting car. Ian and Joe kept track of containers leaving the ship and guests and crew coming and going while the wild, but organized chaos, continued all around them.

Soon it was eleven thirty and the two climbed the stairs to the wheelhouse. It was nice to see the activity high above the deck. From this vantage point, it was quiet with only the muffled sound of the crane cables, whining as they moved back and forth. Ian looked across at the crane drivers and down at the trucks on the dock. In the distance, he could see miles of containers and ships as far as the eye could see lining the port, each busy in the throes of their own cargo operations. Joe looked at Ian and said, "Hey kid, Rotterdam is the busiest port in the world. Can you believe it?"

"Wow … looking at this, I can believe it for sure." Ian's eyes were bright with excitement.

A few minutes before noon, Fritz came through the door. "Goooode afternoon," he said, in his heavy German accent.

The mates completed the turn over and Joe and Ian, both hungry, made their way to the mess for lunch. Ian was starved and tired from the night before. The men sat and ordered hamburgers and fries. Just as the steward left with their order, Larry and Hanna entered. They both looked miserable, dirty, exhausted and flushed. "Larry, you look like hell, what's up?" Joe said lightheartedly.

"We're lucky we made it alongside this morning. We just about lost the main engine. Two of the cylinders are weak and the engine can barely idle."

"Wow."

"We have contractors coming from Zurich but there is word of a labor strike starting tonight," Larry said, as he turned to the steward and ordered two hamburgers and fries for himself.

Ian noticed the dark circles under Hanna's eyes. It must have been a tough watch this morning. She ordered, "Hamburger, no bun and no fries." As the four of them devoured their meals, the captain stuck his head in the door. "Cadets, join the chief and me in the officer's dining room after you've finished your meals. Come as you are," and he turned and left the room.

Ian looked at Hanna and panicked. Did she say something to the captain or the chief? Was he in trouble? Oh shit! She looked back at him and lifted her shoulders, her eyes widened as she bit her lower lip.

Both stared at their plates then pushed them away. Joe and Larry exchanged knowing looks and Joe covered his smirk with his hand. Larry muffled a laugh in his sleeve. Hanna sighed and stood up. "Ian, are you ready?"

"Yes, Hanna"

"Then let's get this over with."

The two cadets stood and left the mess, Joe and Larry chuckled under their breath as they shared a conspiratorial nod.

Hanna and Ian approached the officer's dining room and Ian realized he'd never been there before. Hanna had only been there once.

The captain and chief were sitting together at a table set for four. The captain saw the cadets peeking in from the door and motioned for them to enter. The room was arranged like a nice restaurant found in any American city. The seats were upholstered and the table clothes and napkins were linen. The cadets felt out of place as cautiously entered the room.

The senior officers had finished their meals and were talking over coffee alone in the room. The cadets approached to the table and sat in the two empty seats. Hanna's cheeks were flushed and beads of perspiration clung to Ian's forehead.

 Horne cleared his throat and started, "Ian, so this is your first time in Rotterdam. Are you two planning on going ashore? I ..." he corrected himself, "We hope you are." He nodded at the chief and the chief nodded back."

Hanna said, "Sir, I must help with the machinery repairs ... I don't think there will be time."

The chief set down his coffee and in a kind voice said, "Hanna, going ashore is as important to your sea year experience as working on the ship. We'll manage without you this one time." He smiled. She looked down and then back up at her boss. Her cheeks were blazing red. The chief went on, "Hanna, we have a more important assignment for you." She raised her eyebrows and sat up a little straighter.

"Captain Horne and I would like you to go ashore with Ian and show him around. You will be responsible for teaching him how to be safe in a foreign port. Do you understand?"

She perked up, "yes, sir."

"Good, you are both relieved of your shipboard duties until midnight before we sail," the captain said with a smile. Then he handed each cadet an envelope. "Here is one hundred and fifty dollars for each of you compliments of the chief and me for your hard work. Be safe and stay together at all times."

Ian looked at Hanna and then at the senior officers and said, "Thank you, sirs"

"Get ashore you two," said the chief said and waved his hand as if he were shooing away gadflies. The cadets stood at attention and walked to the door.

Moments before Joe and Larry had quietly followed behind the cadets and stood outside of the door, out of sight but in ear shot. They laughed as the cadets walked between them. Another rite of passage completed. Every academy midshipman went through it.

Still seated at the table, the senior officers smiled. They had continued an academy tradition. John Horne looked forward to sharing this event with Jeanne, his wife, when they spoke later and he planned to open discussions about retiring after his contract was over. He wanted to see how she felt about her husband of twenty years being home for more than a month at a time.

The midshipmen walked back to their cabins and went through their respective doors without a word. Ian, in his room, looked towards the bathroom door. He had looked that direction a lot over the last week as thoughts of Hanna ran through his head. He found himself stepping towards the door as if being drawn there. Just then, he heard a gentle knock from the other side.

Ian froze. There was the knock again. He reached for the door and when it fell open Hanna was there in shorts and a T-shirt cut several inches above her mid-section exposing the curve of her waist and her flat, firm abs.

Ian started to stare then quickly looked away, afraid he would get in trouble again. He hadn't seen her out of her overalls before, and he wasn't prepared for the effect. He stood there, jaw gaping and eyes darting towards anything but Hanna.

"Ian, may I come in?"

"Um, sure," he backed away from the door and ended up against the opposite wall. "I should open the door," he said, glancing at the door to the passageway.

"Don't bother, it's okay," she said, entering the room like a cat, eyeing everything, mindful of danger. "Relax, Ian, I came to talk for a few minutes. Sit down and please don't stand at attention against the wall like a plebe."

He sat on the settee and she sat on the chair across from him, stretching out her long, sculpted legs. It was impossible for Ian not to notice. She rubbed her eyes and said, "So we are going ashore together. I need some sleep first. I didn't sleep last night."

"Neither did I," Ian offered, losing the fight not to stare at Hanna's tan legs and torso. He glanced up to her face and realized she noticed his attention. Her eyes danced a bit and she gave him a half-smile.

"Let's rest for a bit. I'll knock on the door at around twenty hundred. Okay?"

"Okay," he repeated. "What should I wear?" he asked.

"Jeans, a buttoned shirt and jacket. It gets cold here at night." She got up and stood over him, which offered a good look at her. "Good night for now," and she walked back through the bathroom door, pulling it closed behind her.

Ian grinned as he watched her walk away. He crawled into his bed thinking of her until his dreams replaced consciousness.

Chapter Fourteen
Ashore

The cadets had the money the captain and chief had given them in their pocket and Hanna had discreetly slipped a little foil package in her purse as well.

They walked to the ship's brow where they met Joe standing watch. He and Doug were leaning on the rail looking inattentively off into the distance, toward a sea of containers and the city that seemed to go on forever. Doug noticed first and nudged the mate, "Look mate, they make such a pretty couple."

"Knock it off Doug, you know the cadets must go ashore together. Rules, man, rules!"

"Yeah, whatever, mate." His eyes were full of a devilish glint, his eyebrows cocked to one side as he produced a seedy smile.

"Stop it Doug … I'm warning you," Joe growled and Doug's face lost all expression.

Hanna nudged Ian with her elbow as they walked by. "Did you hear them?" She hissed.

"Yup," Ian said, not wanting to face her and walked faster to the brow.

Joe waved them off. "Have fun and stay together!"

They descended the gangway to the dock below. A short walk amidst the commotion on the pier to the terminal gate and they found a taxi waiting for a fare. Hanna looked over her shoulder, "Remember, we are at the Prinses Beatrixhaven Container Terminal near the Maas Tunnel."

"Got it!" The excitement in his eyes matched the excitement in his voice.

They jumped into the cab. Hanna told the driver, "Bitte … Witt de Withstraat … De Witte Aap"

"Ja, Ja." The driver replied and drove his BMW sedan into traffic, headed north towards the Maas Tunnel and crossed under the harbor and surfaced in the center of Rotterdam.

Ian had his eyes focused outside of the car and tried to take it all in. He appreciated Hanna taking the lead. He thought, *I need to make sure I thank her.*

Rotterdam was much like any other large city, but it was different just the same. Of course the signs were in Dutch, almost close enough to English to understand, but then again not. The people on the streets were from around the world, some wearing exotic clothes he'd never seen before. *What an interesting melting pot of culture and people,* he thought.

"The sun is setting," Hanna said. Ian focused on her voice and nodded.

The driver skillfully maneuvered his car through the traffic and in short order was parked in front of the café. Hanna leaned forward and handed him a few bills.

Ian was first out and reached back into the car to help Hanna to her feet. "What did you give him? Those weren't euros!"

"You're right, they are guilders, Dutch money used since the 1400s. They're still used here. They don't shift to euros until 2002." Hanna pointed to the café. "This is my favorite place to eat in Rotterdam. Let's grab a bite here and then we'll do something else. Later if you want, we can come back. There's usually a big gathering of people pouring out onto the streets. It's kind of cool to see. It's a big party and lots of fun to watch."

Ian said, "Okay, I'm hungry."

"Sure, follow me," and Hanna walked into the restaurant where a young blond waiter came running up to her. "Hanna, welcome back. How was America? We missed you here. Oh ... who is your handsome gentleman friend? Goedeavond meneer ..." The waiter said to Ian.

Ian forehead wrinkled. "What?"

"Oh, forgive me, I thought you were a Dutchman." The waiter said, fumbling with some menus. "You see, we Dutch are usually pretty good at picking out Americans a mile away. You fooled me. Please follow me, I'll seat you two." The waiter led them to a quiet table in the back of the restaurant. "There you go, enjoy your meal."

"Thank you, Hans," Hanna said as he disappeared. She looked at Ian and smiled. "Here we are ..."

Awkwardness descended like fog and Ian was unsure of what to do or say. He focused on the menu and ordered. They sipped table wine and waited for their food to arrive with only a few words between them. Hanna shifted in her seat and cleared her throat, found her voice and said, "Ian, I really don't know anything about you. Please tell me about yourself."

His face lit up at the safe topic. He smiled and started his story. He told her about growing up in Bristol. He told her about his sister and her horrible predicament in California. He talked about his mother with respect and admiration and how he thought she and her best friend Maria, were, or at least soon would be, lovers, and it was a good thing because they were so compatible.

Ian spoke of his grandparents and how they, especially grandfather Stanley, were key role models. Ian talked about his sailboat and his first dog, Thor, the black lab, when he was just a boy. As he spoke, they relaxed and enjoyed their moments together.

The meals came somewhere in the middle of the story and were only picked on as Ian continued. Hanna was a good listener, nodding and smiling, and only interrupting to order another bottle of wine. When Ian paused, she asked a question, prodding him to continue. He found himself speaking freely, without censure. Maybe it was the wine, but he sensed it was Hanna who put him at ease.

As Ian was coming to the end of his story, Hanna asked, "What about your father? You didn't tell me about him."

Ian eyes were cast downward. "That's something I really don't know much about," he said. "My father met my mother when she lived in Tampa. He was a mate on a ship called the *Amore Islander*, I think. The ship sank in the Pacific and all hands died."

"Do you know his name?" She said quietly, a slight frown crossed her face.

"Yes, his name was Ian van der Waterlaan. Mom said he was Dutch."

"Have you ever tried to find his family here in Holland?"

"No, I never considered it."

For the first time since Ian began his story, the spell, which had overcome them both, was broken and they noticed it was getting late so they agreed to head back to the ship.

Ian asked for the check and paid in dollars, which the waiter accepted, and brought change back in guilders, surely with a hefty tax applied for his inconvenience. The couple walked into the sobering cold and saw a wild party pouring out into the street.

Hanna grabbed Ian's hand and pulled him around the corner down a back alley to the well-lit street fifty yards ahead of them. There they were bathed in street lights surrounded by pedestrian and automobile traffic. "It's safe here, we can hail a cab." Hanna said.

Still holding hands they waited a few minutes until a taxi pulled up and they jumped into the warm car.

The driver, an honest man, delivered them back to the Prinses Beatrixhaven Terminal without delay or detour for the sake of running up his fare. It didn't matter to the young couple in the back seat. Ian and Hanna were preoccupied holding hands and stealing glances. As the cab stopped, their hands uncoupled.

Ian paid the driver and they climbed out. He noticed it first. "Hanna, there is something wrong." They walked through the security corridor into the terminal. "Hanna, the cargo operations have stopped and the terminal is deserted. Not even a security guard is here at the gate."

"You're right. I guess the threatened strike has happened."

They walked through the abandoned yard, the equipment was silent and most of the work lights were off.

DRAWN TO THE SEA
(First Revision)

It was quiet with the eeriness of a crypt. The only sounds came from the ship, its auxiliary machinery running and the fully lit ship stood in contrast to the darkened terminal.

The cadets came up the gangway and were met by Fritz and Mario. "Did you have a gooode evening in Rotterdam?" Fritz asked.

"Yes, we did," Hanna said, then turned her head and walked to her cabin. Ian stood at the brow and wondered what had just happened. She had been so pleasant and warm when they were ashore.

Once on the ship, she flipped a switch and instantly became cold and indifferent. The air around her became frigid and uninhabitable. Ian reeled back, confused, and a quizzical look came over his face as he headed to his cabin.

The morning watch would come soon.

Chapter Fifteen
The Labor Strike

The next morning Ian had every intention to talk with Hanna about the abrupt change in her attitude as they boarded the ship. *Did I do something wrong or is she crazy?* Ian had every right to be confused, all the women in his life, up until now, were stable and predictable.

At breakfast Joe and Larry talked about the strike and tried to figure how long they'd be stuck in port. The officers were in a noisy conversation when the cadets came in, Hanna first and Ian a few seconds behind.

"Well" Joe said, his face animated, "How was your first night on the town? What did you cadets do for fun?"

Hanna looked over at Joe with a serious look and her face and her cheeks flashed red, "I don't want to talk about it." A moment later she had composed herself and in a calm voice said, "Nothing, we went to Café de Witte Aap, had a nice meal, and came back to the ship."

Joe and Larry waited for her to continue. When she didn't they resumed their conversation about the strike and ignored the cadets as they ordered their breakfast. Ian didn't dare say a word. He ate and when Joe was ready followed him like a puppy.

He hoped Hanna was just trying to keep her distance with him for the ship's sake. Even though he was new, he was aware a romance on board would stink like old fish in a drawer.

On her supervisor's heels, Hanna asked, "What are we working on today, Larry?"

Larry looked over his shoulder, "Evaporators … the worst job in the engine room and we have it!" They descended down into the pit.

Meanwhile, Joe asked Ian, "Hey, kid, is everything okay?"

"Its fine Joe, why do you ask?" Ian replied.

"You're awful quiet, that's why."

"Just tired," Ian lied. It sounded lame even to his ears.

For the next four hours Ian was distracted and Joe sensed it. Since there were no cargo operations, no stevedores, no provisions delivered to the ship, the two of them just leaned on the rail and looked off into the distance. Ian tried to process his feelings for Hanna and understand the wild swings in her personality. He was confused, a little angry, and needed to get to the bottom of it. He relived each moment, her visit to his room, the cab ride, the dinner, his story, the ride back to the ship, and the abrupt change when they boarded the ship.

It was twelve when Fritz relieved them on the bridge. The turnover was quick and simple. "Nothing's happening." Joe said.

Ian wasn't hungry so he went straight to his room. He put on his athletic shorts and sat in the chair at his desk. He could hear Hanna next door and he needed to talk to her, but didn't dare. A few moments later he heard the

119

shower. His mind wandered as he thought about her in the shower. He shook his head, snapped out of his fantasy, and focused on his sea project sitting in front of him more than a little embarrassed about where his mind had taken him.

Later he heard the shower stop and muffled noise as Hanna dried herself and moved into her room. He tried to stay focused on his project, when there was a gentle tap on the bathroom door. His heart thumped in his chest. He jumped and started to run for the door and then stopped. *What am I doing?* He thought and he his forehead began to perspire.

There was another gentle knock on the door and he opened it. There she was in the same clothes she wore during her last visit. "Hello, Ian," she whispered.

He stood there, his muscular chest bare and his strong legs visible half way up his thighs. "Yes?" He said, completely unaware his nearly naked body was driving her wild.

You're more perfect than I could have imagined, she secretly told herself as she surveyed his body. Little did she know her short shorts and exposed torso had the same effect on him?

"I'd like to talk to you," she said. "May I come in?"

"Yea, sure"

"Thank you. I hate to ask, but would you mind putting on a shirt? You're making me uncomfortable."

"Okay," he said, feeling flustered. *Maybe she could put on some clothes too! Then I could complete a full sentence without stuttering!* He pulled a T-shirt over his head without taking his eyes off of her.

She said, "Let's go ashore again this afternoon. Nothing is happening on the ship, as least until this foolish strike is over. I want to take you to the maritime museum and I know a great Irish pub not far from there. What do you say?"

"That sounds good to me, but I need to clear it with the mate first. Okay?"

"Sure. When do you want to go?"

"How about one thirty this afternoon? Okay? Oh, one more thing. I'd like to find an international phone to call home and say hello to my mother."

"Sure, Ian, you're a good guy."

"Hanna, what should I wear?"

"Jeans, sneakers, and a sweatshirt for later will be fine."

"Great."

Hanna stared at Ian's T-shirt, and Ian thought she seemed a little sad.

"Is everything alright?"

"Yes, why?" Without waiting for an answer, she closed the door behind her and locked it. Ian stood there for a moment, processing what had just happened. Then he threw on his overalls and shoes and left to ask permission of the chief mate to go ashore.

Ian stood in front of the mate's office and knocked on the door frame. The mate looked. "Yes, Ian, what do you want?" He had started to call the cadet by his first name in private conversations several days ago. He continued to call him, "cadet," in public and still rode him hard to earn his keep.

"Sir, I'd like permission to go ashore with the engine cadet this afternoon to visit the maritime museum and see more of the city, sir."

"Are you keeping up with your sea project?"

"Yes, sir"

"Well, since cargo operations are stopped because of this damn strike, there is not much for you to do onboard. Sure, but you two stay together and get back before midnight. With the strikes, there may be trouble on the streets. Keep your eyes open and take care of the engine cadet. Understand?"

"Yes, sir, and thank you." Ian turned on his heels and ran back to his room. The mate smiled.

"Oh to be young again," he mused, and returned to his paperwork.

***

The agent was with the captain most of the morning discussing the strike and the limited options available to the ship and Horne. The newspapers and television reported negotiations had broken down and there was no end in sight to the general labor strikes which crippled the country. Garbage piled up on the streets, trains and buses sat idle without drivers, manufacturing was at a standstill, and even the hospitals were minimally manned. It was a mess.

Though the pilots were not striking, the tugs, the pilot boat operators were, so ships couldn't leave or enter port. The containers sat on the ship, ship's power kept the refrigerated containers at proper temperature. However, the clock ticked as fruit, vegetables, and meat products reached their shelf life. The insurance adjusters were already sharpening their pencils, anticipating a deluge of claims.

The ship had sufficient food and provisions for three weeks. The engineers worked on the necessary engine repairs without the on-site assistance of the contractor who refused to work during the strike. The Swiss were supportive over the phone with advice and recommendations from their offices in Zurich, but they refused to send any of their mechanics.

Prosser was livid. "These rats won't help us because of the strike, but will answer our questions from their offices in the Alps. These guys aren't even Dutch, why would they care? To hell with them, we'll fix the main engine ourselves. Don't worry, John," Skip reassured his friend during their morning and evening meetings. "Remember when this same fucking thing happened to us as cadets? The whole damn country stopped." The captain nodded and thought, *that was a long time ago.*

Captain Horne's hands were tied. For the time being he could do nothing but wait as his crew became bored and frustrated. Then there was the matter of the prostitutes, drugs and bars. It would only be a matter of time and the crew would take up residence in the local brothels and then the chaos would begin. It was like the *American Spirit* was sitting on a powder keg and a match was lit.

***

Ian knocked on Hanna's door, "The mate said, it's okay for us to go ashore. I'll be ready in twenty minutes."

Hanna smiled, "Okay, see you then."

They left the ship with the remaining money the captain and chief had given them the other day and headed to the terminal where the taxis were waiting. The taxi business was booming without buses and trams to compete with. They had the transportation market temporarily cornered.

The young mariners jumped into a Mercedes Benz with a taxi sign in the front window. An Arab-looking man was behind the wheel wearing a red felt hat with a tassel. *Quite an interesting clothing accessory,* Ian thought. Hanna asked the driver to take them to the Maritime Museum near the center of town. He smiled and skillfully moved the car into the traffic pattern toward the Maas Tunnel.

Ian leaned forward and spoke to the driver, "Sir, that's a very interesting hat you're wearing. What is it called?"

"It's called a fez. It's a customary hat for Turkish men. I'm recently emigrated from Istanbul," the driver said, as he turned to look at Ian and gave a large smile. A few minutes later, the driver delivered them to the front steps of the museum. Hanna reached into her pocket and pulled out more guilders and paid the driver, "Thanks."

"You're most welcome, young Americans."

The couple walked up a dozen stairs and entered the museum. It was a stone building resembling a church, with large rooms and tile floors echoing every step. There were pictures and artifacts, charts and displays. All were interesting and told stories of man's struggle to master the sea. The Dutch were some of the first to venture great distances on ships to seek wealth and the museum presented their story with pride and detail capturing the young mariner's imagination.

DRAWN TO THE SEA
(First Revision)

They found the Mataro model. It was a fifteenth century boat model completely intact and such a significant exhibit it warranted its own room. In the center of the room, under a glass case, the model stood as correct and accurate as the day it was finished six hundred years ago. Hanna and Ian were awestruck with the detail and agelessness of the exhibit.

Young and interested as they were, they were both getting weary of looking at old things.

Hanna turned to Ian and said, "Let's go over to Paddy Murphy's and have a couple of beers."

"Great, I'm getting tired of the museum," Ian rolled his eyes playfully.

"Me too," Hanna gushed.

It was a short walk and they enjoyed the fresh air and watched people on the street. The business executives and their staffs were conservatively dressed in suits and dresses while the shoppers and others were dressed in an assortment of garb.

"Rotterdam is an eclectic city," Ian said as they walked through the business district surrounded by tall office buildings and well-manicured gardens in front of them. Expensive cars and limousines moved up and down the street.

They got to Paddy Murphy's, sat at the bar, and ordered two beers. Paddy's, an upscale Irish pub, was quiet and dark. *This is perfect,* Ian thought. Hanna suggested they move to a table. The bartender nodded as he polished a glass with his towel.

Hanna took a deep breath and Ian could see she was troubled. He acted with the speed of a lunging tiger and reached out and touched her hands, "Tell me about yourself. Last night I did all the talking. Tonight let's talk about you."

Hanna smiled and the apprehensive look on her face vanished. She glanced at the ceiling, then at him and said, "Where would you like me to start?"

"The beginning, of course," and his eyes danced and he chuckled.

"Of course." She rolled her eyes and looked up at the ceiling again.

Ian was an excellent listener and asked questions. He wanted to learn all he could about this woman he was quickly falling for.

She told him about growing up in a California small town called Point Reyes, overlooking the Pacific, a few miles north of San Francisco. Her father owned an oyster farm which his family had run for four generations. It was dirty work, but he continued to do very well. Her brother began taking over the business and her parents looked forward to retirement and traveling the world.

She grew up on the cold Pacific Ocean and loved the sea … that's what brought her to the academy. She was a good student and loved horses too. She spoke about her horse, Joseph, and how he was her best friend growing up. She talked about, Rufus, her Black Labrador. She was a soccer player and a starting forward on the varsity team at school.

She talked about her family, her parents, and how lucky she was to have been raised in such a solid and loving family. She told a number of funny stories about her brother and they laughed. She spoke of the kindness of her mother and strength and security she had always felt with her father. Then she stopped mid-sentence and looked at Ian. Reaching over, she put her hand on his and said, "I'm sorry. I didn't mean to hurt you."

"Hurt me?" He asked.

"You know, your father not being there during your childhood."

"Oh, my grandfather took his place, I guess, please continue." He realized she still had her hand over his as she went on. Hanna continued about her time at school and her first sea year and the other places she had seen. Ian asked, "Do you have a boyfriend?"

"No. Do you have a girlfriend?"

He shook his head. "No."

She blushed and said, "I had a serious boyfriend in high school. What a disaster that was. How about you?"

"Ummmm, no, I'm waiting for the right girl I guess …" He stammered and turned bright red.

She laughed out loud and he saw she was laughing with him, not at him, and he joined in.

It was getting near sunset and they both consumed enough beer for the time being and needed some fresh air. Ian paid the barkeeper and they poured themselves out of the bar. Ian had his arm around her shoulder and it felt good.

As they approached the sidewalk, she slipped out from under his arm and said seriously, but with a playful hint in her voice, "No public display of affection, cadet."

"Yes, ma'am" he cheerfully responded and saluted. They walked down the street in no particular direction. To Ian, it was clear they were now a couple, at least for the evening.

Ian was beginning to understand why she acted differently around the ship and in view of the crew. The difficult conversation he was avoiding wouldn't be necessary. He was figuring out the politics by himself.

Chapter Sixteen

The Statue

The country-wide labor strike continued into its second week. The *American Spirit* sat idle and the crew began to get antsy and signs of trouble surfaced. The night before, one of the engine gang was arrested for brawling in town and the chief had bailed him out after breakfast.

The crew was spending more time ashore and the captain began to get regular requests for cash advances so they could frequent the local brothels and bars. The most popular, The Exotica, was famous for their women. They boasted an assortment from around the world. Their advertisement boasted, *A Cornucopia of Pleasure for the Adventurous Gentleman.*

Hanna asked Ian if he wanted go to see the famous brothel and he said, "no." She appeared relieved.

The engineers had long since completed the necessary repairs to the main engine and the cargo remained stowed as it had when the strike started. The chief steward informed the captain he'd need provisions by week's end, his the fresh fruit, vegetables, and dairy products were nearly expended.

The captain and agent continued to meet each morning and discussed strike resolution. The latest news claimed "Queen Beatrix and the Prime Minister had threatened to engage and force an end to the strike for reasons of national security," the agent reported matter of factly.

"I hope so, this has got to end soon," said the captain. "I need to get this ship back to sea and the crew focused on work again." They nodded their heads in agreement. Skip, the chief engineer, was concerned about his engine gang, too.

That afternoon Hanna and Ian arranged to go ashore for the first time since their evening at Paddy Murphy's. Hanna had gone ashore with Larry and another engineer and Joe had taken Ian to an Indonesian restaurant two nights ago.

Though Ian missed spending time with Hanna, he enjoyed the distance, too. He knew the other night they'd let their guard down and could have easily gone too far. *But that was then and this was now*, he thought. The irrationality of young hearts …

The cadets met in the officer's lounge at two in the afternoon and headed out the terminal gate when the captain and the chief saw them as they got out of a cab. The men had gone ashore to call their wives and had lunch at a local fish restaurant they both enjoyed. The captain smiled as the young mariners approached and said, "Cadets … headed out?"

"Yes, sir" they replied.

"Hold on a moment." He reached into his pocket and peeled off two one hundred dollar bills. He handed one to each of the cadets.

They protested, "No, thank you, sir. You and the chief have already been too kind." They both insisted.

"No, chief and I insist. We had no idea we'd be in port this long. Enjoy the day and stay together." The chief and captain waved to the cadets and walked to the ship.

The cadets said, "Thank you" and proceeded to the waiting cab.

Hanna said, "They're very nice gentlemen."

"Yes, they are," Ian agreed.

The chief and captain smiled as they watched the cadets disappear into the car and move away. "I think they like each other," the captain said.

"Yeah, me too," said the chief. "Good thing the engine cadet's getting off the ship in New Jersey. Romance on the ship is no good for morale." He rubbed his chin. "Not terrible to see once in a while, though." They shared a knowing smile.

Hanna and Ian directed the cab to the shopping district. They wanted to buy gifts for their friends and family back home. The drive into the center of the city was routine by then and they hardly noticed until the driver had them in the center of shops as far as the eye could see within five minutes. All three times they were ashore they ended up in a five square block area.

They went from shop to shop and Ian loved watching Hanna as she looked through the racks and shelves for just the right gift. He wondered if couples like her parents did that and if her father enjoyed watching his wife move through the shops.

Considering the time and energy they expended shopping, they had purchased precious little and Ian was getting tired of standing like a mannequin. Walking between shops they came upon a small park with several benches and a bronze statue in the center.

131

"Hanna, how about we sit for a few minutes before we continue?"

"Okay, old man," she said giggling, and followed him to a bench. They sat for a moment and Ian studied the statue in the park center. The eight foot man was well-dressed, standing tall and proud. His eyes were on the horizon as if he had a vision of the future. He held a pair of fine gloves in one hand and a walking stick in the other.

"He's a handsome fellow," Hanna offered. "Look, there's a plaque on the base."

"I wonder who he was," Ian said, walking up to the plaque. As he got closer, he could see the plaque was in fact two, one side in Dutch and the other in English. "Great, it's in English," he said. A second later, he froze. His mouth fell open and he blanched white.

"Are you alright, Ian?" When he didn't move, she ran to his side. Shaking his shoulder, she repeated, "Are you alright?"

Following his eyes down to the inscription, she cried, "Holy shit!" They both stared at the bronzed words and Hanna began to read.

> *- Hans Christen van der Waterlaan-*
> *He was a great man of vision, entrepreneurial spirit and motivation. A gifted leader, Mr. van der Waterlaan was the driving force behind the rapid redevelopment of Rotterdam after it was leveled twice during the Second World War. His vision and unmatched courage were instrumental in this fine city's rapid*

transformation from ruin to a thriving city
and the epicenter of European commerce.
He is remembered fondly by the citizens of
Rotterdam as the first amongst her sons.
Rotterdam Preservation Society
Erected September 24, 1962

Hanna looked over to Ian. "Do you think he's a relative of yours? Maybe he was your grandfather or an uncle." Her eyes glowed and her voice went an octave higher, "Ian, you said your father was Dutch. Could it be?" She bounced on her toes. "Let's go to the local library and get online. We need to find out about Hans Christen van der Waterlaan!"

"Okay," he replied, but before they left, Ian took a picture of the plaque with his digital camera. Then he asked Hanna to take one of him next to the bronze figure.

They were both excited about uncovering the mystery. Ian realized there was a large tract of his family history that had never been important until then. The potential to learn more about his father and his family fascinated him and scared him.

Sharing this intimate experience with Hanna was even better. Hanna took Ian's hand and they walked two blocks until they found an Internet café.

"This will do," Hanna said, grabbing his hand tightly she dragged him up the stairs to the entrance. She steered him through the door and purchased thirty minutes online time and two lattes. She left the counter to start the search and Ian lingered, waiting for the coffees to be prepared.

With the coffees in hand, Ian joined Hanna who by now had found fifteen hundred hits on Hans Christen van der Waterlaan. "Holy shit, this guy was famous," she said, as Ian stood over her looking at the screen.

He set down their drinks.

"Look Ian, he was one of the wealthiest men in Holland in 1959. Look at this picture. Hans is standing next to a beautiful woman and a young boy. The inscription is in Dutch. Hold on …" She got out of her chair and walked over to a person three computers down and asked him to translate the article for them. The young man with a scraggly beard and tired eyes agreed, and with some trouble, got up and came over to the computer.

He looked at the screen, "Hans Christen van der Waterlaan, pictured with this wife Margareta, and their son Ian, picture taken in August 1960." He laughed at the two Americans who looked like they had just seen a ghost. "Anything else," he asked. They shook their heads and thanked him. He got up and returned to his computer and resumed rattling the keys with his fingers.

Hanna and Ian shook their heads. "Ian, that little boy was your father!" They scrolled to the top of the recommended sites and the top twelve had murder in the title. Hanna opened one written in English.

"Hanna tapped the screen. "Your grandfather was murdered by a disgruntled employee in his company's board room. He was murdered two days after that picture was taken with your father and your grandmother. See? Your grandmother was a concert pianist and a rather famous classical musician."

"Can we get information on the boy in the picture and see if it is my father?" Ian asked, still stunned.

"Sure, let's try." Hanna said as she typed in a query - Ian van der Waterlaan. "Wow, there are two thousand and twenty one hits." She opened up one of the top three recommended sites. "Here is a picture of him about your age. Geez, you look just like him."

"I see," said Ian, peering closer just as the computer went dead. Their half an hour was up.

"Do you want to look some more, Ian?" Hanna asked.

"Nah, I've seen enough for today," Ian said. They agreed to go get a beer and digest what they had just learned. This accidental discovery had completely upset his life and he needed time to think. What would he tell his mother? Would this discovery change his life? He wondered.

They found a local pub down the street and Hanna ordered two Heinekens. The couple watched as the bartender poured the beer from the tap tilting the glass, the golden liquid running down the side. As the glass filled and the foamy head rose over the lip, he used a wooden spatula and removed the excess foam. It was a fine display and each glass perfectly filled when he delivered them.

"To uncovering your family history," Hanna said, as she raised her glass to toast Ian. "Do you realize you may be wickedly wealthy and don't even know it?" She smiled and winked at him.

He was still dazed. They drank their beers and ordered two more rounds. Hanna was talking a mile a minute. Ian was numb as his mind raced in no particular direction. He'd never felt this way in his life. His body felt heavy, yet his mind worked at warp speed, pondering endless questions and their possible answers. All at once he felt the pub closing in on him and he struggled to breathe. He put down his beer. "Hanna, I want to go back to the ship. I need to sleep." He felt a little sick from the excitement.

"Sure, let's go," Hanna said.

***

They got back to the ship and went straight to their stateroom doors and said good night as they passed their respective thresholds. Ian took off his shoes and shirt and sat on his bed. He tried to process what had happened since he'd read the statue plaque. *Was it fate or luck?*

A few minutes later, Hanna knocked on the bathroom door. He stood up, walked over, and opened it. "I came to check on you Ian. Are you alright?" She asked, concerned.

"A lot has happened to me today."

"I'm here for you. I'm right next door. Call me if you need anything."

"Thanks, Hanna. Good night."

"Good night, and she passed back through the door and closed it.

They undressed and crawled into their beds. Ian noticed she hadn't locked the door when she left and he knew it wasn't an accident. Who would be the one to come through the door? He lay in his bed and wondered. Not wanting to chance being rejected, he rolled over and fell asleep.

His mind was humming like a machine.

Chapter Seventeen
The Wealthy Dutch Woman

The next morning, the eight to twelve watch standers gathered in the officer's mess for breakfast. As was the case every day aboard ship, the steward's department had been up since four preparing food, baking, inventorying stores, and doing laundry. Since they'd been up early, they knew the labor strike had been settled at midnight and all labor services were scheduled to resume at eight across the Netherlands.

Joe was the first to notice the steward named Luis was smiling more than usual and very light on his feet. He was an older man who normally shuffled as he walked, but not that morning. He was stepping like a young man in a dance contest. "Okay, Luis, spill the beans. Why are you so happy?"

"The strike is over, the strike is over." He smiled and left to the galley to retrieve Joe's breakfast.

"Well I'll be damned, the strike is finally over," Joe said.

"It about time," Larry chimed in.

The topic started a conversation and after a few minutes the conversation died-out. Then Hanna said, "Yesterday, Ian and I found his grandfather's statue in a park in the financial district in Rotterdam. He was a very important guy according to the inscription. It was a complete surprise! Right, Ian?" She said as she looked over at him.

"Yea … enough Hanna"

"Really?" Joe looked at Ian. "Did you know anything about your father's family before this trip?"

"No."

"Hey, kid, since the strike is over you better spend your remaining time ashore and try and find out more. That's if you want to know more? I expect the sailing board will be set for tomorrow morning."

Ian had no appetite, he just looked at the eggs and sausage sitting on his plate and pushed it way. *Why would she say that?* He looked over and gave Hanna a hurt look of betrayal.

Ian got up and left the table intending to meet Joe on the bridge at the watch turnover. He was still unsure of how he wanted to deal with the information they'd stumbled upon yesterday.

It really didn't change anything, but, then again, it really did.

Ian got to the bridge five minutes before Joe. The off-going mate was sitting on the chart table patiently waiting for Joe to relieve him. A few minutes later, Joe walked through the door. The outgoing mate spoke, "Nothing happened on the ship last night. The strike is over and the stevedores and longshoremen will be turning-to at zero eight hundred this morning. The captain had me post the board for zero nine hundred tomorrow morning. Looks like you get the departure watch." He smiled and said, "that's it."

"Thanks, I have the watch," and the off-going mate disappeared down the stairs to get breakfast before the mess closed. Joe and Ian were alone on the bridge. Joe looked at Ian and said, "Hey, kid, what gives? Yeah, Hanna has a big mouth. Don't you want to learn more about your family history?"

"Yeah, I guess so. I just wasn't prepared to bump into it in a park, and then in an Internet café we saw a picture of my father as a kid days before his father, my grandfather, I think, was murdered."

"Holy shit, we didn't hear about that part of the story over eggs this morning. Isn't it just like a woman to tell half the story?" Ian smiled at Joe's attempt at humor. Joe went on, "Kid, you should go ashore today and explore the city, and if the mood suits you see if you can find out more about your father's family. If not, enjoy the city. You can always do a web search later and find out more if and when you want. Let's tell the mate you'll be ashore today. Then I need to keep track of the cargo operations. They should start any moment."

Out the bridge windows, they saw workers arriving at the gate, trucks moving, and crane operators climbing the gantries. The stevedores came up the gangway and took their positions and all around the terminal was alive with activity.

Joe and Ian walked to the mate's cabin where the tired old man sat at his desk. Joe knocked on the door frame. The chief mate looked up from his paperwork. "Yes," he said squinting over his reading glasses.

"Mate, cargo operations will resume momentarily. Say, mate, since this is the last day in port and Ian has some family here he just found out about, can you give him the day off to track them down?"

"Why would a kid with the family name Blooker have family in Rotterdam?"

"Sir, the family name is van der Waterlaan," Ian said.

"No shit." The chief mate leaned back in his chair and whistled, "That's a famous name here in Rotterdam. I remember when the old man was killed in his office building." He continued, "You just found out you're a van der Waterlaan?"

"Yes sir," replied Ian.

"Cadet, go ashore but be back aboard by midnight. And take someone with you. Joe, ask the first assistant if the engine cadet can have the day off to keep Ian out of trouble."

"Yes, mate," Joe replied.

Ian noticed a few seconds ago the chief mate had called him by his given name in public. That was a first. It had always been Cadet or Midshipman Blooker or 'kid'. Joe walked Ian to the first assistant's office and presented a case for Hanna to have the day off to go with Ian ashore. The engineer called down to the engine room and asked the engine cadet to come to his office. He turned to Joe and Ian, "Please sit."

Like the chief mate, his office was full of papers and publications. His job was mainly an administrative job. Like most true marine engineers he missed working in the engine room and looked for any excuse to get his hands dirty. Hanna knocked on the door frame and entered. She saw Ian and Joe, and a confused look crossed her face.

"'First', you called for me?" She addressed the engineer.

"Yes, Hanna, I'd like you to take the rest of the day off and escort Ian ashore. He's looking for a branch of his family tree. But then, I understand, you know more about that than I do."

"Yes, sir." She glanced over at Ian. "Sir, I must tell the watch engineer I won't be standing watch today."

"Don't worry, I have already told him." The first assistant said and then added as he looked at the two cadets. "Get out of here, you're wasting daylight. Be back on the ship by midnight."

The cadets spun on their heels and were out the door headed to their rooms whispering to each other,

"What just happened?"

"Hell if I know."

Joe and the engineer smiled and nodded. Joe made his way out on deck as the first container came over the rail. He jotted a note for the logbook. *Cargo operations resumed at zero-eight-thirty- six. Holds two, four and six.*

Hanna and Ian stood in front of their doors in the passageway. Hanna said, "I'll knock on the bathroom door when I'm ready to go, say about fifteen minutes?"

Hanna rapped on the door just as Ian had finished dressing. He stuffed the last of the money the captain had given him and a little more in his pocket. Grabbing his coat, notebook, and pencil, he opened the door for Hanna. Ian noticed she had put on makeup and lipstick. That was a first. "Hanna you look very nice," he commented.

"Thanks so do you," She replied, "Let's get going, it'll be ten o'clock before we get there."

They hurried down the main deck and were ashore in no time. The activity of containers moving quickly overhead, truck traffic moving within the terminal, and the men scurrying about, was a far different experience than the graveyard of silence they'd seen in the terminal during the strike. Now it was a dangerous place and they maneuvered to the terminal gate with caution. A taxi waited and they climbed in. Ian looked at the driver in the rear view mirror and said, "Please take us to the public library nearest the financial district."

In a few minutes the driver had them in front of the library on the Leliestraat. Ian handed the driver fare and tip and they emerged from the BMW sedan and stared at the large modern building. "Good hunting," Ian said and led the way.

Today he was the alpha in the group and Hanna seemed fine with it. She trailed behind him as he headed to the front desk.

He engaged the librarian who acted delighted to demonstrate her English proficiency. "Where would be the best place for us to find information on the van der Waterlaan family, specifically Hans, his wife Margareta, and their son, Ian?" The librarian, who was in her mid-forties and still an attractive woman, stood back from the counter and looked at Ian over the top of her reading glasses. "May I be so bold as to inquire why?" But she already knew why ...

Ian said, "I believe Ian may be my father according to my mother."

The librarian flushed and recomposed herself. "That could certainly be so. You look very much like Ian."

Hanna jumped into the conversation and asked, "How would you know that?"

"Well, it's none of your business, but I was Ian's girlfriend for a short time when we were in school. I was just a short stop as he moved from girl to girl. He was the most handsome and wealthiest young man of his time here in Holland. I guess he may have been a bit spoiled as you Americans say, because his father was murdered when he was quite young. It was said, his mother and his uncle pretty much let him do and go as he pleased. Let me show you where the information is located. I'm afraid most of it will be in Dutch, but I'll be happy to give you the gist of any article that may interest you. Oh, my name is Greta, Greta Bols." She stuck out her hand to initiate a hand shake.

Ian met her hand with his and said, "Ian, Ian Blooker, my mother's name, and this is my friend, Hanna Thorton. We're from the American container ship *American Spirit*."

"Your father went off to sea and I never saw him again," she said. Her voice was wistful and she had a dreamy look in her eye. It was clear even after twenty plus years she was still in love with the man. "Where does your father live these days?"

Ian looked at her and said, "My mother told me he died at sea in the Pacific when his ship sank. The whole crew perished in the storm. He died before I was born."

"Oh, I'm so sorry to hear that, forgive my curiosity." She blushed and her ears became bright red and she started to wring her hands. "Here, let me show you where I'd recommend you start your search." Then she walked them to a corner marked "History of Rotterdam."

The left side was marked "Ancient" and the right "Modern". Greta recommended looking in the modern portion circa nineteen forty five onward to present.

She pointed to her left and said, "There are computers over there that are free to access the Internet, too. Anything else? Please let me know."

She returned to her desk, then looked back for a moment and said, "You're the image of your father when he was your age. Oh, and look under classical musicians, Netherlands. Ian's mother was an accomplished concert pianist of considerable notoriety."

Ian and Hanna got down to work. The two poured through books and magazines and occasionally found something of interest and Greta, as promised, provided the Readers Digest version of the story in English for them, Ian took copious notes the entire time. They found out about his grandfather's rise as a real estate mogul and his shift to shipping and the large corporation which became the spokes of the transportation and distribution system in Northern Europe.

It was not all good news. It appeared he was ruthless in acquisitions and was responsible for many careers and corporations being destroyed when they got in his way. There were also rumors he was a smuggler and an underground figure but was loved and respected, because his vision and drive had provided thousands of jobs and money to rebuild the city after the war.

It was a happy and sad story of his rise to power. Not surprising, he was murdered. He freely left bodies in his wake on his quest for power and control, and some called him a crook.

On the other hand, Ian's grandmother appeared to be a beautiful woman from an elite family. She was a gifted musician and in great demand to perform with the symphony and at classical concerts. She had a notable career herself, but when she became pregnant with Ian, her only child, she stopped performing and focused on being a wife and mother to her son.

When her husband was murdered, she became a recluse and only attended selected events and even more performed infrequently. She appointed her brother Johan to run Hans' companies. Johan had the reputation of being a fair and gifted leader and he took the family fortune much further.

"Wow, Ian, it looks like you might be rich!" Hanna said jokingly.

"Nay, stop it."

There was much written about Ian's father, but little of it flattering. He was a notorious ladies man and constantly in trouble with the law. They found pictures of him in front of expensive sports cars with beautiful women or in night clubs, drunk and out of control.

"Ian, you have bad boy genes in your blood." Hanna said with a wink. "Just remember, that doesn't mean you have to act on them!" She giggled, but it sounded hollow.

Ian read and, when needed, asked Greta for translations and madly scribbled in his notebook. At times, when Greta read the articles about Ian, she would become emotional. Turning her head, she would swipe the back of her hand across her eyes.

They worked tirelessly until ten in the evening when Greta came to tell them the library was closed and they would have to come back tomorrow.

"We can't," said Ian. "We sail in the morning."

"I'm sorry, but I must close the library."

"Come on, Ian, we have enough for starters. Thank you for everything, Greta. You have been really helpful," Hanna said.

Ian agreed, "thank you Greta."

Greta walked them to the door and handed them both her personal card. "Let me know if I can help you in your research. Good night."

The cool air was refreshing and the young couple were invigorated by the chill and dampness in the air. "We have a little less than two hours before we need to be back. How would you like to get a beer?" Ian asked.

"Great, and we can compare our notes on your family."

Around the corner, they found a pub across from the Lutz Theater. They ordered two Heinekens and watched as the bartender performed the same ritual they'd seen in other Dutch bars. It was a careful pour, wooden spatula, and a perfect delivery. "The Dutch take beer drinking seriously," Ian said, as he raised his glass to toast.

Hanna countered, "To our discoveries about your father's family – your family! Cheers!"

"Cheers!" Ian repeated. He was overwhelmed with emotion.

They drank the beer, checked the time, and ordered one more. They finished their second beer, paid for the drinks, and left the bar.

DRAWN TO THE SEA
(First Revision)

Just as luck would have it, the Lutz Theater was disgorging its patrons at the same time and the streets became a mob of people scurrying like ants in many directions. Hanna and Ian stopped to watch the commotion. The cab drivers targeted the well-dressed people coming down the theater stairs. Side by side, Hanna slipped her hand into Ian's.

In a true Dutch tradition with order and efficiency, the bulk of the theater goers were dispersed in twenty minutes. Hanna and Ian walked across the street to the taxi stand in front of the theater.

As they looked to hail a cab, they noticed a Mercedes Benz limousine pull up to the front of the theater. Behind them, they saw an older woman elegantly dressed, her hair tastefully styled, as it sat high on her head. She wore expensive jewelry around her neck, her wrists, and two or three large diamond rings on her fingers.

She was escorted by two enormous bodyguards and a handsome man at her side, clearly her aide. She made her way with dignity and grace to the limousine. The driver got out on cue and moved around the car to open the door.

Ian and Hanna stood at the taxi stand watching as the elegant woman walked in their direction. "She must be really important," Ian whispered to Hanna.

The woman nodded at them and then froze. She stared at Ian, her jaw gaping. Then her eyes began to tear and she began convulsing. The bodyguards gave Ian and Hanna measured looks then one of them said, "Madam, what is the matter?" The other yelled to the driver that they would be going to the hospital.

As they tried to guide her into the car, she didn't budge. She kept staring at Ian and slowly raised her hand and pointed her bony and bejeweled fingers at him. Ian didn't move either, his eyes wide. The old woman struggled to form her words, "Ian, Ian, my son, you've come home."   The men tried to force her along and she stopped them with a firm, but direct order. "Take your hands off me, gentlemen, I am fine." She regained her composure and grinned, "Ian, my son, say something."

Hanna was the first to figure it out, "Madam, this is Ian Blooker. His dad was your son Ian. We are Americans from a ship here in port." Madam van der Waterlaan looked at Ian, then Hanna, then back at Ian. "If so, young man, where is your father?"

"My mother told me he died on a ship in the Pacific just before I was born. The ship sank with all hands lost." Ian finally spoke.

Her face confirmed the story. The guard interrupted, "Madam van der Waterlaan, please get into your car and out of the cold." She ignored the large man in a dark suit next to her. Her focus was on Ian. "Where are you young people headed?"

"Madam, we must get back to the ship. We have a midnight curfew," Ian said.

"Yes, well jump in and I'll take you there and we can talk on the way."

"Um, yes madam." Ian sensed Hanna's panic. It was against academy policy to get into a private vehicle overseas. But just once, and they were together, they looked at the kind old woman and nodded.

The limousine left the theater district and headed to the terminal, Madam van der Waterlaan reached over and hugged Ian and then held his hand. She turned to her aide and said, "Hans, I'd like to make a short detour to the financial district to show my grandson and his lady friend." He nodded and directed the driver.

She pointed out the three large buildings Ian's grandfather and her brother after him had built. Still holding his hand, she asked about where he and Hanna lived and what they were doing. She asked about Ian's mother and his sister and her family. The woman said little about herself or her son, preferring to listen to her guests.

They told her of their chance finding of her husband's statue which led to the day they'd spent at the library learning what they could about Ian's father. The woman's eyes shed a tear and she softly said, "Your father was a good man. Yes, he may have had some demons, but then again don't we all? Losing his father really affected him. The poor dear, his father, my husband, was murdered in the boardroom as Ian and I sat in his office next door eating ice cream waiting for the board meeting to end. We were supposed to go to the theater. Your father heard the gun shot and saw his father's body lying on the floor in a pool of blood."

The aide interrupted, "Madam, please, this will only upset you."

"I'm just fine, thank you," she said, straightening her spine.

The limo pulled up to the terminal gate and they continued to talk for another fifteen minutes. Ian looked at his watch and said, "Thank you so much. We must leave now to get back to the ship before midnight."

"Yes, dear, here is my card. Please write to me and tell me all about what you're doing. I'll write back young man." She looked at him again, hugged him and kissed his cheek. "You're the image of your father," she said as she reached for his hand and held it again for a moment. "As for you, young lady," she said, turning her attention to Hanna, "You take good care of this young man … do you hear me?"

"Yes, I will, madam. Thank you for your time and hospitality."

"You're welcome, dear." She looked back at Ian. "You take care of her too, she is a keeper."

Ian and Hanna kissed the lady on the cheek and promised to stay in touch, then left the limo. They waved as the expensive car pulled into the empty traffic pattern and soon the red tail lights disappeared in the distance. The cadets smiled at one another. Their hunt had been more than successful. They made it back to the ship just as the clock struck midnight and went straight to their rooms.

In the passageway in front of their staterooms, they put their respective keys in their locks and looked at each other. In perfect cadence, they said, "good night," then crossed the thresholds and the doors closed.

A few minutes later, there was a gentle knock on the bathroom door. When Ian opened it, Hanna said, "Thanks for a great day. I appreciate you letting me be part of this wonderful discovery. This was the best day I've had in a long time. Good night."

As she turned away, Ian said, "Good night, Hanna. I'm glad you were there with me. I wouldn't have wanted it to be anyone else." They smiled and Hanna closed and locked the door, then leaned against it for several minutes. Ian was on the other side of the door, leaning against it too. It had been a good day in Rotterdam.

DRAWN TO THE SEA
(First Revision)

Ian wondered what else the future had in store for him.

Chapter Eighteen
Back At Sea

The seven thirty wake-up call seemed early. Ian felt groggy and his head throbbed from processing all the information that bombarded him the day before.

> *1. I found out my grandfather was a*
> *famous and wealthy man and he was*
> *murdered by one of his employees.*
> *2. My grandmother was a professional*
> *classical pianist.*
> *3. My father saw his dad murdered and*
> *after that he grew up a spoiled brat.*
> *4. I, by chance, met my grandmother*
> *and we chatted in her limousine... a*
> *relative I didn't even know existed until*
> *hours before.*
> *5. Oh and I think I'm falling in love*
> *with Hanna.*

After compiling the list in his head he said to himself out loud, "You had a fine day for yourself, Mr. Blooker, or, should I say, van der Waterlaan!"

He heard Hanna in the shower and wondered for a moment what it would be like to join her. He shook his head and started to get dressed. As he buckled his belt, he remembered the ship would be getting underway at nine in the morning and he'd be on the bridge detail. That was a bittersweet thought.

He'd have liked to stay in port a while longer to learn more about his father and talk to his grandmother, but at the same time, he was glad the ship would be underway again. They had been in Rotterdam for nearly two and a half weeks and he, like the others onboard, were ready to get back to work.

He heard Hanna finish in the shower. The door closed behind her so he entered the bathroom and started his morning routine. He held onto the basin and looked deeply into the mirror and thought, *I wonder if my father used to do this.* What Ian didn't know was that's exactly the way his father had started every morning. It must have been in the genes. Next, he brushed his teeth and wet and combed his blond hair which by then had grown out from academy standards. Hanna had commented it looked good a little longer.

He lathered his face and drew the razor over its edges and curves and he hoped to avoid the inevitable cut here and there. Ian was good at many things, but shaving himself wasn't one of them.

He finished the ritual without a nick and silently congratulated himself. It would be another day he wouldn't get ribbed over breakfast for cutting himself. He finished dressing and made his way to the officer's mess. When he rounded the corner and could hear them as they carried on and the noise of their voices echoed down the passageway. He walked into the room and there was instant silence. All eyes were upon him and he became

153

uncomfortable with a sea of faces staring back at him without a sound. He saw Hanna, Joe and Larry at the usual table. Today the other two tables were full too with all the mates and engineers present.

Ian looked to Joe and then Hanna for support. Joe smiled and cleared his throat, "Sir, we would be honored if you'd join us for breakfast ... Mein Herr van der Waterlaan." He smiled and the whole room roared with laughter. Ian looked confused.

Hanna looked at Ian and blushed. "I told them about yesterday."

"Oh Hanna, you didn't."

"I'm afraid I did," she said, turning pink as she looked down at her plate.

"Your highness, can you pass the hot sauce," someone from another table said in the direction of Ian. Ian thought this was getting out of control and there was nothing he could do to stop it. The room was alive once again and he could hear some of the conversations and most of them were about him and his newfound nobility status. Carlos, the steward, addressed him as your highness. "Please stop it, Carlos, I'm only a cadet," Ian said. The room erupted again with laughter.

Ian's stomach felt queasy but he ordered eggs and bacon anyway. Across from him, Hanna fidgeted in her seat, flashing him an occasional apologetic smile. Ian looked around the room at the officers and engineers as they joked and chatted. Fortunately, a minute later Ian was no longer the topic of conversation and he started to relax. He surveyed the room and noticed that Fritz kept looking at him without saying a word. It was the look of a man who'd unlocked a memory and he wasn't happy. *What was it he saw or remembered?* Ian wondered.

Breakfast was shoved down, Ian and Joe made their way to the bridge, as Larry and Hanna dove into the engine room, but not before Hanna said, "Ian, I'm really sorry."

"It's okay," he responded, and gave her a reassuring nod.

Joe and Ian prepared the bridge for sailing. Ian was getting the knack of it and Joe turned some of the preparation over to him. Together they got the ship ready for the zero-nine-hundred departure and were so busy they hadn't noticed the pilot had come up the brow. The pilot was an older gentleman who had been a Rotterdam pilot for twenty years and before that, a ship's captain for twenty more. He was nearly seventy-five but still physically and mentally agile and regarded as the best pilot and ship handler in the pilot's association.

The pilot carried a package wrapped in brown paper tied together with twine under his arm. He presented himself to Joe and Ian as he entered the bridge, "Good morning, I'm Captain Adriaan van der Meer, your pilot this morning." He stood erect, then slightly bowed from the waist, and clicked his heels.

The pilot looked at Joe and the mate introduced himself. Then van der Meer's watery, bright blue eyes looked at Ian and he smiled as if he recognized the young man. Ian stood at attention and introduced himself, "Midshipmen Ian Blooker, deck cadet, sir." The older gentlemen studied Ian as he sized him up and the young man became uncomfortable; in fact, the day had been uncomfortable since he walked into the mess deck earlier that morning.

The pilot put his hands in his pockets and looked deeply into Ian's face. "Young man, I knew your father very well. You look just like he did at your age. I was the man who took your father to sea and convinced him he should be a ship's officer. I was a good friend and old business partner of your grandfather. He loaned me the money to purchase my first deep sea ship. It was a hundred fifty meter coastal freighter that got me started. Hans Christian was a kind and generous man and a good friend. I still miss him, lad."

"Your grandmother is a close friend of mine too and she told me I'd find you aboard. Here, she sent this along for you." The pilot took the package out from under his arm and handed it to Ian. Ian stood there speechless. Joe watched with a widened and amused grin. Ian held the package and slowly his eyes went from the pilot to the package, back to the pilot as if asking what to do.

"Open it when you are ready. Knowing your grandmother, it'll be a wonderful gift," van der Meer said. Then he looked at Joe, "Mate, please let the captain know I'm aboard and on the bridge. We'll have two tugs today. *Rotterdam No. 2* will be forward and *Rotterdam No. 26* aft."

"Yes, sir, Captain van der Meer," Joe said as if shaken out of a deep dream. He rushed to the ship's phone and dialed the captain. "Sir, the pilot is on the bridge, two tugs coming along side soon."

"Very well, I'll be up in a minute. Please have the steward bring coffee and pastry to the bridge," Horne said and he hung up the phone. He glanced at the chief mate in front of him and said, "I heard about the celebrity status of one of our cadets."

The chief mate said, "I told you these damn kids have a silver spoon in their mouths and this one has a lucky horse shoe crammed up his ass to boot."

The captain smirked, "Now mate, let's give the young cadet a break. I bet he's as surprised as any of us at the news. Now, if you please, let's get back to sea."

"Yes captain," the mate said, still shaking his head as he left the office.

Captain Horne grabbed his foul weather coat, gloves and his walkie talkie. He rubbed his chin and mumbled, "I knew that kid was something special. I can't wait to tell Jeanne."

Captain van der Meer sipped coffee and checked the weather as he waited. Captain Horne came through the door and the two men shook hands and made small talk. They'd worked together many times before and had a sincere professional respect for one another.

At zero nine hundred the conversation shifted abruptly to ships business and Horne called over to Joe, "Shift the engine telegraph from *STANDBY* to *ALL STOP*. Ready for engine and rudder orders."

"Aye aye, captain," Joe responded. It was all business now. Ian was grateful he was no longer the center of attention. In short order, van der Meer had the tugs where he wanted them and the ship backed out of the terminal berth and lined-up in the shipping channel.

The pilot called into the wheelhouse, "*DEAD SLOW AHEAD,* Steady Two Seven Eight." He and Horne were on the starboard bridge wing in the damp cold Rotterdam weather. Van der Meer released the tugs and had the *American Spirit* at the Rotterdam sea buoy thirty minutes later. Horne turned the ship to the north, created a lee, and stopped the engine. As the pilot boat made its approach to the starboard side underneath the pilot ladder, van der Meer shook Horne's hand and they bid each other farewell.

Both were old mariners and would retire or cross the final bar soon so they took a long look at one another. It might be the last time they would stand on a ship's bridge together in this lifetime.

Ian stood ready to escort the pilot down to the pilot ladder as the captains bid one another farewell. Van der Meer turned to Ian and said, "After you, young man," and Ian led the way down the ladder to the main deck. As they walked out through the water tight door onto the main deck, they could see the able body seaman standing near the ladder. Ian checked the ladder like Joe had taught him, "All set, Captain van der Meer."

"Thank you, young man. Margareta, your grandmother, is excited she found you. She is a good woman. You would be well served to get to know her and your Dutch family. You come from a very important family. Ik zie je rond junger." The pilot jumped over the rail and lowered himself easily down the side of the containership to the deck of the waiting pilot boat.

Once aboard, the boat operator maneuvered clear and was moving full speed in the direction of an inbound tanker as it came up from the south. Horne ordered the helm to the left and rang the engine telegraph to *SLOW AHEAD*.

"Steady on Two Eight Five," he ordered.

158

Horne called to the engine room, the chief answered.

"Chief, get ready to bring her up to sea speed."

"We just dropped the pilot." He looked at his watch. It was ten twenty-four.

"Let's call departure ten thirty."

"Aye, captain." The chief said as the phone went dead. A few seconds later the engine telegraph rang full ahead. The chief answered the bell and told the first assistant, "Bring the engine up to one hundred and three RPM(s) … Sea Speed!" Then he said, "First, we're headed home."

Up on the bridge, Ian returned to stand the remainder of the watch with Joe. The captain had long since left the bridge and the navigation of the *American Spirit* to his capable mate and young cadet. Ian tried to focus on the tasks at hand. There were a number of ships coming in and out of Rotterdam and the English Channel.

The visibility was reduced to approximately four miles but the traffic was all moving at their respective sea speed regardless of the severe rules of the road warning to reduce speed in poor visibility. The demand that schedules be kept routinely pushed mariners to the edge of safety.

Ian's eyes kept drifting to the still wrapped package the pilot had delivered earlier this morning. *What is in there?* He couldn't wait to open it after his watch.

Today the watch felt like it dragged on forever as Ian eyed the clock. Usually, he was focused on learning and the four hours flew before Fritz was on the bridge to relieve them. Not today.

Finally, Ian thought as Fritz came through the door and the watch was turned over a few minutes later. Joe picked up his coat and turned to leave. Ian was right behind him. As he walked towards the door, he grabbed the package and put it under his arm. He still had his coat on. The off-going watch standers left and descended to their staterooms two decks below. He and Joe didn't exchange a word.

In his room Ian dropped the package on his desk and fell into the chair.

He thought, *What's inside?*

Chapter Nineteen
Family Introductions

Ian looked at the package neatly wrapped in plain brown paper and tied together with a hemp cord. The cord was fastened together with a tight knot and a bow similar to the way a shoe lace is secured. It was effective, simple but clearly done with purpose and care. Ian took the package and set it down on his desk.

What am I afraid of? He thought to himself as he began to panic. Just then there was a gentle knock at the door. He knew it was Hanna. He went to the mirror and ran a finger through his hair before answering.

She stood leaning to one side, balancing herself against the door frame. "I was wondering if you were here." She had removed her coveralls and was wearing a sweat-stained cutoff T-shirt. The fact that she wasn't wearing a bra was apparent. Her running shorts were cut up the side of her thighs. Anything but a thong would have peeked below the cut.

There was still some residual grime the hand cleaner hadn't quite removed and her left elbow was dirty. Ian thought, *she must have missed it when she cleaned up after her watch was over*. The end of her petite nose had a cute little smudge. Her hair was still wet and her cheeks flushed from the heat in the engine room. She was in her socks.

Ian looked at her and he could feel passion beginning to stir. She cleared her throat and started, "Ian, I understand the pilot brought you a package this morning. What's in it? Can I see?" She said as she walked over the threshold that had seconds ago so nicely framed her young body and she moved toward the package on top of the desk. "Good you haven't opened it. Let's do it together. What do you think is in it?" Hanna said.

Ian's eyes were glued to her body.

"Well open it," she demanded.

Ian sat down with care in front of the package and reached into his right front pocket and removed his pocket knife. He was proud of the knife his grandfather had given him and he kept it sharp for just such an occasion. He opened the knife, put his left index finger under the twine and lifted it. With the knife in his right hand, he drew the blade over the hemp.

The twine cut in two and fell limp on the desk next to the package. The brown paper that enclosed the surprise opened slightly around the edges. They both looked in anticipation. The partially opened package was about eight inches wide, fourteen inches long and four inches high.

Ian just looked at it. He was frozen by the excitement of the unknown. After what was probably only seconds, although it seemed like hours, Hanna got impatient and reached over and tore the paper away.

Ian's first instinct was anger. He could feel the rage as it began to rise in his body, then it quickly subsided. He was relieved she'd done away with the suspense by taking action. They looked at each other and then again at the desk. On the top of the stack of items inside the brown paper was a sealed letter addressed to Ian.

He reached out and gently picked up the letter and looked at his name written in perfect penmanship. By then Hanna was standing behind him with both her hands on his shoulders. She nodded and he picked up his knife and opened the envelope.

His hands trembled as he removed the folded letter. His first observation was the perfection and beauty of the penmanship. Every word spelled correctly, no edits, perfectly spaced and correctly formatted in every way. His eyes ran over the words on the page. As he began to understand the tone and purpose of the letter, his enthusiasm vaulted.

MvdW

van der Waterlaan Estate
Amsterdam, Netherlands
27 Jul 2002

Dearest Ian,

Our chance meeting last night was truly providence. The good lord has given me one last gift as my days must surely be numbered. Until last night, I had no idea I had a grandchild. My heart was twice broken when your grandfather was murdered, and then your father perished at sea so many years ago. I thought our blood line would be lost forever. It is the most horrible of tasks to bury one's child. Another, almost as painful

*thought, was knowing your family lineage
would end with me.*

*This was my existence for all these years.
Seeing you gives me renewed hope and life. I
now look into the future with excitement and
promise.*

*There is so much I want to know about
you and your American family, and there is
so much I want to share with you about your
Dutch family. I hope, in time, you'll come
back and allow me to introduce you to your
Great Uncle (my brother). Unfortunately
your cousins died in an accident years ago.*

*I'd like, at the earliest opportunity, to
come to America and spend time with you
and your family. Forgive this old women's
insistence but I fear I'm running out of time
and there is a lifetime of things I want to
share with you.*

*Of course, you are most welcome to
return to the Netherlands anytime you wish.
I'll be happy to arrange for you and your
family to fly here and stay with me, and the
invitation is extended to your pretty young
lady friend, Hanna, too.*

*In closing, if you've read this, you have
met my close friend Captain Adriaan van der
Meer. The dear man was a close friend of
your grandfather and me and was a mentor to
your father.*

*Please consider my request and let me
know your thoughts. I anxiously look forward*

*to learning more about you and telling you
about your family history and more.*

*Enclosed I have provided you some
clippings, important papers, and pictures of
your Dutch family. Be careful on your ship. I
know you love the sea like your father did.
Come back to us. I could not bear … Need I
say more?*
With love and sincerity,
Margareta van der Waterlaan
(Your maternal grandmother)

"Wow, Ian, looks like you hit a home run," Hanna
said as she read the letter over his shoulder. "Your
grandmother even invited me over, too. I think she thinks
we're going out together. Are we?" From the look on her
face, the forwardness of the question seemed to shock her
as much as it did him. The words just hung in the air for a
moment as Ian considered them.

"Sure, if you'd like, Hanna. I'd like that. How
about you?"

"Yes, I would too." She sat down on his lap and
put her arms around his neck. "Let's get this over with."
She brought her lips to his, lightly at first, and then
urgently. As their mouths explored each other, she pressed
her body against his. Then she pushed him away and stood
up. "Let's look at the rest of the stuff." Ian stared up at her.
His heart was pounding and his breath jagged.

Getting to his feet, with quavering knees, he
kissed her with the desire that had been building for
weeks. He enclosed her in his strong arms and kissed her
again. She responded with equal passion.

Their forbidden love was now 'complicated'. Neither one could hide it or pretend it didn't exist any longer. After a few more minutes, they pushed back a few inches and looked into each other's eyes, "This could get really difficult, Ian."

"I know." Changing the subject, he said, "Let's look at the papers."

Ian reached for the stack of papers and sorted them into piles. He moved the photographs to the left and news articles and documents to the right, and then there were a half dozen or so hand written letters addressed to "Mum." They were clipped together with a paperclip and there was a small piece of expensive stationery with a handwritten note with the same perfect penmanship as the letter he'd read moments before.

MvdW

van der Waterlaan Estate
Amsterdam, Netherlands
27 Jul 2002

Ian,

Here are the last letters I received from your father. I hope they'll help you know and understand him. He was a gifted and wonderful man who was tormented by demons. His demons were not of his own doing but from the pressure and expectations of others.

My child, he loved your mother. Oh how life could have been different for all of us had he not gone back to sea one last time.
Love,

DRAWN TO THE SEA
(First Revision)

Margareta

Ian and Hanna looked at each other and agreed the letters would be the last thing they'd read. Ian put his hand on the stack of pictures and pulled them to the center of his desk. Hanna perched over his shoulder, her hands absentmindedly resting on them.

Ian moved the pictures side by side and a sea of faces and places unfolded before them. Each had a meticulous description of the location, date and people on the back. The references were made for Ian's benefit and the names indicated how they were related.

There was an older grainy color picture of Ian's grandparents and their son taken in 1962, days before his grandfather was murdered. He was a handsome man. Large and powerful of frame and he wore very expensive clothes. He held a pair of leather gloves and a riding crop. His blond hair was oiled back off his forehead and his piercing blue eyes looked like those of a 'bird of prey'.

Margareta stood next to him, tall and slender. She wore a colorful summer dress perfectly tailored. Her long blonde hair framed her face and accentuated her class and attractiveness. Her eyes were alive and her radiant smile lit-up her delicate face with genuine happiness. She glanced at her husband with love and respect in her eyes.

Between them was Ian's father. His clothes were neat and fit well, but his messy hair and the mischievous glint in his eyes telegraphed he was a boy constantly in trouble. In the background stood a stable with horses that looked like thoroughbreds with slender legs, shiny coats and handlers holding them in place. Ian turned over the photo. The inscription read,

> *Your grandfather, grandmother*
> *and your father. August 24,*
> *1960 at the Polo Tournament,*
> *Delft, NL. Your grandfather's*
> *team won.*

Ian carefully set the first picture to the side and reached for the next picture. It was of a young man and his parents. The picture was faded to a dull black and white. The clothes were from the turn of the century. "Remember the movie 'Titanic'?" Hanna commented, "They're wearing clothes that look like they did on the ship in 1903."

Ian turned over the card and read,

> *Your grandfather and his*
> *parents, Joop and Ana van der*
> *Waterlaan, circa 1923,*
> *Amsterdam, NL*
> .

Then their attention was drawn to the next picture of about the same vintage with a couple, the woman wearing a large hat, and two children flocked around them.

> *Your grandmother's parents*
> *Will and Stella van Winkle and*
> *your grand uncle (my brother)*
> *Johan and your grandmother,*
> *circa 1926, Amsterdam, NL*
> .

Next was a recent picture. There was a small sailboat with two young boys and a girl gathered around. Behind them was a striking woman Ian recognized as his grandmother standing next to a gentleman with balding hair and a slight belly. The man in the picture was more casually dressed than his grandmother and seemed to be laughing.

"I wonder who he is," said Ian.

"Turn over the picture and see silly," Hanna prodded.

Again, the perfect penmanship and attention to detail answered the question,

> *Your grand uncle Johan, your grandmother, your father (middle), Johan Jr. (left) and Trudi (right), summer 1968*

"Mystery solved, Ian." Hanna said smugly.

Ian looked up and noticed the time was already fifteen hundred. "Fire and Boat drill in fifteen minutes. Let's stop this for now."

"Okay see you later," and she disappeared through the bathroom and closed the door behind her.

Ian's eyes followed her and he sighed. He wished she hadn't had to leave.

Chapter Twenty
Watch

Ian caught a short nap and prepared for dinner. He went to the officer's mess and sat with Joe, Larry, and Hanna as he had for every meal since he joined the ship. He enjoyed the steak, potatoes, cheesecake and hot chocolate for dessert.

They were nearly eight hours out of Rotterdam and the North Atlantic was up to its old tricks. The sky was grey and gloomy. A veil of dark clouds gave the sensation of being indoors. Without direct sun, the sky seemed dark and ominous. The sea was set in a cold pewter color with the tips of each wave torn off by the biting wind. The men worked on deck, wrapped in their winter coats and gloves. Their wool hats snugly pulled down over their ears and neck.

Inside the deck house was pleasant, but the steady rolling reminded the inhabitants they were at sea. The men had settled into their routines and up in his cabin, the captain wore a satisfied smile. His crew once again had purpose and morale already rose even as the barometric pressure dropped with the approaching storm.

Down in the officer's mess, Ian nearly finished his dessert when the chief mate stuck his head in the door.

"Cadet, come to my office when you have finished your meal."

"Yes, sir," Ian said, wondering what he had done or not done this time. *Why does the mate ride me so hard?* He wondered and looked over at Joe as he searched for a clue.

"Don't worry, kid, it's going to be okay," Joe said with a wink.

All of a sudden, the last few bites of dessert didn't seem to taste as good and Ian pushed himself away from the table. "Excuse me," he said and he left. He couldn't help himself and he wondered why the mate wanted to see him so urgently.

He entered his room and fear struck him and nearly knocked him over. *The mate knows how I feel about Hanna. I'll get fired off the ship and be disenrolled from the academy.* His mind ran a mile a minute. He broke out in a cold sweat and he felt his heart pounding away. He began to feel queasy and leaned on the chair for support. He felt hollow and detached. *How could I have allowed this to happen?* He walked over to the head and grabbed the basin and looked at himself in the mirror and said, "You're so screwed!"

He ran a comb through his hair and brushed his teeth. He put on deodorant and straightened out his uniform. He glanced in the mirror and shook his head. "Damn!" he said to himself before heading out.

Ian stood in the hallway outside the mate's office and looked in. He was outlined by the door frame as the mate pulled his head up from his paperwork. "Come on in, Ian."

Ian?!? He stood at attention in front of the desk. The mate leaned back in his chair. "Sit down and relax." Ian thought, *Relax?!?*

The mate took a moment before opening the desk drawer and grabbing a pipe and tobacco. He took his time as he loaded his pipe and tamped the tobacco into the bowl before he lit it. The pipe came to life and the smoke filled the air. It smelled good, like cherry and whiskey. The mate settled back in his chair and stared at Ian. Ian squirmed in his seat a little while the mate drew on the pipe and released a puff of smoke.

"The captain and I have been watching you closely … and quite frankly…"

Oh shit here it comes! Ian was screaming inside.

"We like what we've seen."

"I'm so sorry, sir, I'll try and do better …" Ian said with fear and disappointment in his face.

"What? Did you hear me cadet?" said the mate, scrunching up his forehead. "We like what we've seen. That's a good thing."

"Yes, sir."

"Joe has provided positive comments on your watch standing and the bosun is really impressed too. Keep up the good work, Ian. You won't stand watch with Joe this evening, you'll shift to the twelve to four with Fritz starting at midnight. The mates both know. You'll turn-to with the bosun from zero eight hundred and secure at eleven thirty to eat and prepare for watch. Understood?"

"Yes, sir."

"That's all and get some rest, kid," the mate said as Ian stood and turned to walk out the door.

"Yes, sir," *Thank God I wasn't in trouble.* Ian was giddy with excitement as he raced back to his room. Once inside, he leaned against the wall and stared at nothing in particular on the ceiling. The sound of his doorknob rattling brought him back to reality. He heard it again and as he unlocked the door he thought, *I should just leave the door unlocked so she can just come and go as she pleases.*

She rushed in. "What did the mate want?" she demanded. "Was it good or bad?"

Ian laughed. "I can only answer one question at a time, madam. "Well, please come in and I'll tell you all about it," he requested and bowed deeply. She stepped through the threshold still in her stained overalls. Ian's eyes filled with excitement, "The mate and captain are pleased with my performance so far and I have been moved to the twelve to four starting at midnight tonight."

"Oh, that's great! Congratulations! I was wondering, if you'd like to continue looking over the papers your grandmother sent?"

"Not really, I need to get some sleep," he said, distracted by her eyes and the features of her young and striking face.

"Okay, maybe tomorrow then." She turned to walk through the bathroom, looked over her shoulder and said, "Good night."

"Good night," he responded as she disappeared behind the door. The lock rolled closed and the room was silent. Ian undressed thinking about Hanna next door and crawled into bed. He reached for the light switch and the room was dark. On his back, he looked at the ceiling and waited for his eyes to adjust to the dark. The whole time his mind was next door with the girl he was sure he was in love with. He drifted off to sleep.

Twenty-three thirty came fast as he woke to a knock on his door. Half asleep he said, "Ummm ... Okay ... I'm up." The footsteps of the AB could be heard moving down the hallway. Ian reached for the light switch and the overhead light instantly threw out a bright, retinal-burning glow. As he lay in bed, he became aware the ship was rolling heavily and the papers he'd left on his desk had shifted and fallen onto the floor and slid across the deck with each roll of the ship. "Damn," he mumbled and got out of bed, knelt and gathered them up, and then he put them in a desk drawer.

He moved with purpose, walking towards the head in a left to right to left direction following the pitching of the deck. In a few steps, he was in the head braced against the basin and looking into the mirror. He was tired and would have liked to return to the bed and sleep for a few more hours but there were only fifteen minutes left to dress, get a bite to eat, and get to the bridge. He washed his face, brushed his teeth, and put on deodorant, and intentionally left the bathroom door open. *A surprise for Hanna when she wakes in the morning,* he thought. Back in his room, he dressed and put on a warm coat and headed for the mess and a sandwich.

He climbed the stairs and stood before the wheelhouse door. He took a deep breath and quickly passed through. Up until tonight he would have been finishing up now, not reporting for watch.

Joe had finished up his log entries and Ian addressed him and walked over to the chart and looked at the twenty four hundred position. Joe completed what he was doing and turned to Ian, "It's pretty quiet here without you, kid. Doug and I kind of miss you."

"Thanks, Joe. Did you know about me being shifted to the twelve to four?"

"I'm afraid so," Joe said and smiled. The door rattled and Fritz walked through and made his way to the coffee machine and filled his cup. The coffee was steaming and smelled good to Ian. Then he realized he had never had a cup of coffee in his life. He watched Maria and his mother empty one pot after another at home growing up, but never had any interest in the drink until this evening. He thought, *Maybe I'll have a cup later.*

Fritz looked over the chart and the ship's position, walked over to the radar and looked for a moment at the screen. Next he verified the course being steered and surveyed the horizon from the starboard bow looking ever more to the left until he had surveyed the horizon three hundred and sixty degrees. He turned to Joe and listened to him as he turned over the watch.

"Ja Jooooe I have tis watch, guter nacht," Fritz said in his heavy German accent.

Joe and Doug walked off the bridge together. Joe hollered over his shoulder, "Hey kid, have a good watch."

"Thanks," Ian replied. The door closed and it was dark with the exception of the green hue thrown to the ceiling by the radar screen reflecting upward in a cone shape and the red lights in the adjacent chart room. The red light didn't affect night vision.

With the exception of those two light sources, the bridge was dark. Ian was still amazed at how well he could see in the dark when his eyes became accustomed. Soon, he could see the outline of the able seaman standing in the corner and Fritz incessantly pacing back and forth, his hands clasped behind his back and his soft soled shoes padding along the deck.

Fritz moved to the port bridge door, stopped and looked out the window off to the horizon to the left of the ship. Seeming satisfied there was nothing to be concerned about as he turned and walked to the starboard bridge door he kept open to allow transfer of air. Fritz stopped and surveyed the horizon on the right side of the ship. Again, appearing satisfied, he turned around and walked back to the port side and repeated the routine. On every third cycle, Fritz stopped at the radar and peered into the scope to see if anything had changed.

The radar looked out twenty four miles and the screen resembled acne on an adolescent boy's face. There would be fifteen to twenty ships on the radar as they headed towards or away from the English Channel. The lights on the horizon around the ship confirmed the radar picture.

Ian made his own assessment of the traffic situation and determined all the ships were doing what they should, and there was no immediate need for concern aboard the *American Spirit* as she sped back to New Jersey with all but the watch standers asleep in their beds.

Ian noticed there was a slight green hue outside of the starboard wing and the running light burned powerfully. The same was true on the port side. Its red hue confirming the running light was lit. The bridge was quiet with the exception of Fritz's movement and the low level hum of the steering motor inside the helm station. The able seaman was propped up in the corner and could have been asleep he was so quiet. Ian watched as if detached from the scene.

It was never like this with Joe. They spoke to each other and occasionally joked. Joe taught Ian about ship handling and navigation and Doug had taught him how to steer the ship, decipher navigation lights on the horizon, and the proper way to report sightings to the mate on watch. Joe's watch was animated and busy. Fritz stood a completely different watch. It was a tomb, not a short order diner.

Ian watched and decided to try coffee for the first time. He walked over to the coffee machine in the rear corner and reached for a Styrofoam cup. He poured the steaming black liquid into the white cup, breathed in through his nose and smiled.

With the starboard door open, the bridge remained cool, and Ian was glad he had worn his heavy coat. He brought the cup to his lips slowly and sipped the liquid. It was hot, bitter and he decided it was an acquired taste. Not one for him just yet. He discreetly poured the remainder of the cup into the sink and reached into the refrigerator and pulled out a Pepsi and thought, *Hmmm, that's more like it.*

He refocused on his surroundings and noticed the mate had moved to the chart room where he was putting a position on the chart. With the precision of a Swiss clock, Fritz fixed the ship's position each hour in the open ocean and then made a few entries into the log book. Afterward, he returned to his pacing back and forth in the wheelhouse. This went on for the entire four hour watch without a word. It was quiet until they were relieved by the second mate at four o'clock. From the time Joe and Doug had left for the night, all Ian had said was, "Good night" to Fritz as they left the bridge four hours later.

It seemed like twelve hours instead of four and Ian rubbed his tense shoulders. *What's wrong with Fritz? He ignores me or when he does look at me it's like he hates me. I don't think I like this,* Ian thought as he entered his room. For the first time since he'd reported to the ship, he dropped his clothes on the floor in a trail from the door to the bed. He was sound asleep before his head hit the pillow.

Chapter Twenty-One
Words from the Grave

Ian rolled over and saw the clock reading ten o'clock. "Oh shit!" He overslept and missed his first day with the bosun on his new schedule.

He looked around the room and saw his clothes all over the floor. He rushed out of bed, threw on his boiler suit and shoes and ran out on deck looking for the deck gang and the bosun. He found them chipping paint on the port side forward. Ian's face was burning and he hung his head. The bosun, a heavy set Filipino with a weathered and rutty face, had a smile absent a few teeth. He looked at the cadet and started to laugh. "Come here, cadet," he said and turned to walk aft. Ian followed him.

"Kid, walk with me," and Ian ran to catch up with him. The strong man put the cadet under his powerful arm and pulled him in tight. "I covered for you today. Don't let it happen again … Okay, kid?"

"Yes, sir. I'm sorry," Ian said, his shoulders slumped, "and thank you, sir. Thank you very much!"

"Aw forget it, kid. Now, get out of here. See you at eight hundred tomorrow morning. Right!"

"Right." Ian retreated from the working party and snuck back to his room. Then his thoughts turned to the stack of papers in his desk drawer.

"First things first," he told himself. He undressed and entered the head where he shaved, showered, and took a few minutes to look at his face and thought, *who are you? I thought I knew who I was until a few days ago and now I really don't know anymore.*

He left the head and again left his room door unlocked as if inviting Hanna to come in without knocking. He thought about her, shook his head, and focused on what information could be in the pile of papers. He dressed, combed his hair, and was ready for the watch in another hour and a half. Lunch was thirty minutes away. His gaze returned back to the papers on his desk.

As if drawn by an overwhelming power, he walked over to the desk and sat down. He scanned over the pictures again and set them in a neat pile on his left. He picked up the papers and news articles that told a story of a dynasty of wealth and power. His grandfather was a man of exceptional talent and wielded tremendous power as he became incredibly wealthy. He was a leader with vision and he was in the right place and time. Following the Second World War in Europe, Rotterdam had been destroyed by both German and American bombers.

Ian's grandfather was one of the men who rebuilt Rotterdam and developed it into the transportation hub of Europe. He was loved and hated for his success. The last article told the story of how he was murdered in his boardroom by one of his own employees. The article mentioned his grandmother was left as the sole executor for the massive fortune and her brother, Johan, was made the Managing Director of the corporate dynasty.

"Holy shit." He was rich and powerful. Super rich and powerful!

DRAWN TO THE SEA
(First Revision)

Ian re-read each of the articles. His family history began to come into focus. He gathered up the articles and organized them into a neat pile next to the pictures. Next, he focused on the pile of letters his father had written to his grandmother. His hands began to tremble as he reached for the one on top.

The first letter was written to his mother in Amsterdam days before he left to return to his ship, the *Amore Islander*. He wrote to his mother in English. Ian began to read,

1 June 1978

Dearest Mother,

It is once again time for me to return to sea. I have spent every guilder I have and will continue to refuse to accept your generosity. I am a spoilt reprobate and have made a mess of my life. I know you'd do anything to help me, but I must figure this out for myself. I will ... trust me. I have found a woman in America who is good for me, and in time, will help me climb out of my hell. Someday I'll make you and father proud, that I promise.

I leave in the morning to return to work. My ship is in Tampa, Florida. The 'Amore Islander' is a tired whore of the sea. She is neglected, tired, and has been raped for years by her owners. That said, I've found a family of like-minded souls in the crew aboard. We're an international group of men. To the outside world we're losers, fools, and possibly some would call us human garbage.

181

But we are a family and together we exist and survive. I don't expect you to understand. You and your family live so far the other direction as proper and correct elites. I'm sorry that's a destiny I'm not ready to embrace yet.

I'm eternally sorry for the pain or disappointment I've certainly caused you. I love you with all my heart. Yes, I have demons I must excise before I can return into your world. Give me time. I'm confident Susan will help me navigate back into your world. I know you'll approve of her.

With all my love, your devoted (albeit troubled) son,
Ian

The young cadet set the paper down and considered the intimacy he had just experienced. This was a private letter from a troubled son to his mother. It was not a letter between two anonymous people, it was his father reaching out to his mother. Ian realized he'd just read words formed and considered by his father. They were his final words, words from the grave. A cold chill ran down his spine.

He closed the letter and pushed away from the desk realizing it was time for lunch and then watch. He set the papers in neat piles and took a quick look in the mirror and ran a comb through his hair. Another glance in the mirror and he froze. For a second he thought he saw his father standing behind him. He was tall and handsome with blond hair and piercing blue eyes. Ian looked again and realized he must have imagined it and made his way to the officer's mess to grab a bite to eat. He wouldn't mention the vision in the mirror to a soul.

The officers and engineers who ate in the mess were completely different now that Ian was on the twelve to four. He missed Joe, Larry, and Hanna. Sitting at the table was Fritz and Carl, the twelve to four watch engineer, Ian asked permission to join them. Fritz nodded as he took his focus off his bowl of soup.

"Suit yourself junger," Fritz said, and returned to his soup. There was no conversation at the table. Carl seemed content to eat his sandwich without a word, too. This was a far cry from the eight to twelve team who enjoyed each other's company and talked and joked during each meal.

Ian ordered his lunch. He thought *a bowl of tomato soup and a ham sandwich would do.* The soup was in front of him in an instant. The stewards were as efficient as ever. The sandwich was next to his bowl a moment later and the ham and melted cheese aroma teased his nose as he finished his soup.

With the absence of conversation, Ian found he could consume his meals as if he inhaled them. His soup was finished in several minutes and the sandwich consumed in half-a-dozen bites. *I'll have to eat more slowly from now on,* he thought.

When he finished, he asked permission to leave and made his way to the bridge. Joe was there putting the noon position on the chart and finishing his log entries. As Ian walked through the door, Joe looked over his shoulder, "Hey, kid. What's shaking?"

"Well, to be honest, I miss standing watch with you and Doug."

183

"Is everything okay with Fritz?" Joe asked.

"Yea, he is just really quiet. He didn't say a single word last night until he turned over to the second mate."

"Well, why don't you talk to him? See if he'll open up a little. Don't worry, kid, he'll warm up to you."

The door opened and in walked Fritz. Just as he had done the night before, he put his personal bag on a shelf, walked over to the coffee pot, poured a cup of coffee, walked over to the chart and looked at the noon position, and walked out onto the bridge and looked around the horizon. He looked into the radar hood and then at the true and magnetic course written in chalk on a board. Fritz moved over to Joe and they conducted the watch turnover.

"Ja I have tis watch," Fritz said. Joe and Doug gathered up their belongings and headed to the door to the stairs towards the rear of the bridge. "See you later, kid," Joe said, as they passed through the door and descended to the mess deck to eat lunch before the galley closed.

Ian looked at the seaman in the corner of the bridge where he had stood during the watch last night. He was an average sized man with long hair pulled back in a ponytail. He wore Levis that were torn in the knees and had seen many wash cycles. His shirt was made of wool with long sleeves and paint stained, but it was clean. He stood looking out the window as if in a daze.

Fritz resumed his pacing from left to right with a constant eye outside the ship. He scanned the horizon, periodically checked the radar and put a fix on the chart each hour. Both men knew their jobs and neither one spoke a single word more than was necessary.

DRAWN TO THE SEA
(First Revision)

Two hours into the four hour watch, Ian spoke. "Fritz … during our port call in Rotterdam, I found out I have relatives who live in the Netherlands. It seems my father was a merchant marine officer who sailed on Liberian ships. His family name was van der Waterlaan."

Fritz stopped his pacing and turned to face Ian. His eyes screwed tightly and his face twisted and became dark. "Your father was Ian van der Waterlaan?" Something was erupting within him. "Shiza, I knew it!" Fritz yelled.

"That is what I have been told. I never knew him. He died at sea. His ship sank."

"Ja, the *Amore Islander,* the damned ship!" Fritz said.

"Then you knew the ship and my father?" Ian asked.

"Ja, I knowed the ship and I knowed Ian van der Waterlaan." He turned and resumed his pacing without another word. Ian stood there with his mouth open, amazed this German would be so cruel. Ian was heartbroken and angry at Fritz for his reaction and silence.

The moment the second mate relieved them on the bridge, Ian left without saying goodbye and nearly ran to his stateroom. He would ask if he could be transferred back to the eight to twelve in the morning. Working with this stoic German was uncomfortable and downright creepy. "But then again, he knows something about my father and the ship he died on. I need him to tell me," Ian said, to his reflection in the mirror.

The letters on the desk once again drew his attention and he sat down, staring at the three other unread letters. He reached for and opened the second letter.

3 June 1978

Dearest Mother,

I am back aboard the 'Amore Islander'. I joined the ship at Hooker's Point in Tampa, Florida. Tampa is a nice city. The weather is always warm and there is energy among the people that is light, free, and forgiving. I often wonder if I could settle down here and start anew. There is a strong Latin culture which adds a wonderful dynamic to an already eclectic community. I hope someday I'll be able to show you this part of the world through my eyes and experiences, and not from the manufactured perfection your handlers insist you experience anywhere you go. Do you ever feel like shedding your title and the expectations placed upon you, Mother?

Of course, I know you can't. You're part of the critical glue which keeps our society together. The elite have rules they must live by and the masses expect (no, demand) the excesses of royalty and the elite. I hope you still consider your life a privilege and not a prison. I had to run from the dungeon of privilege. I hope you'll understand one day.

Yesterday, I spent the evening with Susan. She is a lovely woman who is smart yet uncomplicated. She has a beautiful daughter, Sarah, whom I adore. Susan and I

*can spend hours without a word and feel
content and connected. She is in every way
my soul-mate. I guess I've known this for
years.*

*But our relationship is complicated and
I fear if I open up too quickly about the
conflicts that torment my soul, she may run. I
could never bear to lose her completely so I
enjoy the time I have with her when I can. I
do hope to make a life with her and her
daughter. They're good for me and I know
you'll like them, too. Maybe I'll bring them
with me to Amsterdam around the holidays. I
still keep secret my family and the van der
Waterlaan dynasty. I prefer it that way. To
the world, I'm just a simple Liberian seaman.
Your loving son,
Ian*

Ian set the letter down on the table and thought
about what he had just read. His mother was mentioned in
the letter, *Smart and uncomplicated ... Sarah (his sister)...
I adore her. Our relationship is complicated. No one
knows about my family or the van der Waterlaan dynasty.
Dad, why were you so haunted?* Ian asked the letter.

Again a cold chill ran down his back as he tried to
digest his father's words. He walked to the bathroom and
filled the basin and splashed his face several times. As he
opened his eyes and looked in the mirror, he noticed his
father standing behind him. This time, Ian studied the
image and took in every detail. The man's long flowing
blonde hair framed a rugged, deeply tanned, and handsome

face. His intense blue eyes captured Ian's. The man stood tall like Ian and his broad shoulders where identical to his own. The man smiled, his teeth were perfect and Ian could feel the hands of his father on his shoulders. *Son, I have always been watching over you.*

There was a tap on the door and Ian was startled back to reality. The image in the mirror was gone. Ian opened the door and Hanna stood in a buff colored camisole and running shorts.

"I thought I heard you," Hanna murmured. She seemed still half asleep. "Are you okay?" She rubbed her eyes and yawned before coming into his room.

"I was reading the letters written by my father," Ian offered. Hanna may or may not have heard him as she walked zombie-like to his bed and lay down. Soon she was fast asleep. "Hanna, you can't stay here." It was too late, she was already snoring.

"Damn," he said under his breath and grabbed a spare blanket and curled up on the settee for the night. It wouldn't be long and she would be called to watch.

As Ian nodded off he thought, *I have met my father. I don't know how to explain it, but I did, and now I am so close to the woman I love, yet still miles away.* His mind clicked back and forth between Hanna and the image of his father. He had long forgotten about his watch with Fritz.

Chapter Twenty-Two
Fritz Tells

The engineering watch knocked on Hanna's door. Ian bolted off the settee and his head whipped towards his bed. It was empty. His heart pounded and he swung open the bathroom door. Hanna's door was already open and he saw her laying out her uniform. He grabbed his chest. Even with bed-head and sleep in her eyes, she was stunning. "I just wanted to make sure you were up," he mumbled. She nodded and she gave him a bashful half-smile. Their eyes locked and neither spoke. They didn't have to. All that needed to be said was written on both of their faces. Hanna gave him a little wave before she left her room. Ian grinned. When he got into bed, his pillow smelled like her, a mixture of grease, sweat and jasmine. He hugged it as he drifted back to sleep.

He woke up in time for lunch before reporting to the bridge. The noon to four was as quiet as a tomb. Fritz continued his routine without a single word and avoided Ian. For the entire four hours, Ian could have jumped out of his skin. He decided he would approach the chief mate after his shift and ask to be transferred to another watch.

As the watch came to a close, Fritz looked at Ian and said, "Junger, I will tell you tis story during watch tonight. Be patient." Ian vaulted from despair to enthusiasm. He couldn't wait for the evening watch. The second mate came to the bridge, the watch relieved, and Ian bolted for his room.

It was shortly after four and there was an hour until dinner. He cruised down the passageway and opened his door and there she was. Hanna was seated at his desk as she looked over the pictures and papers he had left there. She looked up from her reading, "Hello. Close the door, Silly."

"May I ask what you are doing in my room?"

"You left the door open, so I thought you wanted me to come in and look at the papers. We haven't seen much of each other since you changed watches."

The anger that flared inside of him subsided. He couldn't find it in his heart to be cross with the woman he loved. "Well, what do you think?" he said as he gestured towards the papers.

"For starters, it sounds like your family is rich beyond imagination," she said, with a smile, but then her face got cold and serious, "and it sounds like your father had some serious issues."

"Did you read all the letters?" he asked.

"Yes."

"Oh, I have two more to read." Ian took off his shirt without thinking. Hanna's eyes widened and her jaw dropped as she gaped at his bare chest and muscular arms. Her cheeks flushed and she ran through the bathroom to her room and closed the door behind her. Ian just stood there and wondered what had just happened. He looked over at his desk, took a seat, and picked up the third letter and read,

DRAWN TO THE SEA
(First Revision)

Dearest Mother,

I post this note from Cristobal, Panama. This is a gingerbread town which has a complexity about it which makes it an interesting place to visit, but I could never find a reason to stay. There is a Panama Canal component making it unique. The port adds to the texture. There doesn't appear to be a plan or reason to the way the city has developed. This city needed a man of vision like father when it was being developed. The city will suffer for the lack of a grand design and will forever be without beauty and culture as a result.

We are enroute to San Metalous, Peru by way of the canal. There is a cargo waiting for the ship there. I'm told it's about a hundred miles north of Lima. We'll be loading a new kind of cargo called iron ore pellets for Japan. From there, the ship will go to Taiwan to the breakers. That'll be sad, as I have been working on the 'Amore Islander' for the last seven years.

I should be coming home once the ship is presented to the breakers and it is to that end that I write.

I have given much thought to what I write in these words. I know I love my Susan and I am ready to come home and resume my responsibilities as the van der Waterlaan

191

heir. Through this woman I have found a peace which is genuine and lasting. The demons tormenting me for so long have been exorcised and I'm ready to be the responsible son you, Dad, and Uncle Johan had expected.

This is the first time in my life my course is clear and there is purpose in my decisions. I'll be bringing Susan and her daughter Sarah to the van der Waterlaan castle when I finish this contract.

I write this letter to you from a place of emotional and moral security and happiness. I'm looking forward to returning home and facing my destiny with Susan, Sarah, and you by my side.

Thank you for your patience, understanding, and love as I have looked the world over for the answers to questions driving my restlessness.
With all my love, your son,
Ian

Ian thought, he was going to bring his mother and sister to Holland and include them in the van der Waterlaan family. *I bet mother never knew any of this.*

He reached for the last letter and began to read each word at a time. Tears began to well up as he read,

DRAWN TO THE SEA
(First Revision)

12 August 1978

Dearest Mother,

 A hurried letter as the ship is preparing for the long voyage to Asia. I fear there is something very wrong about this voyage. Our chief mate was just murdered a few hours ago. The circumstances are such, many of us believe the captain may be behind it. The ship has been grossly overloaded and kept secret from even the mates responsible for cargo operations.

 The captain is distant and aloof. The old ship is straining under the excessive weight. Pray for us that we don't encounter a storm. I hope I've misread the situation and the concern comes from my being done with this life at sea. I am ready to start afresh.

 I must end as we will sail in an hour and I want to post this before we leave. Don't worry, I'll be home soon.

Your loving son,

Ian

There was a knock on the bathroom door and Ian wiped his eyes and slowly got up and opened the door. Hanna was there. She had changed her clothes and combed her hair. "I have read all the letters my father wrote," Ian said. Hanna walked over and kissed him hard on the lips.

"Next time you undress in front of me, I will attack you," she said in a raspy voice.

"Okay, I'll remember that." His smile revealed all thirty-two teeth. They sat down and compared their

193

impressions of the letters they had read. They spoke about each one of the letters. Hanna sounded like a television detective as she considered the letters from many different perspectives. It was helpful to Ian to hear her viewpoint and insight.

The time flew and Ian had to prepare for watch. Hanna got up and kissed him on his cheek and left to go back to her room. This time she left the door open to her room and she climbed into her bed and turned off the light.

Ian washed his face, the door to Hanna's room still open. He looked in and after a moment, walked in, leaned over, and kissed her on her cheek. Her eyes opened and she smiled.

He walked to the mess and opened the refrigerator and made a sandwich and drank a glass of milk, then headed up to the bridge. He was there a few minutes before Fritz so he and Joe struck up a conversation and killed the time. Fritz entered, and in a few minutes, Joe and Doug left the bridge.

Fritz poured his coffee and started his pacing routine as he had done every night. Ian poured himself a cup of coffee, and this time, he poured two tablespoons of sugar into the black liquid.

It was two in the morning and the *American Spirit* was alone in the Atlantic with a "bone in her teeth" as she made twenty-one point five knots headed back to New Jersey. The horizon was dark and there wasn't even a single bleep on the radar screen out to twenty four miles. It was cold and the seas were steady and the ship rolled easily in the northeast swell. The sky remained overcast and there wasn't a star or planet with enough light to penetrate the dense cloud cover. The air was moist, yet visibility was excellent.

The able seaman was propped up in the corner with his coffee mug. Fritz was pacing, then he approached Ian, stopped, and looked at the young man. With a serious look on his face he said, "I will tell you what I can. Come with me to the wing of the bridge."

Fritz led the way through the open door on the port bridge wing. It was the lee side of the ship tonight and somewhat protected from the wind. There were some machinery exhaust sounds in the background, but other than that it was quiet.

Fritz walked out on the wing about ten feet to be out of ear shot of the seaman. He put his coffee mug on the rail behind the dodger and leaned against the rail, his head just behind the dodger, deflecting the wind up and over the heads of the lookouts. The clever device created a protected place where the lookouts could stand and be shielded from the wind and rain without blocking visibility.

Fritz looked hard off into the distance ahead of the ship as he appeared to gather his thoughts. Ian slid in beside him. Not too close, but close enough so he'd be able to hear every word.

"Junger, I worked on the *Amore Islander* and I was once a close friend of your father's. I will only tell you what I can. What do you want to know?" Fritz said, never taking his eyes off the horizon. He spoke and stared as if he was hypnotized.

"Sir, can you tell me about my father? What was he like?"

Fritz didn't respond for a moment then he spoke, "I met your father sometime around nineteen seventy two. We were both assigned to the *Amore Islander*. It was our first time on the ship. He was assigned the eight to twelve and I the twelve to four. We were both young and had recently completed our maritime educations. A German and a Dutchman, but regardless we became close friends, or so I thought."

"There was always something about your father, some dark secret. He would be friendly until questions came up about his family and he'd get dark and quiet. I had my secrets too so that didn't stop us. We used to go ashore together and buy nice dinners, drinks, and dates in the ports we were visiting. Our favorite was Tampa and the ship was there nearly three or four times a month. So we had our favorite bars and in the bars were girls, and it was there that your father and I went our separate ways."

He scanned the horizon for a moment then continued, "There was a pretty young girl named Susan we both were in love with. She dated me, then him, and then me, and so on. I was really nuts about her but she wouldn't get involved. Yes, for money she would spend the night, but then that was her business. It wasn't long and Ian got the upper hand with Susan and she became his exclusive girl and left me in the cold."

"This went on for four years and I got so angry one evening we fought over her. Your father and I never spoke a word again. I was fired from the ship and went back to the union hall and found another job. I never returned to Tampa. I wonder if Susan is still working the waterfront."

Ian's blood was boiling. "Susan is my mother, mister."

"Yes, I figured as much." Fritz spoke, never taking his eyes off the horizon. "Don't be upset. That's the way it was. We all do things we wish we could take back."

Ian took in the cool air and his anger subsided little by little. "What was he like?" Ian asked.

"He was a complex and intelligent man but he was haunted by something or someone he wouldn't talk about. I really liked him until we fought over your mother, then it was over forever."

"What about the *Amore Islander*?"

"It was a broken down and neglected ship in nineteen seventy four. I can only imagine what it must have been like by the time it sank." Fritz turned to look at Ian for the first time during the conversation. "Your father liked the ship. It was his home and he loved the crew. He was happy there."

Then Fritz grabbed his coffee cup and turned again to Ian, "Tat is all I know and will talk about. Ja?"

"Yes, Fritz, and thank you."

"It's a quiet watch and we'll be arriving in New Jersey in the morning. Why don't you go to bed, I'll see you tomorrow afternoon for watch. Ja?"

"Thank you, Fritz." Ian said as he grabbed his coffee cup, took it to the sink and washed it, then headed down the stairs.

He tried to be quiet when he came into his room so he wouldn't wake Hanna. Without turning on the light, he fumbled out of his clothes and in the dark he quietly brushed his teeth and used the face cloth to clean his face and his body. He moved to his bed. The cool sheets felt good on his naked body. He lay there and looked at the ceiling as he waited for his eyes to adjust to the dark. He heard movement in the bathroom. It was Hanna in a sheer gown as she walked over to his bed. "Did you lock the door?" she asked.

"Yes."

"Shhhhh," she said and put her finger on his lips, then bent over and kissed him. Her mouth opened and she slid her tongue into his mouth. She slipped out of her robe and slid into the bed next to him. He pressed himself against her thigh as the kisses became more passionate. It was his first time and he knew she didn't have much experience either. They spent the night together as if there were no tomorrow.

What Ian didn't know was Hanna was leaving the ship the next day for an internship assignment. This would be their one and only night together.

When she had received the news back in Rotterdam, she had decided she would come to his bed their last night together.

Chapter Twenty-Three
The Next Morning

When Ian woke he was alone in the bed. At some point, Hanna had left and returned to her room. In fact, by the time Ian was awake, Hanna was already in the engine room standing her last watch on the *American Spirit*. He still felt her and smelled her cologne on the pillow. Still half asleep, he thought about the night before and how good it had been. Gradually, he became aware of his surroundings.

The ship was rolling heavily and the curtain covering the window struck the bulkhead in rhythm to the ships movement. The papers he'd left on the desk were still there, but had shifted a little.

His clothes were where he discarded them the night before. He imagined her filmy, white nightgown entangled with his clothes, just as their bodies had been intertwined. It was Ian's first experience with a woman and he felt like a changed man. He'd stepped off a cliff and could never return back. He was glad it had been Hanna who had shared the once in a lifetime experience. Ian smiled and climbed out of bed when there was a knock on his stateroom door.

"Cadet, mate wants you on the bridge for arrival. Its zero nine hundred … report to the bridge by zero nine forty five."

"Yes, I've got it." Ian responded through the door. The footsteps moving away indicated the able seaman was satisfied the message had been relayed and acknowledged.

Ian was up and started to clean up his room. He took a quick shower, shaved and looked at the mirror hoping to see his father's image, but no one was there. In less than fifteen minutes, he was dressed and making his way to the bridge. He'd have a cup of coffee and that would have to suffice for now. He wasn't hungry, his mind was caught up in his first experience and the complexity of finding out a little about this father and his Dutch family.

His mother came to mind and he realized he hadn't mentioned anything about his father to her yet. In their last conversation, she indicated she and Maria wanted to come to New Jersey and see him during his port visit, but nothing was finalized. He wondered if they would be at the dock on arrival. He realized he was standing in front of the door to the bridge. It was time to focus on the job at hand.

He walked through the door and there was his friend, Joe, standing at the chart table putting a position on the chart. Joe looked over, "Hey kid, good morning. It's nice to have you back on my watch. Keep an eye on that tanker on our port side. Let me know if it looks like he is closing."

"Yes, sir!"

"Kid, cut the "sir" crap for the thousandth time!" Joe smiled. Ambrose Light was visible to the port and Sandy Hook and Long Island were breaking over the western horizon. Joe knew this approach well, having made it a number of times. He called out from the chart room, "Ian, did they teach you about the famous collision between the *Stockholm* and the *Andria Doria* in your navigation classes at school? Well, this is almost the exact location where it happened."

"Wow, really? That was one of the worst collisions ever, um?" Ian said over his shoulder as he walked out onto the port bridge wing and took a bearing on the tanker to see if it was moving ahead or falling behind. He rather expected the latter as tankers are naturally slower than containerships moving at sea speed. He watched and confirmed his suspicion, then came back into the wheelhouse. "Joe, the tanker is falling behind. The relative bearing is opening up."

"Thanks, kid," said Joe. "You're becoming a fine navigator." He looked up from the chart, "Hey, kid, call the captain and tell him we'll be at the sea buoy in thirty six minutes. Then call the engine room and tell them the same. We'll need to be at maneuvering speed by zero nine thirty."

Ian called the captain. Horne thanked the cadet for the call and said he'd tell the chief as he was sitting in his office. Next, Ian called down to the engine room and Hanna answered, "Engine room." Ian froze and just stood there. She repeated, "Engine room." Ian remained frozen. Joe noticed Ian was just standing there with the receiver in his ear.

"Hey, kid, you alright?"

"Yes," Ian said, and then regained some composure. "Maneuvering speed by zero nine thirty, please. We'll be at the sea buoy in thirty minutes."

"Oh it's you, Ian, good morning. Maneuvering speed at zero nine thirty," she said and hung up. Ian's heart was in his shoes. *So this is what love is all about*, he thought and he slowly hung up the receiver. He walked back out on the port bridge wing and felt the cold air on his face and kept his distance from Joe until he recomposed himself.

About the time Ian returned to the wheelhouse, the captain came through the door and said, "Joe, I look forward to returning to Port Elizabeth. My wife, Jeanne, is always there waiting for me. It makes this life more bearable. How is your family, these days? Your daughter must be getting tall by now."

"Doreen is almost eight years old and more the young lady every time I see her. Heidi, my wife, is fine too. It takes a special woman to marry, or should I say, stay married to, a mariner." His voice tapered off, "But I guess you know that, captain."

"Yea, we're the lucky ones, Joe. Guys like us are truly blessed. Will Heidi and Doreen come to the ship this trip?"

"No, captain. Next trip falls during school break and they are thinking about coming down for the day." Joe said with a broad smile on his face. Thinking of his family had that effect on him.

The captain thought for a moment, *Jeanne and I are a one-in-a-million couple too. Everything is easy and in twenty two years together, never an argument.*

Captain Horne looked out the bridge windows at New York far off in the distance. *I'll have a long talk with Jeanne this afternoon about swallowing-the-anchor and*

*coming home for good. I'm ready and this trip, with the
labor strikes, has convinced me it's time to go for good.*

The ship approached the sea buoy as if it had a
mind of its own, like a horse returning to the barn after a
hot trail ride. Off on the grey horizon, the pilot boat
approached at high speed. The boat pounded in the seas
and the spray flew off the bow as it dove into each
approaching wave. The deck gang had already rigged the
pilot ladder and Ian was making his way down to the main
deck to meet the pilot.

The agile boat came alongside the ship. Captain
Horne made a proper lee and the pilot climbed and jumped
over the rail. Without a pause, he was on his way to the
bridge, Ian in tow. Pilot and captain exchanged greetings.
The pilot was armed with a cup of hot black coffee and
began to direct the ship into New York Harbor.

A left turn after the Verrazano Bridge and Port
Elizabeth was dead ahead. The team of the pilot and tugs
had the ship alongside. Before the ship was even secured
to the dock, the longshoremen were coming aboard and
containers lifted off the ship.

The captain called into the wheelhouse,
"FINISHED WITH ENGINES," and came in from the
inshore bridge wing. He walked over to Ian, "Ian, I have a
surprise for you." The captain spoke with a smile from ear
to ear. "Your mother and your Aunt Maria are waiting
with my wife at the visitor's office and will be aboard in
fifteen minutes or so. I'd like you to feel free to meet your
family at the brow and you have the run of the ship. Show
them everything about the *American Spirit*. I hope the
three of you will join Jeanne and me for dinner this
evening in the Officer's Salon."

"I have some other news." The captain told Ian and he looked down indicating it was bad news, "Unfortunately, you will be assigned to another ship. You'll be paid off in the morning and I guess go home until the ATR contacts you. We, especially me, will miss you." The captain said as he held Ian in his eyes. "You are a special cadet and I know you'll make an excellent captain yourself someday. Now scoot and wait for your family on the brow." Captain Horne lightheartedly shooed him away with his hand.

Horne thought, *if Jeanne and I had been blessed with a son, I would have hoped he would have been like Ian.* The pilot stood in the corner of the bridge and caught the captain's attention. There were a myriad of things the captain would need to tend to. The first was sign the pilot's chit that would later become an invoice addressed to the owners in Manhattan. Containers moved in the air and the activity inside and outside the ship became a blur.

Ian ran to his room and this time he knocked on the bathroom door, excited to tell the news to Hanna. She opened the door and Ian peered inside her room. He could see her suitcases were on the bed and she was nearly packed.

"Where are you going?" he asked.

"I got the news in Rotterdam. I have been assigned to an internship in Boston. I didn't want to tell you because I knew that we were falling for each other and I didn't want it to ruin our last few days together. I love you, Ian, and I don't have a single regret about last night."

"I love you, too, Hanna." Ian responded and his eyes began to tear. "I have news, too," he said. "My mother and Auntie Maria will be aboard in a few minutes.

I just found out I'm being reassigned to another ship and so I'll be leaving in the morning, too. Will you come and stay at my home for a few days before reporting to your internship, please?" He nearly pleaded.

"I was planning on taking the train to Boston and staying in a hotel for the rest of the week. I guess I could, if it's okay with your mom and Maria."

"Great, I know they'll love you too," he said with genuine excitement. Hanna reached in, grabbed him, and kissed him hard and deep.

"Now listen to me carefully," she said. "Cool the lovey-dovey stuff on the ship. We don't want word getting back to the academy. Okay?"

"Right," he said, knowing she had a point. This time he leaned in and gave her a soft, sweet, and tender kiss. He felt his knees weaken. He whispered in her ear, "Ik hou van jou."

"What?" she questioned.

"It's Dutch for 'I love you'. I figured based on what we've uncovered about my family's past it would be appropriate."

They smiled and he turned around and headed out the door down to the brow. He arrived just as a van came into sight. It pulled up to the gangway and several new crew members climbed out, grabbed their sea bags, and gathered together at the foot of the gangway. Two of the three lit-up cigarettes and smoked before climbing up to the main deck.

A moment later, three women climbed out. Ian immediately recognized two of the three. The third was obviously, Mrs. Horne. Mrs. Horne took the lead and coached the others on how to climb the ladder and how to hold on.

A moment later, the ladies emerged onto the main deck. Ian hugged his mom and then Maria. Mrs. Horne introduced herself to Ian and then excused herself. "I'm anxious to see my husband," she said with a wink and a smile. Ian brought his guests into the deck house and brought them to the bridge to start the tour. He talked and walked with his family for three hours until they were exhausted. He brought them back to his stateroom and gave them an opportunity to freshen up and rest for a few minutes before dinner.

There was a gentle knock on the bathroom door. Susan and Maria looked at each other with curiosity. Ian spoke, "That's the engine cadet. We share a bathroom." Ian walked over and opened the door and Hanna looked into his room. Ian invited her in and made introductions, "Mom, Maria. I would like to introduce Hanna. Hanna, this is my mother and my Auntie Maria."

The ladies gathered and shook hands and then hugged and Ian watched with a delighted grin to see them get along well. *That's good… This will make asking if she can stay with us in Bristol easier. Then there is the thing… we love each other.*

The four of them made their way down to the Officer's Salon to meet the captain and his wife for dinner. The Horne's were already seated and were joined by the chief and his wife, Dottie. She was a woman from the islands and wore bright colored clothes and large earrings. Ian made introductions and the captain stood briefly, welcomed them aboard, and asked them to be seated, a perfect gentleman.

DRAWN TO THE SEA
(First Revision)

The meal was served with the elegance and pride of a fine restaurant. The stewards were dressed in their best and the meal was outstanding. The only thing missing were cocktails and wine, but as an American working ship there was no alcohol on board.

Stories were told and the chief and captain told the guests positive and endearing stories of the two cadets. They made it clear that Ian and Hanna were highly regarded on the ship. After the extended meal and conversation, the captain and his wife excused themselves and retired for the evening. A moment later the chief and his wife rose and left. Ian saw his mother and Maria were worn out from the day's events and took the initiative.

"Mom, Hanna is leaving for Boston to do her internship starting next week. Could she come home with us for a few days until she needs to report?"

Susan and Maria exchanged knowing smiles. Maria spoke for them both, "Of course she's welcome. Let your mother and me get back to the hotel. We're exhausted and we'll meet you at the visitor center tomorrow morning at eleven, okay?"

"Thank you, Auntie, I love you," Ian said with dancing eyes. Maria and Susan smiled at him and then at each other.

Hanna thought, *these ladies have a wonderful yet strange relationship. They are more than longtime friends and there is an intimacy and trust that's beautiful but forbidden.*

Together they walked to the brow, kissed each other good night as the van waited for the ladies to come down the long gangway. Ian and Hanna watched them from the main deck and kept their eyes on the van until it was out of sight. They looked at each other and walked to their staterooms, locked their doors, met in the bathroom between their rooms and began to undress one another. It would be another wonderful night in each other's arms.

Two decks up, Jeanne Horne came out of the bathroom in her nightgown and joined her husband in their bed. She reached over and turned off the light and leaned over and gently kissed her husband on the lips and said, "John, you know that your cadets are madly in love with one another."

"Of course dear, that's why they are both getting off the ship before something happens. Now let's get some sleep," he said as he leaned over and kissed her.

"I think something already has happened. Good night," she said and they snuggled in tight with one another and slept as they only did when they were together.

Chapter Twenty-Four
Remarkable

Ian and Hanna said their goodbyes to their friends the next morning. With the other sailors signing-off the ship, they made their way to the captain's office, forming a line outside the door. The captain sat at his desk, his wife stood behind him with her hand placed on his shoulder.

One at a time the sailors came into the office and signed their discharge papers and the articles, having completed contractual service. The captain reached into the top drawer of his desk and pulled out an envelope with the sailor's name written on the front. He opened it and pulled out a summary of earnings and read it to the sailor.

"Johnson, you were aboard for six months and four days. You were assigned as able seaman watch, correct?" He waited for a response then said, "Your earnings, less draws and direct deposits leaves you with … Please confirm this is your direct deposit, account," as he pointed to the individual's account number.

Soon it was Hanna's turn and then Ian's. The captain spent a few additional moments with the cadets to thank and encourage them to continue their progress in school. His wife stood quietly by his side and beamed.

Joe, Fritz, and Larry were at the brow waiting for the cadets to leave the ship to say goodbye. The first assistant and chief mate came around the corner and offered their best wishes, too. Doug, the able seaman on watch, took their bags down the gangway and waited for them on the dock.

The bus was running, the driver waiting at the foot of the gangway. Doug threw the bags in the bus and shook Ian's hand as he approached. "Take care, kid. You too, missy," he said to Hanna as she climbed into the shuttle. Their chests heaved as the driver maneuvered away from the ship through the container yard avoiding trucks, cranes and stevedores. They looked over their shoulders at the *American Spirit* with tears in their eyes. Doug waved then began to climb the gangway.

A few minutes later, they stepped out of the shuttle with the other sailors who parted company and made their own way to their next adventure. Ian and Hanna waited for Maria and Susan at the terminal visitor center. The wait was only a few minutes when they saw the ladies drive up in a dark red sedan. Just as the car came into sight, Ian reminded Hanna, "Let's not mention what we discovered about my father in Holland until the time is right and we're home in Bristol."

"That's gonna be tough, but I agree," Hanna said. "It's a lot to put on your mother all at once."

The bags were loaded in the trunk and Ian and Hanna climbed into the back seat. Maria had them headed up the I-95 back to Bristol moments later. She had just purchased a seven hundred series BMW so everyone was comfortable with plenty of room. Maria concentrated on the road, Susan sat by her side and the young lovers were content in the back with their hands entwined. Occasionally, Ian would lean over and kiss Hanna on the cheek and smile. Maria watched in the rear view mirror and smiled to herself. She looked over at Susan and squeezed her hand and the five hour trip flew by.

As the sedan approached Bristol, boredom and drowsiness was replaced with enthusiasm and excitement. Ian began to tell Hanna all about his town as they entered the city limits. Maria maneuvered the car into the driveway and turned to the two in the back seat and said, "Welcome home."

The four got out of the car, stretched, then walked back to the trunk as it automatically opened. Ian removed the luggage while Susan turned to Hanna and took her under her arm. "Ian will get your bags, dear. Come with Maria and me," and she steered Hanna to the house. "We'll get a bite to eat and have a cup of tea. We're so glad you'll be with us for a while." Susan glided towards the door.

Maria looked over at Ian, "Looks like your mom likes her too. She is a nice young lady. Take care of her, young man."

"Yes, Auntie, I love her, you know?"

"I didn't just fall off the turnip truck, Ian. It's pretty clear to your mother and me. Will you bring your mother's and my bags to our room?"

"Yes, Auntie." He thought, *'our room'!*

Maria smiled, turned and walked through the front door the other two ladies had left open. She would catch up with them inside. Susan walked Hanna through the home and pointed out each of the rooms.

Susan completed the tour and stood in front of Sarah's room. "Dear, this'll be your room. It's Ian's sister's, but she is grown and living in California with her

211

husband and children. She won't mind." She smiled, she knew where Hanna would spend her nights and she was fine with that. She already was well aware of the chemistry between this pretty young lady and her son.

The three ladies adjourned to the kitchen. Susan began to prepare a meal and tea for the ladies. Maria and Hanna sat at the table after both asked to help and were told, "No, relax and visit." Maria started by asking a number of soft-ball questions to break the ice. "Where are you from? Brothers, Sisters?"

Hanna told about her family, her home town and how she had ended up at the merchant marine academy. Susan and Maria listened with great interest. In ten minutes, Ian joined them and as he sat down his mother brought freshly brewed tea and four mugs to the table. "How do you like your tea, dear?"

"Just a little sugar, please," Hanna replied. Ian smiled as he watched them interact. He sat quietly and carefully watched the two most important women in his life get to know each other. He wanted Hanna in his life and needed their support. He smiled and thought, *it looks like they're off to a good start.* He watched them talk and become comfortable with each other. Ian became aware that he had his fingers crossed behind his back. He smiled and moved his hands into his pockets.

Ian's grandparents came in the back door and Stanley walked over to Ian and gave him a bear hug, "Welcome home, son. We're sure proud of you." He looked over as his wife slid in beside him and hugged her grandson.

"Ian, you look so grown up," as she held him at arm's length and looked at him. Stanley saw Hanna, looked at Susan and then Ian.

"Who is this pretty young lady?" he said.

Ian, a little embarrassed he'd not already made introductions said, "This is Hanna Horton, she is my girlfriend. Hanna, these are my grandparents, Stanley and Ellen Blooker." Stanley approached Hanna and stuck out his large hand, "Hanna, it's a pleasure to meet you. I hope we will see you here often, I can tell my grandson is smitten with you."

Ellen approached Hanna, with tears of joy in her eyes she embraced Hanna.

They all wanted to know more but the answers would come with time. One look at Ian and they knew he was happy and there was comfort in that. Each thought to themselves as they drank their tea,

Stanley thought, *Ian did a good job finding her. She is a keeper and she'll make him happy.*

Ellen was relieved and she thought, *Hanna is such a nice girl, intelligent, pretty and confident.*

Susan was glad; *Ian has found a good woman to love and she loves him.*

Maria was as happy as any parent could be.

Later, as if on cue, Ian's sister called from the west coast. She, too, had heard from her mother that Ian was coming home and had a girlfriend.

After talking with her brother for twenty minutes, she spoke with her mother and Maria. Their secret had been shared with Sarah months ago and she was fine with it. She had her own secret she'd shared with them, too.

Sarah spoke with her grandparents then asked to talk with Ian's girlfriend. Ellen looked confused for a moment as she stared at the receiver then said, "Why, yes, my dear. Hanna, it's for you," and she handed the phone. Hanna took the phone and looked at it for a moment. It was one thing to meet Ian's family one-on-one and in person but she wasn't prepared to get the third degree from his big sister. "Hello?"

"Hanna, my name is Sarah. I've heard such wonderful things about you from my family. I only ask one thing,"

"Yes," Hanna replied more as a question than a statement.

"Take care of my little brother. If you cross him, you'll have to deal with me, understood?"

"Yes."

"Great. Then welcome to the family. I'll be coming home in September. I hope to meet you then. You and Ian can come to the west coast too, you know?"

"I'd like that," Hanna said.

"Enjoy your stay and ask Maria to make some Portuguese and Italian food. She is a wonderful cook. Bye for now," and the phone went dead. Ian looked at Hanna as she handed the phone to him. "Your sister really loves you Ian."

"I know, she has always been very protective too."

"You think!" Hanna blurted out, and the room erupted in laughter.

Soon it was time for Stanley and Ellen to leave. The family walked them to the door and watched as Stanley's old pickup truck which he'd called his 'green horse' for years, disappeared down the road, then they turned and walked back into the house.

Ian had waited all day for the right moment. The news about his discoveries in Holland were busting out of him like an alien creature hiding in his body, spying for the opportunity to explode through the host's mouth and consume the innocent victim standing before him. He sensed the time was close and he could hardly contain his excitement.

Maria, with something equally monumental on her mind, suggested they move to the living room, open a bottle of wine, and relax before going up for the night.

"Susan, will you walk with me to the wine cellar to pick out an appropriate wine for the occasion?"

"Of course."

Hanna gazed at Ian, "A wine cellar?" she said as she thought about the possibilities with him surrounded by neatly stored bottles of expensive wine.

Maria and Susan were in the other room whispering to one another,

"Are you sure this is the right time to tell Ian?" Susan asked.

"Susan, we should get it out in the open since he is living under our roof again. We talked about this already. Let's throw it out there and deal with how he responds."

"Should we say anything in front of Hanna?"

"Trust me, he'll tell her anyway. Those two are in love." Maria looked over at Susan and kissed her on the cheek, "Let's go. You look beautiful Susan."

Susan smiled and said, "So do you," and they walked out of the kitchen.

Ian and Hanna were conspiring in hushed tones in the other room, "This is a perfect time to tell them about what we discovered in Rotterdam," Ian said as he took the opportunity to put his lips against Hanna's ear and nibbled her lobe.

She shivered with his attention and said, "Do you think so? It's been a long day and, well, do you think Maria will be okay with the information. She may get jealous or something?"

"Na, my father is no threat to her. Let's tell the story." He looked into her eyes for encouragement and she nodded, "Okay, you know best."

Maria and Susan returned to the living room, one carried a tray with an expensive bottle of wine and four delicate glasses, the other a tray covered with crackers and cheese. Maria opened the bottle and poured the wine and handed a glass first to Hanna. When everyone had a glass, she offered a toast, "Hanna, welcome to our home. Ian, welcome home." She turned to Susan, and teary-eyed, she said, "Thank you, my dear, for making my life complete."

They all raised their glasses and spoke in unison, "Cheers."
Susan cleared her throat and leaned forward. "Ian, Maria and I have something that we need to tell you."

Ian said, "That's funny, Hanna and I have something that we want to tell you, too." The room got quiet.

"Is she pregnant?" Maria questioned in an accusatory voice. Ian's jaw dropped and Hanna's face got bright red.

"No, we are not pregnant." Then it exploded out of Ian's mouth before he could control himself. He forcefully projected the words as he spoke in a staccato rattle, "Hanna and I met my grandmother in Rotterdam and learned about my father and his family. I have letters and pictures of him and his family. We've been asked to come back to Holland and meet the rest of the family and we hoped the two of you would come with us." He took a quick breath and continued, "She is a wonderful woman. She was a concert pianist and, not that it matters, but I believe she is very wealthy."

Exhausted, as if he had just violently expelled every last morsel from his stomach, he gasped for breath, his face bright red.

Susan was thrown off balance and felt as if she were falling, a skydiver without a parachute. She was frightened, scared and confused. Her mind numbed and she felt the room closing in around her.

She had long ago let go of Ian's father and started a new life with Maria. In a fit, her son had brought it rushing back and she wasn't prepared, nor able to cope with the memories bombarding her again.

Maria was caged in her worst nightmare. She'd lost control, what was supposed to have been Susan's and her coming out moment was shattered in pieces on the floor. She pulled three deep gulps from her glass and emptied it, poured again and swallowed it in one swift motion. She watched Susan devastated by the news and she was powerless to protect her lover.

Hanna was quiet and watched as the room spun like a dreidel. She set down her wine glass and examined each of the emotionally tapped-out people in the room, searching their faces for clues and answers.

Finally, Susan leaned forward, tears in her eyes and without a word, set down her glass, got to her feet and left the room. She climbed the stairs like a woman of eighty making her way to the bedroom.

Hanna excused herself and found her way to her room without a sip of the expensive wine.

Ian, by now was no longer angry, just disappointed. He had waited so long to tell his mother and it came out wrong and even mean-spirited. He didn't know how to undo his outburst.

Maria, out-of-character, sat without a word and consumed the bottle of wine, staring off into the distance wondering, *would this news undo my relationship with Susan?*

Chapter Twenty-Five
Emotional Disclosures

Ian made his way to his room and couldn't
believe he had blurted out something so important without
carefully discussing it to see if Maria and his mother
would even want to know. He had long ago come to grips
with their relationship. All that mattered to him was that
his mother was happy and was taken care of. Maria was a
good friend, they loved each other, and she had provided
well for him, his sister, and his mother. What more could
he want? He would have to address it with his mother to
clear the air if she was uncomfortable with her lifestyle
around him and Hanna.

But what he couldn't forgive himself for was how
callous he dropped the bombshell on the table and out of
some sense of anger. *Why the anger?* He couldn't figure it
out. All he knew was his mother was going through a
personal hell right now and it was his fault. He lay in his
bed and hoped his father would help him figure out how he
could atone for his horrible mistake.

Hanna mindlessly looked at the pictures and dolls
that adorned Sarah's room. She thought over the day and
how close Ian's mother and Maria were. She decided they
were lesbians, and who really cared? They were good
together and it was clear they loved and respected each

219

other. *Does Ian know? He never mentioned it but then again we are still getting to know each other.*

If Maria and Susan are stressing over their relationship, maybe that's part of the dynamics. She nodded her head. Hanna slipped off into a fitful sleep and hoped the problem would be resolved quickly in the morning and injured feelings repaired. As she fell asleep she wondered if there was anything she could do to help repair the damage. The engineer in her needed to fix what was broken.

Maria came in the master bedroom and she was brooding, angry and worried she may have undone in three words what had taken her nearly eighteen years to create with Susan. Maria had always chosen her words well, *how could I have been so far off the mark this evening.* Her alcohol infused emotions were charged and moved her from rational thought to self-pity and baseless anger. She couldn't remember being so emotionally confused and upset.

She crawled into bed and looked at Susan and hoped they would be able to overcome the tidal wave that had crashed down on their perfect Camelot. With bloodshot eyes she watched as Susan pretended to sleep next to her. Susan could feel the tension in Maria and fought not to come to her. Susan was working through her own issues.

Susan lay in bed with the memories of Ian's father surrounding her. She felt like she was drowning in the pain buried long ago in order to move forward with Maria. She knew her relationship was a compromise compared to what she had with Ian, but she would never utter that to a living soul. Maria had given Susan and her children a warm and loving home.

She was a strong and supportive partner and Susan knew she loved her. Yet Susan had compromised in love, having lost her one true love to the sea twenty years ago. Now all the memories were there. His deep blue eyes, his long, flowing blond hair and his perfect smile haunted her once again.

Ian made contact with his Dutch family and she'd be expected to engage with them. There would be questions she was unprepared to answer. He'd been exhumed from the recesses of her mind and the memories were painful and tormenting. How would she balance his memories and Maria? Would it be fair to expect Maria to live with his memories or would the jealousy drive them apart?

Her stomach twisted in knots and there was a sense of loneliness, fear, and emptiness sucking the life from her body. She lay perfectly still in her own private hell.

Then he came to her in a vision as real as if he were standing in front of her. She didn't move, just looked at the figure as he approached and sat down on the bed beside her. She studied his features. Kind, deep blue eyes, his hair was a little longer than she remembered but it framed his face like the mane of a lion. His face was tired and weather worn, his smile warm and perfect.

She looked over at Maria's back as she slept on her side, facing away from Ian. He sat there for a long moment staring into Susan's face with a tear forming in the corner of his eye. He reached out and held her hand

and began to speak, *Susan, there is so much I wish I could tell you.*

I knew for a long time before my death I loved you and wanted to tell you, but I had so many things I was wrestling with, I didn't want to involve you in, that kept me from telling you then, when I could have.

It was in my death I was finally free of all my pain and I could love you and our son without distraction. But without having had the opportunity to tell you, I haven't been able to rest in peace.

Yes, I have been watching over you and guiding our son when I could. I have spoken to him on several occasions and I am proud of the way you and Maria have raised both Ian and Sarah.

I'm here, my love, to tell you I love you and will for eternity. But you must feel free to move forward with your life and love again.

Maria is a good woman and she loves you with the passion and completeness I once could. She is the right person for you to give yourself selflessly to. Please, I implore you to not let my memories interfere with the two of you.

Remember me through the eyes of our son, but never let my memories affect you and Maria. Promise me ...

My time here is short, so let me make a final request. Please go with Ian and meet my mother, Margareta. She is a kind and wonderful woman who I caused so much pain in life and death. Maybe you and your family can bring her happiness in her remaining days?

Promise me ...

DRAWN TO THE SEA
(First Revision)

I must go, the light is bright and I am being called to it. He stood, leaned over, and gently kissed her lips. Then he turned and walked towards the window and disappeared.

Susan buried her face in her pillow and sobbed. The weight and emptiness which consumed her just moments ago melted away. Her soul, her conscience, and mind were free of torment and guilt. Ian had helped her and at the same time, told her what she always hoped had been the case. He loved her unconditionally and forever. Susan would now be able to move on with her life with Maria. She rolled over and looked at the woman next to her. Maria rolled over and their eyes met in the dim light and Susan crawled into Maria's arms and whispered, "Hi there."

"Susan, I'm sorry about tonight." They kissed, comfortable their relationship was intact.

The next morning, Susan was tired, but felt lighter, as twenty years of pain had been erased from her heart. Holding hands, she and Maria made their way to the kitchen where they created a special breakfast for Ian and Hanna. Maria prepared eggs and bacon, Susan made coffee and pancakes and set the table for four. She came up behind Maria and put her arms around her waist and kissed her cheek. She whispered, "I love you. Thank you for being so patient," and she kissed Maria again.

A few minutes later, Ian and Hanna came down the stairs. "Something smells delicious," Ian said. "You two always knew how to get me out of bed before I was ready."

Maria tossed her head back and laughed.

Susan, with the coffee pot in one hand, moved around the table and filled their mugs and smiled. "Good morning. Sit down and get it while it's hot."

The four sat down at the table and Ian blurted, "Mom, Maria. I'm sorry I was such a jerk last night. I hope you can forgive me and I haven't hurt you too much with what I said."

Susan said, "Ian, not at all. Maria and I want to hear all about it. But first we have something we want to tell you."

The announcement Susan and Maria had so long worried about telling Ian was after all a non-event. "Mom, I'd guessed it for years." He got up and kissed her cheek, "I love you, mom." Then he walked over to Maria and kissed her and said, "Can I still call you auntie or would you prefer, mom?" He smiled and Maria started to cry.

"Auntie is fine, you meat head!" They all laughed and finished their breakfast. Each knew, it was the other story, the story of Ian's discovery, which held excitement, intrigue, opportunity and even danger.

Susan wondered, *what does the future hold for Ian?*

Chapter Twenty-Six
Family

Gradually, the showers could be heard, and one by one, they washed away the night and the scent of intimacy from their bodies. It was eleven before they gathered in the living room with their hair still damp and their cheeks rosy. Maria looked at the others, "Shall we try it again? I'll get another bottle of wine and we'd like to hear your story."

"That's a great idea. I'll make some more crackers and cheese to nibble on." Susan said as she reached over and squeezed Maria's hand.

The women left the room almost like the night before and in a few minutes returned with wine and cheese. Ian and Hanna waited and looked at each other. Their fantasy of slipping off to the wine cellar still called them.

With the wine glasses charged, everyone leaned forward in anticipation. Ian, seeing his cue, reached for a pile of papers and photographs he'd placed next to his seat and set them on the coffee table in front of him. With a deep breath, as he had rehearsed, he began his story. Ian was sure he gave Hanna more than a fair share of the credit. Susan and Maria stifled giggles when he went on and on about Hanna's helpfulness.

Ian started with how they accidentally found the statue of his grandfather. He told them about the near magical force which had driven him to the location and the statue. Ian continued his story, the Internet search, his grandfather being murdered in the board room, as the wife and son watched him bleed out on the floor in front of them. They stood there frozen in fear as he died.

"That explains a lot about your father," Susan said, her eyes aimed out the window and off in the distance. "It must have been traumatic to see something so horrible when he was so young."

Ian told his audience about the library and Greta, one of his father's 'old flames', who helped them research and interpret the articles they found. Stories of his father's youth and young adult life seemed reckless and excessive. He was a flashy, rich playboy with no restraints. Then he just disappeared off the social roster and nothing more was heard of him. "I think that was the time he left for sea." Ian deduced. "He left title, privilege, fame and fortune for the sea."

Susan's voice cracked when she said, "He never talked much about his family or his past. Now I understand why. He was a tormented soul. More than anything, he talked about his love of the sea. I always sensed he was running from something, but never guessed it was his destiny to run the family business." She paused and shook her head. "The same business took his father's life. The poor soul …"

Ian told the ladies about the grandmother and her fame as a classic concert pianist and a woman of title, old family, and class. Then he went on about how they met his grandmother as she was being escorted to her limousine by two body guards and aides outside of the Lutz Theater. Hanna sat on the edge of her seat as if she were living this for the first time. Much to Ian's surprise she didn't say a word the whole time.

Ian provided a detailed account of the time they spent talking in the limousine outside of the terminal. He told of the things the old woman shared and, of course, the invitation to be part of her life. Lastly, he told the part of her story to visit Holland to meet the other members of the van der Waterlaan family.

Ian talked more quickly, he was excited. The ladies set down their wine glasses and leaned forward. As if riveted to their seats, they listened to every word. Maria took Susan's hand and held it on her thigh. Ian reached for the papers and photographs in front of him and told of Captain van der Meer and how he delivered the brown paper wrapped package that contained these items. "Captain van der Meer was a close friend of my grandparents and a mentor to my father." Ian said with a sense of pride.

Ian picked up the pictures and handed them one at a time to his mother and told its story. The pictures moved from one person to the next. He gathered the letters and explained they were the last four letters his father had written to his mother before he died, Ian handed them carefully to his mother. "Mom, you'll want to read these. You are the focus of each of his letters. He loved you very much." Susan clutched them to her breast and started to cry. Maria wrapped her arm around Susan's shoulder and pulled her closer.

Finally, Ian mentioned he had met Fritz, a shipmate of his father's, from the *Amore Islander*. Susan's face crumpled and her spine became rigid. "The *Amore Islander?* You met people from the ship?" Her cheeks grew crimson.

Ian paused, realizing what she was fearful of. He continued the stories and carefully avoided parts that would embarrass his mother and Maria. The fact she had been a hooker years ago was not relevant and he would never mention it to anyone, not even his lover and soul mate next to him on the couch.

"And there it is," he said. *Except for the parts that don't need to be mentioned,* he thought. *Hopefully, my mother's secrets will stay buried forever.*

Chapter Twenty-Seven
Reaching Out

Several days passed and Ian and Hanna kept themselves busy exploring Bristol. Ian took Hanna sailing and they roamed the streets stopping to chat with an endless stream of folks who were curious about what Ian was doing and, of course, the pretty young lady by his side.

"I feel like I'm hanging with a local celebrity today," Hanna joked. "When the autograph signing starts, I'm bailing on you!"

"Cut it out," Ian said, his face reddened.

Susan and Maria returned to their routines and Stanley and Ellen dropped by with regularity to check in on everyone. The August weather was warm and pleasant but their Camelot came to an end when the phone rang and Captain Mann spoke into the receiver. He called for Midshipman Hanna Thorton. Ian handed the phone to Hanna.

"Midshipman Thorton?" Mann asked

"Yes, sir," she responded and stood at attention out of reflex. Ian noticed and chuckled to himself.

"Your internship has been changed and you will need to be at T.F. Green airport in Providence tomorrow morning. You'll intern with ABC Shipping in San

Francisco, California. That should be good for you. This assignment puts you home for a couple of weeks."

"May I ask why?"

"The company in Boston went into receivership yesterday."

"Yes, sir. Yes it will be nice to be home for a while, sir."

Ian could see she was looking for paper and a pencil, so he handed them to her as he observed every move. She sat down at the kitchen table and began to scribble notes as she listened to Mann on the line. Occasionally, she would respond, "Yes, sir," and continued to scribble. Several minutes later, "Thank you, sir, and here is Midshipman Blooker." She handed the phone to Ian.

"Midshipman Blooker, sir!"

"Well, Blooker, you had a very productive first assignment and I have your sea service report back from Captain Horne. Did you know he's a classmate of mine? He reports you ..." Ian's mind went numb. *They know about Hanna and me, shit, we're dead."* In the background Mann's voice continued to drone on. Ian concentrated on the voice again. The worried look on his face as he stared at Susan caught her attention. "And Captain Horne has requested you back by name for another assignment on the *American Spirit*. You'll catch the ship the week after next in Rotterdam. You'll be there three days early, so enjoy yourself."

Ian's eyes went from concern to excitement. "Really, sir? That sounds great!"

"Kid, you must have really done a great job aboard. I've never seen a captain ask for a cadet back by name. The travel details will be sent to you by email later today."

"Yes, sir."

"Then goodbye," said Captain Mann, said and the phone went dead.

Hanna asked, "Well, what just happened?"

Ian smiled and looked in her eyes, kissed her and said with a slight bow at the waist, "ladies first."

"Okay, if that's the way you want to play, it." She responded with a hint of mock annoyance in her voice.

Ian winced. "Ouch!"

She laughed and leaned in and kissed him.

Hanna told Ian of her change in orders and she'd be catching a plane in the morning for San Francisco to do her two week internship with ABC. They looked over the notes she'd written and realized this moment was what they had known would happen but really hoped would never come. They would go separate ways for a while.

"Okay, hot shot, your turn," Hanna said.

Ian got a serious look across his face and said, "Well, it seems Captain Horne has asked for me to return to the *American Spirit* and the company will fly me to Rotterdam the week after next, three days prior to the scheduled arrival of the ship. What do you think of that?"

"A three day paid vacation. Hmmmm," she said, pouting and crossing her arms. After a few seconds, her joy and excitement bubbled to the surface and she smiled and hugged him. After the long embrace, she abruptly pushed him away. "We need to write to your grandmother today and arrange for you to spend time with her and your 'Dutch family' during your layover."

"Great idea Hanna," Ian said and then ran out to retrieve stationery and a quality pen.

"What's that for?" she asked as he walked back into the room with the heavy bond paper and a fountain pen. "Why not send her an e-mail?" Again she looked at his hands.

"Hanna, a proper lady, such as Madam van der Waterlaan, must be corresponded with in proper fashion. Remember the letters she wrote me?" Ian put on a bit of a hoity-toity voice for show.

"Why yes, dear Ian, now that you mention it," she responded in an equally lofty voice and they giggled.

Another minute and they were back at the kitchen table. Ian had the paper in front of him and the pen poised in his hand ready to write. Together they prepared the letter on the first try, a feat unto itself.

Ian looked up and scowled. "I hope she was serious about me coming to visit and not just being polite."

Hanna eyed him. "Get real. She's going to be thrilled."

"You never know," Ian said, tapping his pen on the table. He read the letter out loud,

3 August 2002

Dearest Madam van der Waterlaan (I hope you will allow me to call you Grandma),

Hanna and I write this letter, first to thank you for your time and the trust you bestowed in me by sharing your photographs and letters from my father and also for your

gracious offer to open communications between our families. Although I appreciate all three very much it is the latter which compels me to write this letter.

We are currently at my mother's home in Bristol, Rhode Island. Today we received our next assignments. Hanna will be flying to San Francisco, California and I have been reassigned to the 'American Spirit.'

My orders have been written for me to fly to Rotterdam in two weeks and board the ship for the return voyage. I understand I may be arriving up to three days prior to the ship. If it would be at all possible, I would like to meet again and spend time with you.

I do not wish to impose in the slightest and can only hope this letter will find you well and with an interest in meeting me.

Please forgive the haste with which I write but I want this letter to arrive quickly. I can only imagine you're a very busy woman and I'll fully understand if you're unable to spend time with me on this short notice. I promise to continue to write and look for future opportunities to visit.

My mother's home address is:
17 Gibson Terrace
Bristol, RI
02809
USA
Home phone is: (401)283-5112 (My mother's name is Susan and her roommate is Maria).

With sincere respect and admiration, your
loving grandson,
Ian Blooker
PS: Hanna is sitting next to me and sends her
regards and best wishes

Ian finished the letter. He reread it and signed it. Hanna said, "You even write like an aristocrat. I hope you send me love letters with aristocracies and loftiness so I can read them aloud to all my girlfriends." With that he chased her around the table and easily caught her the second time around.

"I love you, my Hanna."

"I love you too, my Ian."

They found his grandmother's address with the package of photographs and letters and drove to the post office and sent it First Class Airmail. By the time they returned home, his mother was in the kitchen and Maria was coming through the door. Maria dropped her purse and keys, kissed Susan, and greeted Ian and Hanna. Maria asked if anyone would like a glass of wine as she continued to the wine cellar. All three chimed-in with enthusiasm. She came back with two bottles in hand, a Cabernet from California and a Chardonnay from Australia. Without the formality of the other night, she pulled the corks and poured the wine into the four glasses Susan placed in front of her.

Susan whispered in Maria's ear, "Is everything okay?"

"Everything is fine," Maria said, with a *please don't ask again* look Susan picked up on.

Ian took the opportunity to change the subject and tell of the day's news. "Mom, Auntie ... Hanna and I got orders today!"

Susan and Maria eyed him with curiosity. "Do tell," Susan said.

Ian continued, "Hanna will fly out of Green Airport tomorrow morning to San Francisco to do her two week internship with ABC Shipping."

"Hanna, isn't your home near San Francisco?" Maria asked.

"Yes, just about twenty miles north on the coast." Hanna responded, her pride for her home and family reflected in her sparkling eyes.

"Mom, I'll take her to the airport if that's okay?"

"Sure son," Susan smiled with a hint of sadness with Hanna leaving.

Maria swallowed a gulp of her wine and then said, "Ian, you said 'we' got orders and how about you?" She took another deep swallow of red wine.

"Yes, Auntie. I have been reassigned to the *American Spirit,* but this time I'll fly to Rotterdam to catch the ship. I leave in two weeks."

Maria stared, as if the wine had already gone to her head, and then she smiled and the tension in the room lifted. "Will you look up your Dutch family?"

"Well, I hope to. Hanna and I wrote to my grandmother this morning and posted the letter First Class Airmail. I told my grandmother I'd be coming and hoped for an opportunity to meet again. Mom, Auntie, I hope you don't mind I gave her your address and phone number as contact information."

Maria walked over to Ian, kissed him on the cheek, and said, "Sweetheart, this is your address and phone number as much as any ones. I'm glad you did. I hope she'll call and soon."

With Maria's mood mellowed the evening was calm and relaxing. They ordered Chinese takeout and watched a mindless movie. Susan carefully tucked under Maria's arm on one couch and Ian's head rested on Hanna's lap on the other. Wine glasses slowly emptied and refilled as all four stared at the images on the television. Not one of them watched the movie. Each one of them lost in their own world.

Ian wondered about the things to come. *Will Hanna and I be able to continue our relationship when we are on other sides of the world? And what's going to happen in Rotterdam when I get there?*

Chapter Twenty-Eight
The Invitation

The next morning Ian and Hanna were up early, she had her bags ready by the front door. They sat in the kitchen around the table enjoying their first cup of coffee. Neither drank coffee before they were assigned aboard the *American Spirit,* but now looked forward to morning coffee as much as anyone.

It wasn't long before Maria and Susan came down the stairs together. Maria said as she poured herself a cup, "Hey, how are you young love birds?"

Susan kissed Ian and Hanna, "Good morning, kids. How did you sleep?"

"Just fine, thank you," they responded.

Susan followed Maria over to the counter and poured the remaining coffee into a cup and made another pot. As she did, Maria found a seat at the table and settled in with the cup held tightly between her two hands as she always did in the morning.

Susan had the coffee brewing and was scrambling eggs and crisping bacon as the others sat around the table talking.

After a long goodbye, Maria and Susan climbed into their cars and drove off to work. Just as Ian and Hanna were loading the luggage, Stanley and Ellen came around the corner to say goodbye to Hanna and extend their personal invitation to return to Bristol any time she'd like. More hugs and good wishes and finally Ian and Hanna left for the airport. On the twenty minute transit, they promised to call and write often and find opportunities to get together before they returned to the academy later in the year.

Ian pulled up to the curb and Hanna got out and retrieved her bags. They held each other for a long moment and kissed gently. She pushed away and picked up her bags, turned, and was gone. Ian, with a heavy heart, returned to his running car and drove back to home. He was experiencing the feeling of missing someone for the first time and the feeling was both painful and pleasant.

Six hours later, Hanna called. "Ian, I arrived okay. My parents picked me up at the airport and we just got home here in Point Reyes. I hope you can come and see it for yourself. It's really beautiful here. They're dying to meet you. I told them we are in love with one another. I hope that's okay?"

"Of course it is. It's true and my mom and aunt already know too. I love you and miss you very much."

"Me too, I've got to run. My brother is coming through the door now."

Ian held the receiver for a moment. *So this is what it's like to have a long distance relationship,* he thought to himself.

The phone rang often and Ian and Hanna talked about everything, and the days flew by. Three days after Hanna left, the postman came to the door with a letter. Ian answered the door somewhat surprised to see a letter being hand delivered. "Hello, Ian." said, Perry, the postman.

"Hello, Perry."

"I have a First Class Airmail with EXPEDITE instructions on it. I have only seen two of these in my thirty years in the postal service. Someone really wanted you to get this immediately. Here, sign the receipt and she's all yours." Ian did as he was instructed. The letter from Holland was placed in his hand. Perry turned and headed back to his post truck he'd left running at the edge of the driveway.

After Ian watched Perry drive down the road, his attention was drawn back to the envelope in his hands. He examined it carefully and read the affixed certificate of highest priority delivery. The envelope was of the finest paper and the penmanship was familiar. As was the case with all the letters and notes his grandmother prepared for him, the hand writing was perfect. He walked into the house and looked for his pocket knife to open the envelope. It was so perfect he couldn't bring himself to carelessly tear it open.

He found his knife, cut the envelope, and removed the contents and walked over to the couch, sat, and began to read.

MvdW

5 August 2004

My Dearest Ian,

Of course, I insist you call me Grandmother, Oma or Grotmoeder, if you prefer. I'm excited to hear you'll be returning to the Netherlands so soon. Please let me know when you'd like to come and I'll have

239

*the family jet come for you. I want to
sincerely extend the invitation to your
mother, her friend, Maria, and that includes
your lovely young lady, Hanna. There is
ample room for all of you.*

*Please accept this offer to bring you to
and from Holland. I want to spend as much
time with you and your family as the good
Lord will allow. Please contact me directly at
the following number and I'll dispatch the jet.
I am told we can get there in 7 hours, health
permitting, I'll make the trip.*

*Your Dutch family is looking forward to
your visit. Please come as soon as you can
and stay as long as you can. There is plenty
of room and you don't need to bring a thing.
We'll pick up what you require when you
arrive. All you'll need are your passports.*

*Please call me directly at 001-31-
027789756. I look forward to sharing your
family history and your birth-right with you.*

*Finally, I re-read this letter and there
may appear to be some desperation and
urgency in my words and requests. Please
forgive this old woman. I have so much I need
to tell you and show you before I die, and at
seventy-eight years, I know time conspires
against me. I so want to meet your family. I
hope they'll come.*

I wait for your call, my grandson.
With all my love,
Grandmother Margareta

DRAWN TO THE SEA
(First Revision)

Ian re-read the letter and reached for the phone to call Hanna.

Hanna was in the backyard with her dog Rufus, her loveable, but terminally dumb black lab. Her parent's new wireless phone sat on the table next to her. She glanced at the caller ID and drew in her breath as she spilled her lemonade trying to push the right button.

"Hanna, you won't believe this." He read the letter to her and they discussed it for a few minutes.

"I am so excited for you, Ian! You must be thrilled!" Her voice cracked when she said, "I only wish I could come along. My internship starts tomorrow. Hopefully your mom and Maria will be able to go."

"I hope so, too,"

They talked for twenty minutes and then Rufus began to bark and nip at her pant legs. Hanna acknowledged the dog and said, "I have to go Ian … Rufus is hungry. Good luck and keep me posted. Send my best to your grandmother."

"I will," he responded and they said good bye.

When Susan came home, she roughed up his hair and said, "You know, I'm getting used to having you around. It's going to be tough to have to let you go."

"I'll always come back, mom," said Ian. "It's going to be hard for me to leave. I'm getting used to all your good cooking." He shot her a wink. When she didn't respond, not even with a smile, Ian said, "Hey, are you alright? You look like something is bothering you."

Susan put on a smile that appeared to be pasted on. "I'm fine. I don't know. I'm a little worried about John. John Gates, my boss. You remember him, right? He just

241

seemed a little off today and was very quiet. I just hope he's not catching a cold or something."

"Of course, I remember Mr. Gates," Ian said. "It's kind of weird to catch a cold in August, isn't it?"

Susan's back was turned when she mumbled, "Yeah, I suppose it is." She shook her head and continued making tea.

As she came to the table with two steaming mugs Ian had the letter in his hands. "What's that, darling?" she asked. Ian handed it to her. She took it and read. After a moment, she glanced up and smiled. "You scared me. At first I thought you were showing me a 'Dear John' letter from Hanna. I should have known better." She finished the letter and looked at Ian.

"Remember I told you Hanna and I wrote my grandmother a letter last week?"

"Yes."

"Can you believe she has a family jet and want us to fly in it? How awesome is that?" Ian's face glowed.

"Yeah," Susan said with eyes focused on her mug. "It's unbelievable. I wonder how long she's had it."

Ian arched his eyebrows then frowned. He realized his mother was probably sad his father never asked her to meet his family on the jet. Shifting in his seat, he blew out a sigh of relief when Maria came in the door. It broke up the awkwardness of the moment. Then his shoulders slumped. Maria didn't appear to be very happy. Not angry, just preoccupied. *I wonder what's up?*

After dinner, as they drank wine, Ian told Maria the news of his grandmother's invitation.

"Her jet," Maria repeated. "Wow, and when?" she asked.

"Anytime we'd like, auntie."

Maria turned to Susan, "I can't leave the pharmacy, but I hope you'll travel with Ian. I think it would be good for you to get away and meet Ian's family. By rite they are your family too."

"I'd like that if I can get leave from work."

"I'm sure John will give you the time off, Susan." Maria offered and then a funny expression crossed her face.

It was late when they brought closure to the evening with an agreement. Ian would confirm the ship's schedule and Susan would accompany him if she could get the time off. Maria knew that wouldn't be a problem, John could only benefit from Susan's trip. It would allow the star crossed lovers a week to rekindle their passion one last time, and Maria would reluctantly stay behind. Of course, Susan wouldn't know that Maria would discreetly spend time with her old lover.

Perfect everyone would win, Susan hopefully would never know. Maria thought as she fell asleep dreaming of John lying next to her once again.

Chapter Twenty-Nine
Plans

Maria was the first out the door and dialed her cell phone before she left the driveway. The phone rang across town, "Hello."

"John ... Maria, can we talk?"

"Yes, I'm alone, are you?"

"Yes," she said, though she whispered as if someone could overhear her. "I have a favor to ask you, John. I think it is one you may like to help me with." Her palms were sweating and she almost dropped the phone before continuing in a conspiratorial tone.

When Susan arrived at work she went through her morning routine as if on automatic pilot. She hung up her jacket and started the coffee machine. Once it brewed, she poured some into John's favorite mug and added a lump of sugar before carrying it into his office.

He smiled, "Good morning, Susan. How are you?"

"Fine, Mr. Gates. May I ask you something, please?"

"Sure."

"May I please accompany my son, Ian to Europe for two weeks so he can meet his Dutch relatives?"

"Of course, you may. Take as much time as you'd like."

244

He motioned for her to sit across from him and asked her general questions about the trip and how it came about. John watched Susan become more animated as she retold the story. "I hope you have a wonderful time. You deserve it."

"Mr. Gates, you're really a wonderful man and a super boss. Thank you so much."

John's eyes roved everywhere around the room except on Susan's face. His jovial manner seemed forced when he said, "Susan, take the rest of the day off to get ready for your trip. Let me know the days you'll be gone. Oh, by the way, I expect a postcard!"

"Thank you, sir, Thank you." She moved past her desk, grabbed her purse, her light coat, and nearly ran out the door to her car. As Susan left the Prestige Rug and Carpet parking lot on lower Thames Street, she dialed her cell phone. The phone rang up the street. "Town Pharmacy," said the voice on the other end.

"May I speak with Maria please?" Susan asked.

"Just a moment," thirty seconds later, Maria voice came through, "Good morning, this is the pharmacist, may I help you?"

"Maria, it's Susan, Mr. Gates said yes! I can get the time to accompany Ian to Europe and he gave me the day off to get ready. He's really a wonderful man."

"That's great. He is a wonderful man," Maria said, biting her lip. "Susan, I must get back to my customers now. Start packing." She set the phone down and her eyes turned glassy. Flinching when the customer in front of her cleared his throat she said, "Yes, Mr. Russo, what can I do for you today?"

245

Susan pulled into the driveway and Ian met her at the car. "Mom, are you okay?"

"Yes dear, Mr. Gates gave me time off to go with you and told me to go home, make plans, and pack for the trip."

"Great news, let's call Holland and discuss the itinerary."

They walked through the front door arm in arm towards the kitchen. Ian found the letter with the phone number on it and Susan made tea for them. A minute later, the tea kettle was whistling and she poured the hot water into the pot to steep. Ian reached for the phone, "Are you ready?"

Susan smiled and said, "If you only knew how ready I am ..." She laughed. "I can't believe I'm meeting your father's mother twenty years after I had hoped to. I didn't realize until this morning how much I'd always wanted to."

Ian dialed the phone as the letter had instructed. It took a little longer to connect than a local call then he heard it ring. Unlike American phones with their distinct ring, the ring tone was characterized with two short rings followed by several seconds of silence. After three rings, he heard, "Goedenmiddag ... van der Waterlaan Haus."

Ian cleared his throat and timidly said, "Hello, my name is Ian Blooker, may I speak with Madam van der Waterlaan please?"

The man on the other end of the line shifted from proper Dutch to perfect English, "Well, young man, Madam van der Waterlaan has been expecting your call. She is in the parlor playing the piano. Just a moment, I'll see if she'll take your call."

DRAWN TO THE SEA
(First Revision)

A moment later, an elderly voice he recognized answered, "Ian, my dear, this is your grandmother. I hope you and your family come soon to visit Holland."

Ian explained he and his mother would like very much to come, but didn't want to impose and would make their own arrangements.

"I want to send my jet and I'm feeling well enough to make the trip and bring you back myself. Of course, my jet will return your mother to America whenever she is ready. "Ian, you and your mother are most welcome and never an imposition. You are my family! When are you able to fly?"

Ian, with the receiver against his ear, looked at his mother and asked, "When can we go?"

As they were thinking, his grandmother said, "I will fly there this afternoon and meet you at the airport tomorrow morning."

Ian repeated, "Tomorrow morning!" His jaw almost hit his chest.

"Is that okay?" the madam asked.

Ian looked at his mother and she nodded her head. Ian responded, "Yes, ma'am, tomorrow morning."

The older woman said, "My secretary will call back with the details of where and when we'll meet at the airport. All you'll need are your passports and we can buy what you need when you are here," she said.

"But Grandma, I'll need my clothes and sextant for the *American Spirit*."

"Of course you will. Bring whatever you need." She said and then, "I look forward to meeting you and your mother tomorrow. I have always wished I could meet the woman who meant so much to your father. Goodbye, dear, see you tomorrow morning."

Susan said, "Well, I guess we better pack and get ready. Tomorrow morning will come fast."

Stanley and Ellen came over and brought several pizzas from the local restaurant. Later, Hanna called from California to tell Ian about her internship and was excited to know he and his mom were making the trip. She said, "Say hello to your grandma for me."

Ian's grandparents had been to Holland many years ago on a guided tour and talked about what they had seen and remembered of their trip. Sarah called and Ian was able to share the latest events. He laughed when his sister squealed over the private jet. The household was a flurry of laughter and activity.

Only Maria seemed detached from the organized chaos. When anyone said anything to her, she asked them to repeat the question, as if something else weighed heavily on her mind.

At nine o'clock, the phone rang. Maria picked it up, then handed the phone to Ian. "It's for you."

"Ian?" a man's voice spoke.

"Yes sir."

"My name is Hans van der Molen. The van der Waterlaan jet will be at the corporate terminal at T.F. Green airport ready to depart for Holland at nine tomorrow morning. A limousine will pick you and your mother up at your home in Bristol at eight. All you need are your passports and IDs. I'll come in the limousine and escort you to the jet. Your grandmother is looking forward to the meeting. Any questions?"

"No sir."

"Then *Ik zie je morgen*. 'See you in the morning'," and the phone went dead.

Everyone's jaw dropped when Ian repeated the information. He grinned and said, "And we're going in a limo too!"

Stanley turned to Ian, "Son, you must be royalty!" and the room erupted with laughter.

It was getting late and Stanley and Ellen said their goodbyes and left. Ellen shed a tear or two as she got into Stanley's 'green horse'. Ian kissed Maria and his mother good night and went to his room. Who was he kidding, he wouldn't sleep a wink. He was too wound up for that. Maria and Susan walked up the stairs holding hands. At the top of the stairs Susan turned to Maria, "Is everything alright?"

Maria moved in close and kissed Susan. "Yes dear, let's get to bed."

The alarms went off early and the house was aflutter with final preparations for the trip. The long, black limo pulled up out front at eight and Mr. van der Molen knocked on the door. Maria answered and looked at the stunning gentleman. Hans clicked his heels together and slightly bowed. "May I introduce myself, I'm Hans van der Molen."

Maria blushed and in a dreamy voice said, "Please come in."

In the meantime, Susan and Ian moved towards the front door with their luggage in hand. Hans took the bags and easily maneuvered them into the trunk, opened the door and gestured for Susan and Ian to climb into the limousine. Maria stood at the door as she watched this handsome stranger whisk her partner off in a long black limousine. Maria stood on the porch and waved them off. When the luxury automobile was no longer in sight, she rushed into the house. When she glanced at the clock, she said aloud, "I have a lot to do, better get ready," and she ran up the stairs.

Chapter Thirty
The Affair

Being the town pharmacist gave Maria the privilege and burden of knowing people's medical status through discussions with physicians and filling prescriptions. When she filled Susan's boss' medication, her chest constricted and she felt like she couldn't breathe. "No, John, please no. This can't be true," she whispered to herself. When she realized tears were pouring down her cheeks, she hurried to the restroom to compose herself.

When he came to pick up the prescription, his somber expression made her want to start crying again. She passed him the bag and he reached for her hand. "We should probably talk," he said.

Maria nodded. "I can take a break in about ten minutes. Meet me on the bench behind the store. We can have some privacy there."

John nodded, and his lips trembled when he gave her a half-smile.

Maria's heart was fluttering when she told her employees she was taking a break. When she went out the back door and saw him waiting for her, she realized how alone and scared he seemed. He stood as she approached. Wrapping her arms around his neck, she brushed her mouth across his neck. "How bad is it, John?"

He gave her a tight squeeze and said, "Let's sit down." He rubbed his jaw line. "I have stage four pancreatic cancer and the doctor says I only have a few months ... Maybe."

"No!" Maria grabbed his arm and put her head on his shoulder. "I'm so sorry, John. If there is anything I can do ..."

"I can't ask anything of you. Years ago, you were my lover. Since then, you've been a dear friend. A man can't hope for anything better than that."

Maria looked into John's eyes and said in a tender voice, "I was blessed to have you in my life too. You were discreet, kind, and wonderful during our affair. I'm only thankful we were able to remain friends afterward. I'm able to look back on our time together and smile. It was romantic, tender, and special. Thank God we didn't do anything to ruin that."

John brushed a strand of hair off her face. "You know I still have feelings for you. I always have. Some things just aren't meant to be, no matter how badly you want them."

Maria reached in her jacket and pulled out a tissue to wipe her eyes. "I still love you, too. How could I not? You're a good man with a good heart."

John groaned and gave her a wry smile. "Too bad I didn't have a good pancreas." He jostled her shoulder until she gave him a playful push back.

"You're not funny, ya know." She blew her nose.

He stretched out his legs and leaned back, pulling her head into his chest. "Yeah, I know. Please don't tell anyone, though. I haven't even told my wife of thirty-five years. I'm not ready yet. I suppose I'm still a bit in shock.

Things need to be done on my terms now, please give me that dignity." He sighed. "I suppose this is yet another secret for us to share."

Maria sat up and her eyes widened. "You mean I can't even tell Susan?"

John glanced skyward, "For God's sake, no! She'll pity and pamper me every day. I can't deal with that now. She is a good woman and will also be worried about her job. I don't want to do that to her. Somehow, I'll figure everything out where no one suffers because of my problems."

Days after John's admission, Maria was still coping with the knowledge she would be losing John soon. It was hard not to be allowed to share her pain. Trying to act normal while her emotions ran rampant was tiresome, but she couldn't spoil Ian and Hanna's short visit with her worries, although she sensed they suspected something was bothering her.

Hiding John's illness from Susan was a bit tougher. The two of them were so close, hiding anything was almost impossible. Maria was thankful for the invitation to the Netherlands to distract Susan from pushing the issue.

The morning Ian took Hanna to the airport, Maria had spent another sleepless night thinking of John. She couldn't help but remember the passion they once shared, and when she dozed for a few minutes at a time, dreams of her and John's naked bodies entwined filled her head. The sultry images were still in her mind when she arrived to work.

Before lunch, as she was counting out pills, it hit her ... *If I could get Susan to leave for a week or so with*

Ian, I'd have time for John and me to rekindle our affair. I know he wants to before he is too sick to make love and I do too. She kept the idea buried deep in her mind. She and John had discussed making love often since he was diagnosed and they had committed to find an opportunity to lay in each other's arms for a few evenings away from his wife and Susan. *This would be the excuse.* She loved Susan, but she still loved John too and wanted him before he was no more.

Maria knew John could only benefit from Susan's trip and it would allow the star crossed lovers a week to rekindle their passion one last time. Of course, Susan would never suspect and Maria would discreetly spend time with her old lover.

Perfect, everyone would win ... well, Susan hopefully would never know. That night Maria fell asleep dreaming of John lying next to her once again.

The next morning, Maria encouraged Susan to take advantage of the trip to Europe and ask John for the time off. Susan agreed and Maria nodded as her excitement built up.

Maria was the first out the door and dialed her cell phone before she left the driveway. The phone rang across town, "Hello."

"John ... Maria, can we talk?"

"Yes, I am alone, are you?"

"Yes, my love," she said. The sting of guilt seared her conscience as she betrayed Susan, but the unbridled passion for him drove her forward. "John, Susan will ask you for two weeks of leave to travel to Holland with Ian to meet his Dutch relatives. His grandmother will send her private jet soon. Give her the leave and send her on her way with a clean conscience and I'll be yours for the time she's gone."

A few seconds passed before he answered. "I will and I can't wait, Maria. God, I wish I had more time."

I know, my love, I know," she said.

"I must go, I hear Anna coming down the stairs. Goodbye." He hung up the phone as his wife appeared around the corner.

The day Hans came for Susan and Ian, Maria's nerves were frazzled. When she opened the door, she almost swooned. Hans was gorgeous. *What is the matter with me? He is taking my partner off in a limousine and I am preparing to meet an old lover. This is not the time to Lust for another man.*

After the limo pulled out of the driveway, Maria's mind spun. She couldn't believe she had orchestrated a plan allowing circumstances for her and John to reconnect. The memories of him were haunting her daily along with new fantasies of rare passion and forbidden delight. She had a week or two to fulfill her desires.

She dropped her robe and entered the shower. The warm water on her skin felt good as her imagination flitted back and forth between the possibilities of both Hans and John and what each could do for her. Now she felt a stab of remorse for what she was doing to Susan, and felt she was being untrue to John as well.

She turned off the shower and muttered, "Damn you, Hans."

Slipping into a new pair of Victoria Secret lace panties, she focused on John. He was waiting for her eight miles up the road in a hotel room. She owed it to him and herself to be an attentive and passionate lover and give her body over to his wanton desire.

Once she dressed and dabbed perfume on her neck, wrists, and cleavage, she grabbed her purse. Soon she was in her car, speeding down the road to John and the Shade Tree Motel.

Chapter Thirty-One
Exciting New World

The limousine pulled up to a closed gate with a sentry. The sentry approached the driver. A moment later, the gate was opened and the black vehicle drove onto the airport tarmac. The driver maneuvered the vehicle toward a hangar at the far end of the airfield. As the car approached, several men in dark suits came out of the hanger. Each was a large and athletic man with dark glasses and a uniform tie of diagonal blue stripes.

As the car came to a stop, one of the men came to the door and opened it. He and Hans nodded to each other. The others came around the car and looked outward. The driver had the trunk open and removed the bags while Susan and Ian were escorted into the hanger. The other athletic men followed, their eyes on everything around the building. Ian and Susan noticed. It was a little uncomfortable for them, as neither had ever been in the center of a security bubble before.

As their eyes became accustomed to the reduced light in the hanger, they noticed a sleek corporate jet. The jet was shiny and a brilliant white with diagonal light blue and dark blue stripes on the horizontal surfaces of the wings and the vertical tail surface.

Hans directed the guests to the boarding ladder and said, "I've taken the liberty of clearing you with the U.S. Immigration Department and we'll depart momentarily. Your bags will be put aboard. Please follow me, Madam van der Waterlaan is aboard waiting for you."

Ian, Susan and the bodyguard followed Hans onto the plane. Once inside the fuselage, Hans moved to the side and as Ian entered, he announced, "Ian Blooker, madam."

She looked up from a book and smiled, "Ian, my dear, I'm so glad to see you again. Please sit by me."

As Susan stuck her head in the door, Hans announced, "Ms. Susan Blooker." Susan blushed. Madam van der Waterlaan stood up, "Let me look at you dear, so you're the one who stole my Ian's heart. Thank you. You were the only one who could have brought him back to me." Her lower lip began to quiver and the stewardess came to her side and bid her to take her seat. She did with some assistance. Behind Susan, the three other bodyguards slipped into the plane and secured the fuselage door as the jet engines roared to life.

With Ian sitting to her right, Madam van der Waterlaan patted the seat to her left. "Susan, dear, please come sit by me. Hold my hand and tell be about my son and all about you. My dear, you are the daughter I never had. I hope you'll grow to understand how happy I am to know I have a daughter-in-law and a grandson." The plane gathered speed, and in seconds, it soared through the air headed for the Netherlands.

As the women spoke, Ian's mind was running a mile a minute. He looked between his grandmother and his mother, then gazed out the window into the bright morning sun. He closed his eyes and felt the sun on his face and thought, *is this a dream or is this real? My grandmother is richer than anyone alive, surrounded by bodyguards and handlers. Why did it take so long for us to meet? She seems nice and generous, but there is a hard and demanding side to her too.* Ian looked at Hans seated at a desk as he worked on something. Ian continued, *there must be a catch, this is too perfect. How will I fit in and what will be expected of me? Can I really hope to finish school and sail for a career? I'm sure there will be expectations. After all I'm the last of the van der Waterlaan family. Where will mom fit in? Our lives are about to change. It could be for the better or for the worst. Only time will tell, I guess.*

The ladies were sipping champagne and he noticed his mother was comfortable with Madam van der Waterlaan. He thought, *that's good, mom and I are in for the adventure of our lives and we have no idea where this will lead us, but I know it will change us forever. How will Hanna fit in? What about Maria and mom?*

Just then Madam van der Waterlaan glanced over at Ian and her ice blue eye gripped him. The power and intensity of her gaze made his heart jump and he squirmed a little.

"Ian, where are you, dear? Join the lovely conversation your mother and I are having as we get to know each other." She smiled and her eyes softened.

"Oh, yes grandmother, I'm sorry I was just thinking about Hanna and how much she would have loved to make the trip." He lied.

The Madam gave him a knowing smile and nodded. As she continued to talk, he listened, but in his heart he knew that instant, she had a grand plan and he and his mother played a part in it. What part and for how long, only time would tell. He leaned forward in his chair and reached for a cracker with a yellow piece of cheese the stewardess had placed on the table.

"May I pour you something to drink Mr. Blooker?" The pretty lady in uniform asked.

"Champagne would be nice, please" He looked at the lady and then engaged in the conversation with his mother and grandmother.

Before the jet reached altitude, the matriarch knew the most nuanced and intricate objective of her life was achievable, *yes, there would be heart aches, but such a small price to pay for the family to survive.*

Susan realized her Liberian seaman was more special than she had ever imagined. *He had been heir to a dynasty and she would have been his queen. Would that destiny now be passed on to her son?* She pondered the possibilities.

Ian thought, *I feel like Alice falling down the hole and landing in Wonderland. I have no idea where this will end, but it will be an interesting journey.*

Madam offered a toast to family, each immersed in their own thoughts as they raised their crystal. *Clink!*

As the sleek jet sped East at four hundred knots, the stewardess poured more champagne and served gourmet meals.

Back in Swansea, Maria and John were tearing away at each other's clothing in a dark hotel room. Both driven by lust, their souls riddled with guilt.

The End
***

The van der Waterlaan family story continues …
pick up *Torn between Destiny and Desire* and *The
Gentleman Pirate*. Read all three!

Death of a Liberian Seaman

(A Short Story)

Book Five
The van der Waterlaan Dynasty

Rex Inverness

***

Other Books by Rex Inverness:

Drawn to the Sea
Torn Between Destiny and Desire
The Gentleman Pirate
Two Warriors Collide
Bonnie Mae
The Cursed Seven
Leviathan

MV2

Maritime Fiction Novels
Bristol, Rhode Island
02809
www.rex-inverness.com

DRAWN TO THE SEA
(First Revision)

The cover is a copy of an original painting by the maritime
artist Bradley Van Vleck

Death of a Liberian Seaman
Copyright 2017 Rex Inverness
MV2 Maritime Fiction Novels
All rights reserved.
ISBN 13:9781546503958
ISBN 10: 1546503951
CreateSpace Independent Publishing Platform
North Charleston, South Carolina

Dedication

To the children of the men that go to sea... they have had to endure much of their childhood without a father. Their father, in most cases, was nothing more than a wallet, an occasional voice on the phone and the author of letters from far away.

Also to my wife... who with incredible patience and understanding encouraged me to write this story.

DRAWN TO THE SEA
(First Revision)

Introduction

The Ship

Ships, like hookers, frequently change names. The ship in this story was the *New World Order* on her maiden voyage. But with each successive owner, she was given a new name. Twenty years later she was called the *Amore Islander.* At which point in her life, she was an abused and ignored old ship. A seafaring lady, whose beauty and grace had long since been stolen from her by years of abuse and unfulfilled promises. Her rotting hull suffered from neglect and the tortures of greedy, self-indulging owners and her crew of pirates, thieves and vagrants. This seafaring whore (a tramp steamer in every sense of the word) quietly slipped from one port to another with little fanfare or recognition. A ship loaded with non-descript cargoes and syphilitic sailors who left left disease and unwanted children behind to challenge the compassion and forgiveness of the port communities they burden. This ship, the *Amore Islander,* was once a lady of class and character and the pride of the seafaring world. Now she is an ugly trick. And all the time, her hull sold to line her immoral owner's pockets with gold. How long will this go on?

The Man

Ian van Waterlaan was born into an educated family of means and political influence. He was raised in the eclectic city of Amsterdam in a beautiful and historic house on the Herrengracht. He was the only son of a prominent and successful businessman and professional musician. He lost his father unexpectedly when he was five. His father was shot to death by a disgruntled board member as he chaired a meeting in Rotterdam. Yet despite this tragedy, Ian remained the product of a loving family of refinement and culture, his should have been a charmed life with family wealth and position. Gifted, with a strong well-shaped frame, blazing eyes, charming smile and locks of golden hair, any woman he desired was quickly and without reservation drawn into his bed. A willing and erotic partner for a moment, an evening or a weekend… but never longer.

Provided the best in education and opportunity, he had it all… yet the unexplainable happened. One day without purpose or reason he slipped the grasp of the privileged elite and entered a life of mistrust, evil and self-abuse. He became a Liberian Seaman…

The Ocean

The ocean is a crafty one. She is bountiful and freely giving to men brave enough to fish her, work her or cross her vastness in search of wealth and freedom. She is even a loving mistress to those who would disappear from a past too horrible to face.

The ocean can be kind, alluring and seductive to all that would venture upon her fair skin of warm emerald green, breathtaking cobalt blue or the cold unforgiving death mask of gray. The ocean, unlike nature's other environs, gently soothes and seduces men for years, making them complacent…even overly confident and just a bit arrogant.

It is then that she will exact her merciless tax. Without warning, she can become unforgiving and torturous. Ominously she will howl with delight as she consumes the helpless fools as they cling to pathetic hopes of redemption. The sea is a heartless witch. In the end, she will have her way with those who have challenged her. The men that go to sea play a game they cannot win.

Rex Inverness

Chapter One
The End Is Near
August 1978 -- Somewhere in the Pacific

THE END IS NEAR ... Ian shoved his life jacket under the mattress to keep from rolling off the bed then curled up with a pillow to keep from being thrown onto the deck. A heavy wool blanket, tightly wrapped around his body, kept him warm.

There he slept as the motion rocked him like a baby in a cradle. He tossed and turned as he dreamt in magnificent colors and erotic smells. His body ached for the touch of a lover, and his fantasy had his heart racing as every detail played out in slow motion. Pouring from his mind the story unfolded something like this:

The Brazilian sun rebounded off her long soft auburn hair while the summer sea breeze gently stirred through its length. Her eyes made emeralds dull by comparison, with the bewitching ability to penetrate the soul at a glance and leave one's innermost secrets exposed and naked, for all to see.

The soft, deeply tanned skin of her face radiated the youth and beauty that few have known, yet many have sinned for. She walked towards him. Her slender, well-shaped frame outlined by the Rio de Janeiro seascape as her body played a symphony of sensuality, poise and eroticism.

DRAWN TO THE SEA
(First Revision)

A minuscule black bikini bottom drove his stare to where her shapely thighs came together. She wore a wrinkled cotton shirt. The fact she had been in the water only moments before left little to one's imagination.

Closer and closer she came as he lay on the beach. Helpless in the presence of this approaching goddess, he rose to his feet.

From behind her ripe red lips, she produced a porcelain smile. Then, to his astonishment, her eyes remained fixed on him. Her sweet lips drew together and launched a seductive and overpowering kiss, leaving him weak and powerless.

Her delicate hand reached out for his and as if hypnotized, he responded ... Just then...

"Third" spoke an old, tired male Filipino voice shattering the young man's dream,

"It's twenty-three-thirty, sir, it's time for your watch."

An instant later, Ian's retinas screamed in pain as the excruciating brightness of the overhead lights pierced his closed eyelids. His first conscience thought was to kill the bastard for ruining his dream.

"Get the hell out of here," he yelled as the door closed.

The able-bodied seaman smiled; his entertainment for the morning was complete.

Losing his woman once again, the angry man wiped the last bit of sleep from his eyes and realized his stateroom was moving violently. The room, his prison, his sanctuary, was small, measuring no more than eight by twelve feet of dark paneling. In the far corner, his treasured eight cases of Holstein Beer were carefully secured and intact.

Good, his muddled mind registered.

Near his beer was the settee with a pile of dirty clothes a week or two overdue.

"Another damn job I've got to do," he muttered to himself.

Next to the settee was the head, its toilet and sink forever clogging, a testimonial to the condition of the vessel and the owner's lack of concern for the crew. To the immediate right was the wooden desk, bolted to the floor. For the last two or three days, Typhoon Diana had faithfully cleared his desk of papers, pencils and his well-thumbed Hustler magazines.

As his ears began to function, his attention was drawn to the deck where the trash can slid back and forth in a sympathetic symphony with the movement of the vessel. Its contents slid across the deck sounding like percussion instruments. The curtains covering the porthole rhythmically brushed the wood trim as the books in the bookcase flopped back and forth in a frenzied dance.

"Damn," he said under his breath as he braced for another watch on this miserable ship. It was twenty-three forty-five and just fifteen minutes left until he'd relieve the bridge watch.

Struggling from the bed got harder each day. "God, I wish I were dead," he said as he shook the grogginess from his mind.

As he weaved a drunken path of least resistance towards the head, the moving deck directed his course from left to right to left. Ian's eyes shut in pain as he turned on the overhead light. He grabbed the sink with both hands to balance against the movement underfoot.

He couldn't believe what stared back at him in the mirror, a dirty and unshaven face. He shook his head and talked to his reflection. "You were born into a wealthy family of position and political influence. You grew up in the finest home in Amsterdam and your mother's family owns a castle in the country. You're the heir to one of the largest shipping companies in the world and what have you become?"

He took a breath and continued, "But then there was the fact …"

"You watched as your father was murdered in his boardroom. You were only five. Your mother is hauntingly demanding and the coldest and most unforgiving woman on the planet who tolerates nothing but perfection and ruthlessly crushes anything less."

"Yes, I should have had a charmed life of wealth and position. I had plenty of expensive toys and beautiful women, and, yes, an irresponsible playboy and family embarrassment the butlers and lawyers cleaned up after. Why did I join this damn ship anyway?" He asks the face in the mirror.

"I don't know but I can't go home just yet."

He looked deeply at the twisted and tormented face in the mirror. Then slowly his face softened and the storm in his eyes cleared. For a moment, he tried to remember what he used to look like. "I can't." he mumbled. "I can't."

He needed to get ready for watch. Ian struggled out of the head when the motion of the vessel abruptly changed from long, deep rolls to a gut-wrenching motion as the vessel plowed into the monstrous Pacific swell. With each swell, the bow dove headlong into the sea and mercilessly slammed. The vessel surged and violently shuddered in protest to the compass course it was held too. It dove again into a wall of water and moaned as tons of seawater covered the forecastle. The ship struggled and groaned while it shed the unwelcome weight.

271

"My God, the old man must be nuts to have us on this course. The damn ship will break her back," he said to himself. "I'll change course in a couple of minutes, to hell with this."

Ian wore his dirty, stained and torn khakis, worn boots and he combed his long unkempt hair with his fingers as he wove his way to the pantry for something to eat. He hadn't used a bar of soap, razor or toothbrush in five days, but he was damn hungry. He had his priorities.

He pulled on the refrigerator door and saw an untouched plate of cheese, cold cuts and a quart of fresh milk. With abandonment, he groped for the bread and made a sandwich.

The sandwich in one hand and the quart of milk in the other, he turned the corner and headed for the bridge. Ian walked down a narrow passageway and climbed the stairs as the violent storm raged on. The walk was a challenge and the trail of crumbs, meat and milk were testimonial to that fact. "Who cares … the damn steward will clean it up."

Up the last flight of stairs to the wheelhouse and there he stood knowing full well that once he crossed the threshold, the vessel and the lives on board were his responsibility. He took a deep breath as the ship pounded and shuddered then reached for the door handle.

Chapter Two
The Beginning of the End
Seven Weeks Before

Ian's plane landed at the international airport in Tampa. Bright sunshine poured through the fuselage windows and assaulted his face. Ian raised a well-read magazine to shield his eyes and groaned. After being in Amsterdam for five months, his eyes stung from the light. They had become accustomed to the dark nightclubs, bars, and brothels he frequented.

His liver had been punished with copious amounts of *jonge jenever,* which the locals described as young gin, and beer. His heart hammered in his chest, still reeling from the cocaine and other drugs in his system. He couldn't remember the names or faces of the women he'd run through in the constant blur of self-abuse.

Ian rubbed his eyes as the plane taxied down the runway. He pulled out his wallet and thumbed through the couple of bills inside. "Shit, that's all I have left?" He sighed and shoved it back in his pocket. Maybe he could change with Susan's help, but deep inside he knew he wasn't ready to become what his family expected – no, demanded, of him.

When the passengers began to exit, he let them rush by and then slowly followed to the baggage claim.

Mindlessly, Ian gazed off into the distance until the flashing red light and alarm brought him back to reality. The jolt of the conveyor belt was immediately followed by a metallic sound and it began to move.

Moments later he saw the sea bag and luggage that contained his sextant, binoculars and other professional accessories each deck officer carried with them. Elbowing his way into the impatient travelers crowded around the moving luggage, he grabbed his bags and walked away from the horde.

With luggage in hand, he made his way outside and spotted the local shipping agent Arturo Sanchez. He'd be hard to miss, with his ever-present toothpick, white suit, and unbuttoned shirt. He smiled when he saw Ian, showing off his crummy teeth with two gold crowns glinting in the sun.

Ian stifled a laugh. "Hey man, good to see you. It's been a while." He put his bags down. "Even though you look like a pimp, you're a sight for sore eyes. You know that gold chain is going to drown you someday. You'll go straight to the bottom with it around your neck."

Arturo puffed out his concave chest. "Dude, I am better than a pimp and you know it. Who does everyone come to see when they need transportation, happy pills, or companionship? Me … Arturo!" He pounded his sternum in a poor rendition of an anorexic Tarzan.

He slid his over-sized sunglasses down his oily nose and his beady black eyes took Ian's measure. "It looks like you've been overloading on the good things in life yourself, my friend."

"I've had my share," Ian said, "Too long in Amsterdam can kill a man."

Arturo chuckled. "I can see that. Come now, I have a driver waiting." He turned and headed to a sedan at the curb. Ian grabbed his gear and followed.

The driver was a rather plain looking man in a dirty white shirt, cheap sunglasses and horrible teeth, his filthy cowboy hat sat on the back on his head. His nicotine stained fingertips drummed the steering wheel.

He lowered the window as they approached and he and Arturo exchanged a glance and a nod. Ian rolled his eyes and got in the back. Arturo slid in next to him and barked, "Hooker's Point – the Cement Terminal."

Arturo's helot responded and put the car in gear and quietly merged into traffic. Ian found the small talk shallow and uninteresting. The peddler beside him pitched his goods … "girls? … drugs? …what do you want?" Ian hardly heard him as the noise of the city sympathetically drowned out the other's voice.

Ian stared out the window. He'd been in this city a number of times and hardly knew a thing about it. *Tampa seems like a town where there may be tolerance for a man like me to start over.* That thought rushed over Ian with warmth and urgency and just as quickly it was gone and then there was nothing. He felt hollow and returned to his private place. A place deeply embedded in his thoughts. He was only semi-aware of the people and places that rushed by the window and the dullards who occupied the car with him.

As the car left the city, the sights became familiar. Beautiful buildings and well-manicured homes were gradually replaced with warehouses, rundown homes, cheap bars and pawnshops. The clean and well-maintained cars were replaced with broken wrecks and burned-out hulks that littered the streets.

It dawned on Ian that every port around the world was the same. They stunk with the promise of quick money, crime, desperation, exploitation and misery. A look into the eyes of those who existed there and it was all the same. There were the few that had learned to exploit these dens of misery through crime and violence. Most, however, carried their burdens until their lives were spent.

Why did he see this so clearly? He feared he had become one of those creatures himself.

Closer and closer to the ship they traveled. Soon in the distance the *Amore Islander* was visible above the buildings and warehouses that lined the pier. There she was … his home, his prison, his sanctuary, and his hell.

The *Amore Islander* was stunningly beautiful yet wretchedly ugly. She was pure of soul, yet tormented. She embraced with love and security then cast away to the devil himself. A rational person would call a ship an inanimate object but to her crew she was as alive as any woman who had graced the earth. She was cold and unforgiving, yet warm and passionate. She was an angel and she was a demon, and so was the love-hate relationship all mariners share for their ships.

The car moved to the gate at the head of the pier. The driver slowed and briefly stopped. They got a disinterested glance from the fat and sleepy guard in his ill-fitting, sweat-stained uniform and with minimal effort his arm provided the go-ahead. Around the corner, the ship came into full view. It was overpowering. All of its eight-hundred and fifty feet dominated the pier and dwarfed everything around. The driver pulled up to the gangway. Arturo looked at Ian and said, "Home-sweet-home, sailor boy," and smiled. Then without a moment wasted he and his driver bounded up the gangway to shake-down the captain for whiskey, cigarettes and a free meal or two.

DRAWN TO THE SEA
(First Revision)

Ian gathered his things and watched as two Filipino crewmembers scurried down the gangway to help him aboard. They were covered from head to toe in grimy and ripped hand-me-down clothing. Long sleeve shirts, long pants, gloves, and oversized straw hats kept the sun off their skin. Their bright and cheerful faces beamed as they excitedly greeted him.

"Third … welcome back, we heard you were coming back! Many good times? Third … lots of parties? Have fun on vacation?" The curious deckhands asked.

Ian's head cleared, he was alert and felt alive once more. This rusty sea whore was his home and the crew his family. The gnawing emptiness that haunted him for months vanished.

He and the two Filipinos carrying his gear walked up the long gangway. It flexed up and down under their feet as they made their way to the top. They reached the deck and boarded the ship. Forty feet above the water, the view opened up and Davis Island, the City of Tampa, and the vast bay were readily visible. *It's nice to be home,* Ian thought. The smells, sounds, and vibrations that are the soul of the ship were assimilated into Ian's body and he and the ship became one. Once again the mother and her child were together and Ian was safe in the warmth of her womb.

With a few friendly conversations, Ian walked along the rusty deck to the house and passed through the watertight door. He casually noticed the watertight gaskets were missing and the door and its hinges rusted and neglected. Inside, the *Amore Islander* was clean and well lit. The stewards department had done a good job keeping up with the hotel services. He walked by the officer's watch mess and saw Herbert, the Third Engineer and Neil, the First Officer. They raised their mugs to him, both with wide grins.

"Welcome back, you old dog," said Neil

"Screw you too," Ian said with a smile. "You two have been around a lot longer than I have, and you guys were geezers when I met you." He pounded them both on the back. "But hell, it's still nice to be back aboard."

Ian suggested and they agreed to go ashore later to the local club and catch-up. Ian bid them adieu and continued down the passageway to the stairs. Up two flights of stairs and he stepped into "Officer Country," where the officers and engineers lived.

With experienced ease he turned to his right and walked down the narrow passageway towards the starboard side and right again, heading aft to the second door on the left. He took a deep breath and walked in. This would be his home for the next six months. His bags were waiting for him in the middle of the floor. To his left was a desk, ahead the bed and to his right the head. This room had been the temporary refuge of every third mate. For twenty years this was where men had slept, cried, written home, lost their humanity and some their sanity. All the time they wasted their lives away ... this was Ian's private hell.

Memories of his previous tours rushed over him and then he looked at his bags and grumbled, "To hell with it!"

Unpacking, he changed into the uniform he'd live and work in until this contract was completed. He had four sets of identical clothes -- khaki shirts and trousers. One pair was clean and unstained, the others tormented with spilled paint, grease and rust.

He put on the clean set, tied his boots, smiled at himself in the stained mirror then made his way up to the captain's office with his merchant marine license in one

hand and his passport and sea service book in the other.
All of these he would surrender to the captain. He
reversed his course to the stairs going up another flight to
the "Senior Officer Country" where the captain and chief
engineer lived. Again emerging from the stairs, he turned
right and then made an immediate left and looked into the
captain's office.

Ian saw the captain seated at the desk, his reading
glasses rested on his bulbous and blood shot nose. The
older man was balding, overweight and dressed in dirty
and wrinkled clothes. Ian stood there for a moment as the
man concentrated on papers in front of him. He shook his
head and smirked. *What a wretched mess of a man you
are, Herr Captain.* Ian straightened his back, squared his
shoulders, and knocked on the door frame.

The captain looked up, leaned back in his chair,
removed his glasses and squinted as he ran his fat fingers
over his bald head.

"Ian … good to have you back … I've been
expecting you." He waved his meaty hand.

"Come in and sit for a moment."

Ian sat in the wooden chair anchored to the floor
and said, "Captain Strauss, thank you for requesting me
back by name. I do like the ship, her crew and the run."

"You're a reliable officer and a pleasure to have
aboard." Ian suppressed a chuckle because he knew the old
man was blowing smoke.

After a few minutes of small talk, the captain grew
noticeably tired of the conversation, leaned back in his
chair and said, "You're assigned the eight to twelve watch
starting tomorrow morning." He shuffled around some
papers. "Enjoy your time ashore with Neil and Herbert."

His vacant stare would have normally alarmed Ian,
but Ian knew this man. He was a drunk, a loner, and

miserable human being. Strauss was a company man, submissive and spineless, and the crew had little respect for him as either a man or a leader.

Ian smiled and handed over his paperwork. The captain grabbed the papers, screwed his eyes into focus with much effort and looked to ensure they were current and complete. Satisfied he set them down and pushed the shipping articles under Ian's nose.

Ian picked up the pen and signed the contract. He was officially part of the *Amore Islander* crew. Once again, his prison sentence sealed until properly relieved. The ink was black but he knew this contract was written in blood.

Chapter Three
Charlie's Bar

After Ian left the captain's office, he thought, *something really bad is going to happen to this ship and the men aboard with such an incompetent in command. If you're smart, you'd cut and run now.* He grimaced and knew he had only one option and that was to go back to Holland and be strapped into the yoke his family had built for him. He shook his head and said, "Not quite yet." Then he walked aft through a watertight door out on deck to clear his head. He looked over towards the center of Tampa. Again, he wondered, *Could I start over in a place like this? Could I live a better life or is this life my damnation for eternity?"*

When Ian was home, he had visited the family priest in Amsterdam as he looked for salvation and a solution to his anguish. The man of cloth offered little hope. Embarrassed and angry, Ian thought, *if a Dutchman can't offer redemption ... there's simply no hope.*

That disaster had fueled his most excessive binge of self-abuse yet. Memories of his five months ashore in Holland were absent, or at best, distorted.

The sun warmed his handsome face and it felt nice to close his eyes and soak up the heat. It was nearly time for the evening meal and he could smell the unmistakable stench of atomized lard coming from the galley fry-o-lator.

It must be fish tonight. Later he would meet up with Neil and Herbert for a night on the town before departure on the morning tide.

Back in his room, Ian pawed through his clothes for something to wear into town. Nothing too fancy. They were only looking for drinks and a good time with the local working girls. He knew Susan would be there.

She'd been his steady for years and the focus of his dreams and hopes for the future. He knew he would be able to fix himself with her love and support, but he couldn't get his head completely around "how" just yet. He grabbed a clean shirt, shorts, sandals and thought, *Might as well be comfortable,* and he headed down for dinner.

The meal was as good as could be expected. The stewards did their best, but they could only do so much with a limited amount of questionable food. Ian saw it in the chief steward's eyes as he fed the crew. Ian and the others knew the chief steward was an amazing restaurant manager and chef.

For many years, Cookie Chavez owned one of the finest restaurants in Manila. He had named it after his mother Isabella. For some reason, he left it all to join the merchant marine and over time ended up on the *Amore Islander* where he'd been the chief steward for years.

Cookie made it no secret things had gone to hell in the galley since Strauss became the captain.

Neil and Herbert were joking while they waited for Ian on deck by the gangway and when they saw Ian walk towards them, the banter started.

"Are you going to wear that clown suit ashore?"

"Screw you too, numb nuts."

"I'm just saying … the girls won't give you the time of day."

DRAWN TO THE SEA
(First Revision)

"I'll give you something," and the ribbing continued.

Neil chimed in, "Hell boys, let's get drunk." With that they smiled and checked the sailing board. Ian thought, *Departure, ten in the morning*.

Down the gangway, they laughed and joked like frat boys and piled into the waiting cab. "Charlie's Bar," said one of them to the sleepy cab driver who sat up and stretched like a cat and rubbed his eyes.

"Are we keeping you up?" Herbert joked and looked at the others as they laughed with him. The driver started his old Chevy, unshaken by soon-to-be-drunken and obnoxious mariners. The faded car was missing three hub caps and the windshield was cracked. The rolling junk squatted as it moved down the road, its shocks creaking and moaning in protest to the three large men in the back seat.

Charlie's was a well-know dive a mile or so down the road from the ship. The owner was a colorful old mariner in his own right. He had spent years sailing around the world as a ship's bosun. He had a notorious, and probably well-deserved, reputation as a hard drinking and wild whoring sailor who found the seediest dives in every port.

After his second heart attack, the Coast Guard took away his seaman's document. Undaunted, he decided to marry his favorite hooker, swallowed the anchor, and bought his own bar. Charlie's was dark and dusty, just like any dive in any port town.

He made no effort to make the place feel warm and friendly. The old bosun knew from experience that mariners and stevedores went to bars for two things … drinks and girls and that's what he catered to.

Tonight the girls had on their war paint, short skirts and poured out of their small blouses as they aggressively hawked their goods. The men cycled through. Some paired up with a hooker right away, others waited until the alcohol took effect and a few passed the time just watching the action.

There was sadness in the air, the *Amore Islander* was well-represented, and the girls knew they needed to make their money from the crew tonight before the ship left in the morning.

For the last nine years the *Amore Islander* and her crew had been a regular fixture at Hooker's Point and at Charlie's. The ship was in and out of Tampa two to three times a month all that time. Tomorrow the ship and her crew would leave and never return.

Thinking back Ian could see the night the ship arrived in Tampa, there were more working girls on the ship than crew. During Ian's first contract, he learned to keep his room locked or visitors crawled into his bed. If he was away from the room, he knew he could expect to be robbed if the door was left unlocked. These ladies were good in bed and stole whenever given the opportunity.

Ian and his friends paid the driver and ran through the bar door. Ian looked around and thought, *this shithole hasn't changed a bit.* Then he saw a familiar face in the distance and smiled. Susan was sitting at the bar. She was nursing the first of many drinks and looked off in the distance, clearly in a dream far away. She turned and their eyes met.

She'd been in the same line of work for about ten years and her youthful beauty was quickly waning. Each time Ian saw her she looked more tired and older. Whether a short-time or the occasional overnight marathon, she knew exactly what he needed and had been his steady for years.

Ian had no claim to her nor she to him … they just seemed to end up together. It was comfortable and satisfied them both. Ian planned to make it more, but needed to control the demons that tormented him first. She was the only one who seemed to understand his struggle with destiny and desire and the pressure, guilt, and regret which lay between the two.

He wasn't quite ready, but with her help, he would be soon. He'd already written to his mother about Susan and told her he would bring her with him when he was ready to come home.

Susan was once a pretty young girl from somewhere up north. Her naturally blonde hair and her blue eyes were striking, but a closer look reveled years of pain and disappointment. Yes, she was pretty, but she had a class about her which reminded Ian of his mother. Class was a rare commodity in Susan's line of work and he loved her from the first time they'd met.

Over the years, Charlie had told him bits and pieces of her story. She followed her boyfriend to Tampa right after high school, got knocked-up, and he ran on her. She was pregnant, pretty, desperate and alone, and became easy prey for the pimps in the area. After the initial shock and horrible guilt subsided, she found it was easy work and occasionally even enjoyed spending time with the men passing through town.

Ian thought, *I want to settle-down with her and start over. We're both so much alike, and yet so different. Would our relationship work or not? I wonder if she ever thinks about me and a possible future together, or am I just another one in hundreds of men that rotate through her bed and soil her sheets?* Ian wanted to ask, but couldn't, and she kept it simple by never offering up more than the money on the table had purchased.

Ian walked up to Susan and kissed her discreetly on the cheek. He pulled up a stool next to her and looked over at Charlie behind the bar. "Charlie, how are you doing my friend? It really sucks that we are leaving Tampa, I really like this town and …" He looked at Susan and smiled and her eyes grew swimmy. "I really like the company." He winked at her and she blushed, erasing years from her face.

Charlie chuckled. "What you drinking Ian? I assume you are buying Susan a drink too, right?"

"Of course, Susan my dear, what would you like?"

"Bourbon on the rocks."

Ian looked back at the man behind the bar, "Bourbon on the rocks for the lady and a vodka martini, make it Grey Goose for me."

Charlie bristled and barked back, "Grey Goose, what kind of a place do you think I run here? If you want that highbrow hootch, go into the city. I've got Smirnoff or Absolute. Take it or leave it."

"Okay … don't get so sore Charlie … Absolute is fine." Ian turned back to Susan and they chatted a few minutes patiently waiting for their drinks. They talked about nothing and everything, as love and passion shone in their eyes. Ian asked about her daughter and she politely told him Sarah was fine and doing well.

Charlie delivered the drinks and waited for Ian to drop a twenty on the bar. Once the money was in the till, Charlie moved to another patron waiting for a beer.

Over the years, Ian had met Susan's daughter several times and loved to watch Susan talk about her and it made him smile. At the same time, Ian watched as she sized him up. Tonight was a money-making night for her and she needed to choose well. They had been in this mating dance many times and Ian knew what she was thinking, *Will he buy me for the night or an hour?*

Ian reached into his front pocket and pulled out a wad of bills, gave her more money than she expected and she smiled. Charlie looked from behind the bar as he stood next to his wife and poured them another round. "On the house you love birds."

After they both had their fill of drinks, Susan brought Ian back to her apartment. They made a bee-line for the bedroom where they consumed each other as lovers do. Later, spent and content, they slipped into a gentle sleep cradled in each other's arms. *Is this what it's supposed to be like?* Ian wondered.

Hours later Susan gently woke him, reminding him he needed to get back to the ship. She poured coffee and they sat around the kitchen table and quietly sipped the hot black beverage. Ian wondered, *is this the way it's supposed to be? A partner to love and one who loves you in return?*

Later she drove to the ship. The sleepy guard recognized her and sent her though. She drove Ian to the gangway and turned off the headlights. Susan turned to Ian with both hands still on the steering wheel, a tear rolled down her cheek and she leaned over and kissed him. They talked and kissed each other for ten minutes in the idling car until Ian asked, "Would you ... ever consider..."

She touched his lips and said, "Don't say anything ... I love you and I'll be here when you return." They kissed again, one long, feathery goodbye and Ian climbed out of the car and walked away. He looked one final time over his shoulder and thought, *this is the first time I've truly loved a woman.*

Chapter Four
Departure

Later that morning, Ian woke and lay in his bed for a moment and thought of Susan. He remembered how she felt, smelled, and responded to his touch. Then he scolded himself and thought, *Who am I kidding? I paid her to respond that way.* Ian slowly rolled out of the rack and headed to the sink to wash his face. There was a knock on the door … it opened, the light came on, and a little Filipino face peered around the door, "Third … it's seven fifteen. We sail at ten." With that, the tormentor was gone.

Ian showered, shaved, and dressed in his better khakis. He remembered they'd have company on the bridge. Dressed and ready to go, Ian walked out the door and headed to the watch mess for a quick cup of coffee and a couple of eggs and toast.

The watch mess stunk of old grease and filthy men. The room was small and this morning it was crowded with mates and engineers gathered for the morning meal. It was popular with the men because the meals were served quickly. Engineers especially liked eating there because they could eat in their dirty overalls and greasy boots. Of course the stewards hated the room because it was so difficult to keep clean.

Mates looked down their noses at the engineers. The engineers had a healthy distrust of mates, and the stewards were everyone's tool. The stewards, in turn, selflessly tended to the interior living spaces, prepared and served four meals a day, and cleaned the officer's rooms.

They tried to ignore their second class status, but carried it locked in their hearts. It burned with such passion that, if unleashed, would result in violence – even murder. Who could blame them? Slavery was alive and well aboard ship and shipping articles as binding as a bill of sale was for flesh on southern plantations a hundred and fifty years ago.

His belly full, Ian smiled and thanked the steward. He didn't want them sharpening their knives with him in mind. Ian moved through the maze of passageways and stairs as he made his way to the bridge to assume his first watch and prepare the ship for departure.

During the early morning, cargo operations were completed. Discharging the ship was far less difficult; therefore, the second mate was left in charge to finish while Neil went ashore. Looking into the deck log, Ian saw the last of the cargo was discharged at four thirty-six. Since then, the watch team had secured the hatches and gear on deck for departure. So routine were the preparations Ian barely noticed as he came aboard earlier.

On the wing of the bridge, the second mate, Dieter, sunned himself. Yes, another German. Ian thought, *I'm surrounded by krauts, yes, and I hate krauts!* His family had suffered a number of times at the hands of Germany. But mainly he hated their arrogance, sense of superiority, and aloofness. *It must be in their DNA.*

They continued to invade Holland in their Mercedes Benz, their modern day panzers, and did their best to dominate and control the Dutch. He smirked as he remembered 'keying' an expensive red sedan with German plates on his sixteenth birthday while several of his friends drank beer and encouraged the vandalism.

Even the Germans aboard the *Amore Islander* had that way about them. Neil and Ian talked about it constantly and tried to look beyond it because 'these' krauts had become family, their shipboard family, *Okay, but they're still krauts!*

Ian looked over the deck log, nothing unusual caught his eye. He walked out to Dieter and they started the watch turnover.

"Good morning, Dieter."

"Good morning. Cargo operations completed four thirty-six and the deck was secured for sea. I contacted the engineer on watch and the machinery was tested and ready for sea. The number four winch is still broken, so the spring line has to be run to a secondary winch to be retrieved. It should be brought aboard first. The starboard anchor windlass was broken too."

He continued and Ian was only half listening, the routine of standing watch had become second nature. Though his first watch of the contract, he was already back-in-the-groove. Dieter droned on and on. Finally he stopped to catch his breath and Ian re-engaged. "Thanks Dieter … anything else?"

"No."

"Then I relieve you," Ian said.

Dieter bid goodbye, clicked his heels, spun around, and headed down to the salon for his morning meal. A proper German, he was always dressed in clean khakis, polished shoes, and had a cleanly shaven face. Most meals he dined by himself in the salon with silverware, linen table cloth and napkins. The only other person who routinely dined there was the captain. Ian thought, *that's too much trouble.*

DRAWN TO THE SEA
(First Revision)

Alone on the bridge, Ian called his engineering counterpart, Herbert, in the engine room and confirmed all was ready for first bell around ten. He confirmed and commented quickly on his experience ashore last night.

"Yeah … I had a good time too," and Ian hung up the phone.

Next, Ian checked the charts and logs. The charts had stains and Scotch Tape repaired several torn areas. Ian carefully placed them on the chart table with sharpened pencils, dividers, navigation triangles, and parallel rulers. The deck log entries were in black, red, and green ink. The captain insisted normal entries be made in black, safety events in green, and key and emergency events logged in red ink.

On top of the other charts was the harbor chart used to transit to the bay's entrance beyond the Sunshine Skyway Bridge. Under it were a few coastal charts marked with the track to Panama.

A quick check of the weather confirmed light winds from the south at five to ten knots, and seas outside were two to three feet in height. Off at the far end of the weather map was a low pressure area that no one was concerned about yet. Ian set the map aside and walked to the bridge wing and looked at the sky. *Alto cumulus clouds overhead, maybe there'd be showers later this morning.*

Ian turned on the VHF radio and called for a radio check. It worked. He contacted the tug company and confirmed they were sending three tugs, the *Alice, Suzie Q* and *Betty*. These tugs were all small so they'd need three instead of the two they usually called for.

Continuing down his check list, he contacted the pilots and confirmed a pilot was on the way.

"Carlos," Ian called on the walkie-talkie to his Filipino able seaman on deck.

"Yes, third"

"Is the gangway ready to bring aboard?"

"Yes, third ..."

"Make your way to the gangway with Juan and standby for the pilot. I'll be down in a few minutes."

Ian continued down the list. Next the ship's whistle and general alarm were tested. It announced to the crew and those on the dock, the ship would be underway soon. The ship came alive and Ian heard auxiliary machinery. Just then, the captain came through the door onto the bridge. *He looked remarkably rested and alert for a change.*

"Good morning," Strauss said.

"Good morning, sir."

The captain looked over the chart, the weather report and the deck log. He asked about the number four winch. "No, it's still broken sir," Ian replied.

"Does the starboard anchor windlass work?"

Again Ian said. "No, sir."

"Never mind," Strauss said under his breath.

"The pilot should be here any moment and the ship is ready for sea, captain."

"Good. Have coffee and pastries brought to the bridge."

"Aye, sir." Ian picked up the phone and called the galley, "Steward ... Bridge ... please bring coffee and pastries for the captain and pilot."

Ian threw a series of switches on the radars, the satellite navigation system and the new navigation tool called LORAN, and efficiently tuned them. He thought, *they work ... amazing!*

A black car came up alongside the ship near the gangway. Ian excused himself and left the captain to his own thoughts as he rushed to the brow to greet the pilot. The old man came up the gangway huffing and puffing as he reached the top. Ian got there just in time to meet him.

"Welcome aboard the *Amore Islander*".

The pilot brushed by asking, "is the ship ready for sea?"

Ian respond, "Yes, and Captain Strauss is on the bridge."

"Strauss, you say," the pilot said, stopping short and looked at Ian.

Ian confirmed with a nod.

"He still has a job … hummm." The pilot turned and continued to the bridge.

Out of courtesy, Ian escorted him even though the pilot had been on *Amore Islander* many times, and knew his way around as well as any of the crew. They entered the bridge, Ian introduced the pilot to Strauss and returned to his preparations for departure. But first, Ian grabbed the *hotel* "H" signal flag, and ran aloft and hoisted it. Back down on the bridge, as the captain and pilot talked, Ian called Herbert, "Start the generator and bow thruster and standby for engine orders."

Ian could feel the pressure beginning to mount as the departure approached. He hung up the phone and rang the engine telegraph from *FINISHED WITH ENGINES* to *STOP*. Up the narrow channel came the three tugs. Ian tested the bow thruster... *It works -- amazing!*

Carlos came to the bridge and assumed his position behind the helm, still in his dirty deck clothes, long sleeve shirt and pants. He removed his hat and stood behind the helm. Ian was busy documenting the time the crew turned too, the pilot boarded, the telegraph shifted to *STOP,* and the locations and time the tugs were made fast.

Ian had Carlos cycle the rudder from left to right and back. Steering system checked satisfactory. The captain and pilot were on the offshore bridge wing looking at the approaching tugs. The pilot was communicating with the boats, and the captain with the mates on the bow and stern each with a handful of deck hands. The decision was made … *Alice* forward, *Suzie Q* aft, and *Betty* amidships. Orders were given and the tugs were made up to the ship.

The crew moved to their maneuvering stations on deck forward and aft. Their job was to retrieve the mooring lines and stow them below deck. As if on cue, line handlers came out of the dock shadows and tossed the lines off the bollards.

Captain Strauss called the mate, "Bring in the spring line forward."

"Aye, captain"

A similar order is given to the mate on the stern for the aft spring lines. Order acknowledged. Ian walked out onto the in-shore bridge wing and watched as the lines were brought aboard. Another task Ian would record in the log. The pilot directed the tugs to "push easy" and they complied. The ship was pinned against the pier as the final lines were brought aboard. The captain called to his mate on the stern to bring in all lines. A moment later the same order was given to the mate on the bow.

The captain called to Ian, "Last Line."

Ian scribbled the time in the log book. The voyage had begun.

The captain and pilot moved back and forth from one bridge wing to the other. The whole time the pilot gave orders to the tugs by walkie-talkie. He yelled rudder and engine commands to Ian in the wheelhouse. The captain was present and engaged but silent.

"Left Full Rudder" the pilot directed. Ian repeated the order. Carlos repeated the order and complied.

"The Rudder is Left Full," Carlos responded after the rudder indicator needle was buried to the left of the gauge.

Ian repeated, "Rudder is Left Full."

And the pilot called for, "*DEAD SLOW ASTERN.*" Ian repeated and moved the engine telegraph to *DEAD SLOW ASTERN.* Another time for the log ... *'First Bell'* ...

Down in the engine room, the chief engineer acknowledged the telegraph order and opened a valve connecting the two story slow speed diesel engine with high pressure air in a series of large bottles. The air turned over the engine until the diesel fuel began to fire the cylinders.

The ship bucked as the engine coughed to life and the twenty-four foot propeller began to thrash the water, and the ship vibrated and began to move. Slowly it backed to the left, away from the dock. All three tugs reversed their thrust and pulled the ship from the pier. The ship was moving.

The pilot twisted the ship in the narrow channel, slowly turning the *Amore Islander* end for end. The tugs pushed and pulled the ship and the rudder and engine were used to help spin the ship. The channel was only eleven-hundred feet wide in the turning basin, and the *Amore Islander* eight-hundred and fifty feet in length overall.

The maneuver was slow and carefully conducted to avoid collision with the other freighters that lined the piers.

By ten-fourteen, the *Amore Islander* was pointed outbound and the tugs sat idle alongside, still made fast.

"Rudder amidships, *DEAD SLOW AHEAD,*" called the pilot as he and the captain moved into the wheelhouse from the port wing.

Orders repeated and the helm placed amidships and the engine telegraph rung-up to *DEAD SLOW AHEAD*. As the rudder indicator confirmed the rudder was amidships, Carlos confirmed, the rudder was centered. RPM indicator confirmed fifteen turns forward and Ian responded, "*DEAD SLOW AHEAD*."

The ship gathered momentum and began to respond to the rudder and the pilot asked the captain to let go the tugs. "Start forward and work aft," he commanded. The captain called his deck mates and the task was accomplished. Ian thought, *Tugs away … another entry for the log.*

Davis Island passed close by the starboard side and the Cement Plant to the left. The pilot brought the ship left to a new course down the "C" cut channel and asked for *SLOW AHEAD*. Ian complied and rang the engine telegraph. The vibration of the ship began to change as the engineers increased the RPMs. The ship moved along at seven knots.

Several minutes later, the pilot asked for *HALF AHEAD*. The same routine and the ship moved along at ten knots. Ian paced between the compasses and the charts marking their position as they continued south down the shipping channel. He noticed how nice the weather was and few ships competed for the narrow channel.

The pilot called for right rudder and settled the ship on a new southwesterly course within the "A" cut channel and the passage out to the Sunshine Skyway Bridge and the sea buoy. The sun was dead ahead, Carlos squinted and put on his sunglasses which were missing a lens. Ian stifled a laugh and handed Carlos his glasses.

"Here you go, you look ridiculous, Carlos."

The captain and pilot chatted and drank coffee while Ian was busy keeping track of the ship's position and documenting the transit, listening for engine orders and Carlos smiled and stood behind the wheel as he kept the ship on course. It was a simple symphony of movement with the chatter of the radios in the background and the vibration of the ship underfoot. *I love this life,* Ian thought.

They passed through "A" Cut, came right again into Gadsden Point Cut, left on "F" Cut, then "E" Cut, "D" Cut, "C", "B", "A" passed under the Sunshine Skyway Bridge and then Mullet Key Cut to Egmont Channel and seaward bound. At the entrance to Egmont Channel, the ship was slowed and turned to the left to make a lee for the pilot to disembark.

The pilot and captain exchanged pleasantries and farewells then Ian escorted the pilot to the main deck and the pilot ladder. The boat was already lying alongside under the ladder. The pilot waved to the bridge and hailed the boat. He stepped over the rail and down the boatswain's ladder to the pitching boat deck below.

With the pilot aboard, the boat operator gunned his engines and sped away, heading back to the harbor. The deck gang stowed the ladder while Ian climbed the stairs back to the bridge. He stopped briefly, to pull down the "H" flag on his way.

On the bridge, the captain had ordered the engine *AHEAD FULL* and Carlos was steering a new course of two-two-three. A moment after Ian got back, the captain left and the watch was Ian's.

He took a hastened look over the horizon, looked at the radar picture and then to the chart. The sun was shining, the sea breeze was refreshing, and they were moving through the water at sixteen knots.

It was nearly twelve so Ian finished the log entries, put a position on the chart, checked the compass heading and again scanned the horizon. Neil stepped through the door at eleven fifty with his usual punctuality and they talked through the morning events, reviewed the ship's position, speed, course, and discussed the transit. "Continue southwest for Cristobal."

Neil took over the watch and Ian was properly relieved. He grabbed his jacket and headed down for the noon meal.

The *Amore Islander* was in deep water making sixteen knots on a steady course. The ship took on a hypnotic sound, vibration, and her own gentle motion as she moved in the loving arms of the ocean.

Down the ladder Ian entered the officer's deck and made his way to his stateroom. He dropped his gear and washed his face as he looked in the mirror – he could already see the change had started. Sun and wind had burned his face, his eyes were irritated and red, and his face had stubble which helped with the rugged look. Ian wondered, *did Bruce Banner have the same thoughts when he looked in the mirror at the "Hulk" lurking beneath his skin?*

His stomach growled reminding him that he was hungry. He sped back into the passageway and down the ladder to the watch mess and ordered his lunch. He made it moments before the galley secured.

"A grilled cheese sandwich and fries would do," He told the steward. Without even enjoying the food, he shoved it down his throat and left. Ian was tired from the night before and decided he'd take an afternoon nap.

Back in his stateroom he stripped off his clothes, left them in a pile on the floor and crawled into his freshly made bed and thought as he sighed, *it's nice to have stewards. I rarely sleep in a made bed at home. I'm just too lazy to make it.*

Ian drifted off into a numbing sleep as the motion and vibration of the ship coursed through his veins.

He dreamt of Susan.

Chapter Five
At Sea

It was late in the afternoon when Ian opened his eyes feeling the vibration of the ship. The muffled humming of machinery below and the constant sound of forced air coming into the room through the overhead vent were all reminders the heart and circulatory system of the living thing called *Amore Islander* functioned properly.

Ian stretched, climbed out of bed, made his way to the head, where he leaned on the sink, braced himself with both hands, and studied the face in the faded mirror. He carefully watched the slow transformation back into a Liberian Seaman. The change was gradual, but profound just the same.

With each contract, Ian observed the same thing. The first and most obvious change was the beard and the abuse the wind and sun had on his skin. Next was the growing length of his hair and his eyes became chronically blood shot. At the same time, his teeth changed color from white to coffee stained and looked neglected.

The final physical manifestation was he'd drop twenty-five pounds or so, his personal hygiene became unimportant, and his hair became oily and untended. His skin became dirty and he smelled of musk and sweat like an animal in the wild. He was not alone. This was a seaman's life and none more profound than those sailing under flags of convenience. They were an international brotherhood of mariners who for any number of reasons could not or chose not to work under their nation's flags.

Their stories all varied but they were all the same. It may be they were hiding from ex-wives, or in some cases, the law. They may have had their mariner documents revoked, for any number of reasons, and found refuge with Liberian documents. It may be they were drunks, druggies, or reprobates who fell below the low expectations other nations held for their seamen.

In Ian's case, he was running away from the uncompromising demands of his tyrannical mother and the rigid plan she had in mind for him. She had told him, "I demand and expect nothing less. You will, with grace, honor, and if necessary, an iron fist rule and with Machiavellian cunning assume control of the dynasty your family has built for generations." He could hear the nagging and persistence in his mother's voice. Instead, he tried to find a sense of peace and distance to balance the pain and failure he felt for not meeting the lofty expectations set before him. He thought, *maybe someday with Susan's support and love it could be different.*

The handsome Dutchman gathered his clothes from the floor, dressed, and laced up his boots. He reached for a cassette tape and loaded his Sony player, pushed the play button, and was surrounded by Journey's, "City by the Bay." Ian drifted into memories of his home, his mother, and the excitement and beauty of Amsterdam. Cobblestone roads and canals encircled the city and boats transited the waterways, painted in bright colors. All this was visible through the windows of his city home. *I miss my youth and how simple life used to be until the walls seemed to close in around me.*

There were still several hours of daylight before the evening meal and he needed the fresh air. Ian left his stateroom and walked around the ship to see if anything had changed since he'd left five months ago.

Ian moved down to the main deck. The ship was empty and rode high in the water. He stood nearly thirty feet above the surface and had a commanding view of the horizon. There was nothing but water and a few fishing boats working off in the distance. The warm sea breeze was invigorating and the bright sun warmed his forehead.

He removed his shirt and felt the warm sun on his shoulders as his eyes were drawn to the deteriorated steel railings lining the deck. Its purpose was to keep mariners safely aboard. Many of the secondary rails had rusted through and been discarded over the side. No apparent effort has been made to replace or repair the dilapidated sections. *Damn owners -- damn captain,* he thought.

The decks were rusted and plate welds pitted and neglected. Deck machinery, like the mooring winches, were heavily corroded, the bearings longed for grease, and the wiring lay open and exposed to the elements.

Ian continued forward to the bow and climbed the ladder to the "eyes of the ship." The foredeck told its own story of neglect and torture. Ian shook his head and thought, *she's a good ship and deserves better. Like a beautiful woman, married into an abusive relationship, the ship is dying at the hands of a violent and twisted partner.*

He continued along the port side only to see more of the same. He quietly accepted his share of the responsibility because he had been a member of the crew for years and had done nothing to reverse the neglect.

By choice, he stayed a third mate never striving to promote. He stood a bridge watch and supervised cargo and ballast operations under the close oversight of the chief mate. It was easy work and allowed him time to reflect and hide with little responsibility.

Ian saw more decay back on the stern. One of the mooring winches had broken free from its mounting, and the deck was covered in orange rust scale. A large section of the railing was missing and replaced by rope which the bosun had hastily made-up. He thought, *she has really gone down fast and the bottom of this trajectory must be close at hand.*

Continuing his walk he moved down the aft deck hatch and through an open door to the steering engine room where he entered the bosun's locker. The locker was filthy, dark, and smelled of damp hemp. The steering room floor was covered in oil from the leaking hydraulic steering system. In the dim light, he nearly fell as the ship moved underfoot.

The space was loud and the vibration excessive from the propeller directly beneath the room. The throbbing sound reported the propeller's rotation as it thrashed angrily through the water. Ian thought, *this is without a doubt the worst place on the ship.*

The machinery growled and hummed as the hydraulic rams moved the rudder back and forth. The steering engine, a large hydraulic system, worked twenty-four/seven when the ship was underway. Without it, the ship couldn't be steered and this system clearly needed a major overhaul. "No money for the engineers, either," Ian said under his breath. "I've seen enough for now."

He walked out of the steering room, up on deck, and with determinate strides moved forward to get away from the sound and vibration. He squinted and let the sun and salty air caress his face.

He was out of the belly of the ship and had a clear view of the rolling waves and vast horizon and all seemed right with the world again.

The evening meal was just about ready and he could smell the food being prepared by the stewards below. *Is anything better than this?* He thought of Susan and the softness of her touch.

He shook his head and thought, *She's a hooker... what am I doing?* Then another voice in his head whispered, *No, she's your soul mate.*

He snapped out of his daydream and knew, he was hopelessly in love.

Chapter Six
Watch

With the heavily seasoned meal of fatty pork and wilted vegetables grinding around in his belly, Ian remembered why he lost so much weight as he shoved down the food one bite at a time. The meal was one step short of disgusting. It was obvious the stewards prepared marginally, even expired food the waterfront vendors sold. The *Amore Islander* bought what no other ship or restaurant would. The steward's imagination made the meals as close to "good" as anyone could, but the poor old man had just about run out of tricks.

With his stomach protesting the meal he'd just wolfed down, Ian got out of his seat, thanked the stewards and retired to the officer's lounge to relax before his watch. The lounge was quiet and an almost forgotten place on the ship long, since abandoned by the officers and left unmaintained or used except for Ian.

A carry-over from another time in the *Amore Islander's* history, it was large, ornately paneled, and appointed with comfortable furniture, now dusty and threadbare.

The room was nearly half of the senior officer level along the port side, with an up-scale wooden bar, mirrors, and empty shelves behind the counter. Stools remained in front of the vacant bar occupied by ghosts of the "good old days" while they killed time together. Only Ian saw them as they quietly conversed among themselves.

Years ago, the *Amore Islander* reigned as 'queen of the bulk carrier fleet'. Her designer was a man of vision in an era when men of the sea, in proper surroundings, conducted themselves as gentlemen of refinement. Each stateroom provided its occupant unheard of amenities. The officer's spaces were large, well-appointed and comfortable. The *Amore Islander* was a maritime social experiment and a credit to the architects' vision and the original owner's commitment to his crew.

Ian had read the articles and awards posted under glass documenting the ship's famous past. He thought, *it must have been unbelievable.* An equal amount of effort was spent to ensure the ship would be a profitable tool with a cutting edge cargo discharge system, too. Ian mused, *a masterpiece for all times*. At least that was the way Ian had envisioned it. With much excitement the then *New World Order* was christened in the builder's yard and entered the limelight, *her original beauty and poise was now just a thing of a by-gone era,* Ian sighed as he thought.

Alone in the room, Ian looked around the once elegant lounge where officers had worn their uniforms and their wives enjoyed a drink and the companionship of others. The room was now dusty, neglected and rarely used except for Ian. It made him melancholy for the times gone by and the life which must have been wonderful.

His imagination danced with visions of the officers conducting themselves as gentlemen, well-groomed, dressed, accompanied by their wives, and occasionally their children. The ship must have had a calmer feel with women aboard. Ian heard soft music in the background, the women's gentle laughter, the smell of cigars and the clinking glasses as toasts were offered. The beautiful women in their dresses alive with color and the warmth of friendship secure their husbands were nearby. Ian leaned back in a dusty chair as he imagined new carpets and comfortable furniture inviting conversation and relaxation.

Ian's attention was drawn to the vision of a steward in a white uniform standing behind the bar busy polishing glasses as he patiently waited to serve his clientele. Ian thought, *I found Camelot years too late.*

Then his mirage faded out to nothing. He was back in a room with tattered furniture, threadbare carpeting, and a moldy odor permeating the air. He liked the room better with the visions and ghosts but that was his secret and his alone. He turned and left and closed the door behind him. He'd be back.

He looked at his watch and said, "Shit, it's time." He made his way to the mess and looked in the refrigerator. He pulled out the night lunch and made an overstuffed sandwich. He kicked the refrigerator door closed with his foot, headed to his room, and grabbed his jacket. Two more flights of stairs and he was on the bridge. Ian stood for a moment in the lighted stairwell then passed through the door into the dark bridge.

Standing in the dark Ian saw the dim lights in the chart room and the green glow coming from the radar screen as his eyes slowly adjusted. A seaman stood in the corner and Dieter, the second mate, was scribbling his entries into the deck log. He looked up. "Hello, Ian."

Ian replied, "Hey there."

"I'll be with you in a minute. Let me finish these entries first."

"Sure"

Ian walked forward and gazed out to the horizon. In the distance there were a number of lights from ships and boats.

His watch partner, Carlos, came through the door. "Good evening, mate," he said. Then he walked over to his counterpart. In the corner they giggled and whispered for a moment in their language. Then the other man approached Dieter and requested permission to leave the bridge. Dieter waved his hand and bid him good night and he disappeared out the bridge wing and down the stairs.

Dieter and Ian discussed the chart and the twenty-hundred (local) position on the chart. Dieter nodded towards the horizon and pointed to the light on the port bow, "That one is going to the east at twelve knots." Ian eyes glazed over as Dieter gave detailed information on each boat in the area. He would figure all that out for himself later.

"The weather seems to be holding and the visibility good." Dieter finished his turn-over and Ian assumed the watch.

Satisfied, the second mate left and Ian and Carlos were alone on the bridge. One more look at the chart and Ian walked over to the coffeemaker where Carlos had just made a fresh pot.

"The coffee smells good Carlos," Ian said. He then stuck his nose in the warm cup and sipped the brew. Ian glanced at the radar and it confirmed what he saw on the horizon.

"It will be a slow watch, tonight, Carlos."

Carlos looked over with an impish smile and said, "We like them that way, right, third?"

"Right!"

Chapter Seven
Panama

The transit from Tampa to Cristobal, Panama was an eight day voyage. The Gulf of Mexico and the Caribbean were calm. The gentle sea breeze kept the temperature comfortable and time passed quickly.

After the Tampa departure, Captain Strauss retired to his cabin and wasn't seen again until the evening before arrival. It was out of character, but it was no secret he was a drunk.

Strauss was sprawled out on his mattress, the floor around his bed littered with liquor bottles. Some days he managed to get out of bed to splash cold water on his face and make a slow attempt at getting dressed. Ultimately, he just made it to the head to relieve himself and make another drink.

No matter, the officers and crew ran the ship with ease as they'd been on this route before and there was no need for concern, in fact things ran better without the "old man" around anyway.

The *Amore Islander* was under a lucky star the day it arrived in Cristobal and the ship was given permission to move directly to the awaiting Gatun Locks. The canal pilot, a commissioner and an immigration officer, boarded the ship at the sea buoy. The pilot was an American with the attitude and confidence of a Texas cowboy. Tall and dressed in white, he walked onto the bridge and took command of the ship. The other officials were Panamanian, wearing ridiculous uniforms with one hand out for themselves and the other out for their agency.

Strauss must have been on his game because by the time the ship crossed the sill of the first lock, the commissioner had assessed the ship and levied the transit fee and immigration had cleared the ship. The Panama officials were very efficient. The commissioner and the immigration officer were off to the next ship, their employers paid and their "personal interests" handsomely compensated.

The pilot commanded the ship through the harbor to the first of three successive locks, sliding the one-hundred and six feet wide *Amore Islander* through the one-hundred and ten feet wide canal. It was a tight squeeze all the way around, as the ship was eight-hundred and fifty feet long and the lock was only nine-hundred feet long.

"The designer of this ship was a genius," Ian mumbled. "If the ship were any bigger they would have to make the long and dangerous passage around Cape Horn." He gazed at the small Panamanian city of Cristobal, admiring the buildings favoring Spanish architecture with stucco walls and bright colors.

The pilot maneuvered the ship to the entrance of the first lock. The crew stood in groups forward, amidships, and aft and received lines from the line handlers on the canal walls. The lines were made-up to tractors called "mules," and the mules, under the pilot's command, pulled the ship into the lock. When the ship was nearly half way in the lock, a second set of mules passed a line to the crew on deck and they helped pull the ship. The mules adjusted line tension to keep the ship within two feet of the lock sides.

DRAWN TO THE SEA
(First Revision)

A third pair of mules connected aft and the ship moved gently into the lock. The gate closed and the lock flooded. The ship gently rose and the mules adjusted the line tension to keep the ship in position. The Gatun Locks were three successive locks that raised ships eighty five feet above the Atlantic Ocean to Gatun Lake.

The process became routine and the crew killed time basking in the tropical sun smoking cheap cigarettes. Gatun Lake was man-made to alleviate the need to excavate the entire forty-five mile length of the transit. In addition, it provided the source of water for the lock system on both the Atlantic and Pacific sides. Ian thought, *it's a strange sight for an ocean going ship to be in a fresh water lake surrounded by jungle.*

Ian and most seamen transiting the canal agreed the most spectacular part of the transit was Galland Cut. As the ship, eighty-five feet above sea level, passed through the Continental Divide and its stately cliffs, Ian had trouble keeping his mind on his job. The *Amore Islander* and her crew were grossly out of place in the face of so much beauty. *I'll have to remember to describe this to Susan,* he mused.

After Galland Cut the ship approached the Pedro Miguel Locks. Again, the pilot with help from the mechanical mules, moved the aging ship towards the lock. The identical procedure was followed. However, this time after the lock was closed, the water was removed and the *Amore Islander* gently settled thirty feet.

The lock opened and the pilot directed the ship to the Mira Flores Locks. Two more locks dropped the ship to the Pacific Ocean level. Thirty hours fifteen minutes total transit time. Ian noted the time in the logbook. Ahead was the vast expanse of Balboa Harbor and the Pacific Ocean beyond it.

Ian looked out at Balboa and it had none of the charm of Cristobal, instead it possessed the seediness of most port cities. The buildings were dull and dirty. The local U.S. military bases ensured there was a thriving dark underbelly with ample bars and brothels.

The ship was maneuvered to the duty-free anchorage. After twenty hours on his feet, Ian's back hurt and his eyes were getting heavy. He spent as much time as he could on the bridge wing with his face in the wind. *No time for sleep now. The crew and I will sleep deeply later.*

Neil and his deck gang were on the forecastle and readied the port anchor. The pilot put the ship in a suitable location and the captain nodded and growled the order to release the port anchor into his radio. Neil acknowledged the command and released the anchor, the fact confirmed by a loud rattle of chain as it ran out the chain locker, through the hawse pipe, and into the teal-colored Pacific. Its violence was controlled by the windless brake. Regardless, a cloud of dust, rust, mud and scale went up the nostrils of anyone in the vicinity. The pilot gave a slight backing bell to ensure the chain didn't pile up on the bottom. Strauss croaked into his radio again, "Six shots at the water's edge."

"Aye, captain," Six shots, five-hundred and forty feet of chain measured from the water's edge to the anchor was ordered and carried out.

FINISHED WITH ENGINES... The pilot and captain went below and Ian took the opportunity to sit for ten minutes in the captain's chair, the only seat in the wheelhouse. Ian thought, *No one sits in the captain's chair but the Captain. Fuck it! I'm exhausted.*

The stay in the duty free anchorage would be short. The prearranged fuel barge came alongside and the weary deck gang tied it to the ship. The engineers, who were just as exhausted, lined up the fuel manifold and coordinated bunkering with the barge operator. The evolution took ten hours.

On the starboard side another smaller boat came alongside and the crew raced to meet it. The boat brought provisions, minimal spare parts, and the crew's orders for duty free alcohol. The owner's one concession was to allow crewmembers to consume booze aboard.

Before leaving Tampa, a list of individual orders for alcohol was compiled by the steward and sent ahead for delivery in Balboa. It would be a long time before the crew could get ashore, so Ian requested eight cases of Holstein beer.

The deck gang used a small boom and winch to bring the cases over the rail one at a time. "Don't drop my beer you devils," Ian yelled down from the bridge wing forty feet above them.

"No worry, mate." The bosun responded, looking up at Ian. Both men were barely able to stand they were so exhausted.

"Hell, I hope so," Ian mumbled to himself, and returned to the chair and thought, *two more hours*.

Later that evening, the steward knocked on Ian's door and delivered his beer.

"Great!" Ian, standing there with a towel wrapped around his waist, paid him on the spot and the steward left to deliver the rest of the crew's orders.

Duty free anchorages were two edged swords. Fuel and food were tax free and benefited the owners, but the crew was stuck aboard, captives kept within sight of land, ladies and booze. The *Amore Islander* crew was especially antsy because they knew the next port, San Metalous, Peru had no town or facilities and the next leg of the voyage was thirty-one days to Japan.

Two months with no liberty and no women.

Chapter Eight
Iron Ore

The ship's clock showed it was one in the morning as it chimed twice. Ian was back on the bridge after a short and unsatisfying nap. The air was still and the sea flat. A small swell moved with no particular speed or direction. Bunkering was completed and the barge released. The rusty barge and its anemic tug made their way back into the harbor. The black smoke belching from the tug so dense it was visible even in the dead of night.

Neil went forward with a few deckhands. The captain and Ian were on the bridge. Preparations were made, the engine room readied and the captain called, *"DEAD SLOW AHEAD*...Rudder amidships.*"*

Carlos centered the rudder and Ian rung up the engine order telegraph. The ship rumbled and came to life. After a moment the captain called, *"ALL STOP,"* and the engine stopped. Ian heard the port windlass grind away as the anchor chain was pulled on deck and deposited into the chain locker. To bring six shots back aboard took twenty minutes.

Ian and Strauss had time for a cup of coffee as they waited on the bridge and the activity on the forecastle continued. After what seemed like an eternity, Neil reported the anchor was aweigh and the chain strained under the weight as the anchor swung under the ship.

Ian marked the time in the log book then turned-off the deck lights and turned on the running lights. This was routine for the men aboard. The radio crackled, "the anchor is clear of the water." The captain turned to Ian and ordered, *"DEAD SLOW AHEAD."* The engine coughed to life and the *Amore Islander* was making way. *It's a good feeling to be moving again.*

Neil called the bridge and reported, "Anchor, secured for sea. Captain, may we secure forward?"

"Yes."

"Aye captain, good night."

A grunt back to the mate was Strauss' response. With that, Neil and the gang moved aft. They could be seen walking back along the darkened deck, their flashlights nervously moved back and forth in rhythm with their footsteps.

It was a dark night. The captain maneuvered the ship out of the anchorage and weaved around ships as they lay at anchor. Balboa was a busy anchorage full of vessels waiting their turn to go east through the canal. The captain turned to Ian and said, "San Metalous … set sea speed for one-hundred-three RPMs. The watch is yours." With that, the captain left the bridge.

Ian looked out at the vast and beautiful Pacific Ocean. *You're a lady tonight.* The ship, in ballast and at sea speed, cut through the water at fifteen point six knots. The *Amore Islander* was nearly motionless except the vibration of her machinery and the throbbing of the propeller as it chewed up the water and pushed it behind. The ocean gently rolled the ship as it cradled her exhausted crew through their first night on the Pacific.

Ian looked over the chart and called for course one-nine-two true and Carlos turned the helm to bring the ship on course. Visibility was unlimited and occasionally they saw ships in the distance ahead or on the starboard quarter as they made their way to Balboa. All in all, it was a quiet watch.

Ian looked up to see Neil waiting to relieve him. They chatted for a moment or two and turned over the watch. Ian staggered to his stateroom, his eyelids heavy. Through the door he stripped off his clothes and dropped them in a pile on the floor. He crawled into his rack and was asleep before his head hit the pillow. The last two days had been hell.

The next port, San Metalous, was located about one-hundred miles north of Lima. There was nothing there except an iron ore mining facility and a minimal port facility to load ships. In the middle of nowhere there were no customs, immigration, coast guard or government agents around and opportunity for the less scrupulous was abundant. To the crew, there were no restaurants, no bars and no girls, and going ashore offered the poor souls nothing but an opportunity to stretch their legs.

It took six days for *Amore Islander* to coast along Columbia and Ecuador and the ship crossed the equator without ceremony. *No pollywogs in this crew*. The Galapagos Islands were barely visible to starboard, and then the ship coasted along Peru until San Metalous rose above the horizon to port.

Arrival was straight forward. At the right moment, the port anchor was dropped under the ship as it headed into the dock to stop the vessel before it ran aground. Two grossly underpowered tugs helped as much as they could. No pilot was present to help Strauss.

Before the ship was tied to the pier, the local facilities' representative boarded the ship. He and Strauss spoke in hushed tones and adjourned to the captain's office. The door was closed and the details ironed out.

The ship would receive a bill of lading for approximately seventy-six thousand tons of high grade iron ore. It would actually carry an additional twenty-five thousand tons of cargo which would go undocumented. For that "miscalculation" the facilities rep had been handsomely compensated by a mysterious visitor the week before.

Everything went just as the visitor had explained to the captain back in Tampa. The ship would be severely overloaded with thousands of ocean miles ahead.

The captain blotted at the nervous sweat streaming down his temples as he and the rep drank Scotch before parting company.

"Oh, by the way," said the rep as he passed out the door. "We have a labor issue going on and there are some snipers in the hills taking pot shots at the workers and ship's crew on deck … nothing to worry about. No one has been hit yet."

Cargo operations commenced and the iron pellets came aboard by conveyor belt and dropped into the cavernous holds. The ore was heavy and dirty and the ship became engulfed in a black cloud. In minutes the crew and the ship were covered in fine black dust.

Forty hours later, the ship would be full and on its way across the Pacific, heading to the Far East.

Chapter Nine
Over Laden ... Storm Ahead

The government nationalized the mining operation at San Metalous in the early seventies. Like everything nationalized by governments, the equipment was neglected, skilled labor lost and management shackled. This facility had become the "poster child" to government inefficiency and business incompetence.

For some reason the bureaucratically installed management fired all of the local labor from the native villages in the region. These were simple men who struggled to provide a meager existence for their families. As a group they had a reputation as honest and hard-working. Ian knew many of them from previous visits and he was left with the impression they depended on the mine and port for work because there was no other employment in the region. The decision replaced all of them with labor from the capital city. *Where was the wisdom in that?* Ian thought.

An ongoing feud ensued between the displaced workers and management. During the *Amore Islander's* port call the feud had notched-up to a boiling point when one of the native women had been run over by a company truck. The truck didn't stop and there was no effort to investigate or compensate the victim's family. The local paper reported some of the locals had claimed the incident was intentional and the accusation fueled up the already angry men who took their weapons and disappeared into the surrounding hills. From behind trees and rocks they took shots at the workers at both the mining and loading facilities. Occasionally they took shots at the crew on deck, too. Their rifles were old and inaccurate and the shooters were neither skilled nor motivated to hit their targets, so it was an acknowledged nuisance.

"Hell," Ian told Neil, "Here we are in this third world shit hole on a third world shit hole ship being shot at by third world assholes. We must have our heads where the 'sun don't shine'." They laughed together, but their eyes were dull as they exchanged knowing looks. The cargo operations continued.

Half way through the loading operations, Strauss called Neil to his office. Neil came directly from deck. His overalls, hands, and face were black from the ore dust. If everyone didn't look the same it would have been comical. Neil stood in the doorway with narrowed eyebrows and a toe-tapping boot. He needed to be on deck managing cargo operations. "What's up, captain?"

Strauss reached for the bottle of Scotch whiskey he'd become too familiar with since Tampa. "Neil, come in and sit. Don't mind the mess. Here, let me pour you a drink." Neil sat fidgeting on the settee as Strauss poured two drinks, handed one to his mate, closed the door to his office and returned to his desk.

"The *Amore Islander* has been sold and headed to the breaker yard after Oita." That much was true but the rest was a lie. "The owner has washed his hands of the ship and the crew. I can't pay you or the rest of the crew. There will be no more provisions and the only money left is the ten-thousand dollars in the safe. The owners won't pay to fly us home. They've taken every penny. There's only one option and I need help." He paused and tugged at the collar of his dirty shirt, as if he was choking. "We're in a backwater port without authority over-site. The transit, thirty-one days and we'll be alone the whole way."

Neil listened, his jaw dropping to his chest. The glass of Scotch remained untouched. The captain continued, "If we load twenty-five thousand tons over our load limit, I've been guaranteed that the freight for the overage will be provided to the officers and crew to cover wages, expense, and travel and a little more for you and me?"

Neil's hand tightened around his glass until his knuckles turned white. "Captain, you know that I have been party to 'overing' several thousand tons knowing we would burn that in fuel before we arrived at the discharge port. But twenty-five thousand tons is nearly thirty-percent overage. That's dangerous and criminal. The ship may sink or break her back if we hit any bad weather. We'll be a long way from shelter in the event of a typhoon. How about the authorities in Japan? What happens if we get caught? It's jail time, captain! I can't do that again!"

"I know," said the captain softly and he went on. "As for the authorities, we'll discreetly meet a small bulk vessel south of Okinawa near an uninhabited island and discharge the 'extra' ore then proceed to Oita." Strauss looked into Neil's stormy eyes and flinched.

Neil stood up and set the untouched whiskey down on the desk and said, "No, captain. I won't be party to this. I must resign immediately. I'll leave the ship at the end of this shift." Neil turned and left the office.

Captain Strauss said, "Shit," and reached into his desk pulled out a small piece of paper and dialed the number his visitor had left.

"Hello?"

"He won't do it."

"I understand, I'll take care of it."

The phone was dead in Strauss' hand.

Neil walked out on deck and shook his head, his fists trembling. He heard a smattering of bullets from the natives on the hillside in the distance. Then a bullet pierced his temple. He slumped and fell forward, dead before his body hit the deck.

The crew was told it was a stray bullet from the native sharpshooters. "An accident, it was an unfortunate accident." Strauss assured the crew.

Neil's body was quietly removed from the ship with the assurance it would be sent back to the Isle of Man and properly buried.

"The owner's agent will tend to all the details," Strauss promised the concerned crewmembers.

Neil's body was carefully placed in the ambulance as the crew watched from the ships rail. The vehicle moved away in a cloud of dust on the winding road toward the distant gate. Later when the ambulance was out of site and long before cargo operations had resumed, the body was dumped alongside the road three miles outside the facility gate and the crew would be none the wiser.

Strauss called the mates together and told them he alone would takeover loading the ship. Dieter and Ian would stand six hour bridge watches in a six-on-six-off rotation until they arrived in Japan and another mate replaced Neil.

Ian's friend was gone. The captain's secret remained intact. The crew's fate sealed. None of them were the wiser as the ship loaded deeper and deeper in to the sea.

DRAWN TO THE SEA
(First Revision)

We must be alright ... Ian hoped but he knew there was more to Neil's death. It was no accident. He wrote a hurried note to his mother and another to Susan. In these notes he revealed his concern and suspicion in rushed thoughts. He mailed the letter to his mother but at the last minute tore up the letter to Susan. He didn't want to concern her.

The next day was calm and departure uneventful. The ship's course was set at two-nine-three degrees. The same monotonous course the *Amore Islander* would maintain for the next month and the crew settled in for the long slow transit.

Typhoon Diana wasn't even on the weathermen's watch list yet. The captain stayed in his office as he falsified the ship's logs to protect the owner under the *inclement weather provision* in the charter to buy time to rendezvous with the smaller ship. If all went well, the Japanese steel maker would be none the wiser, the *Amore Islander's* owner richer, and the North Koreans would have something they desperately needed ... high grade iron ore.

Chapter Ten
As the Demons of Hell Scream

Weeks later the skies were stormy and dark, sheets of heavy rain fell from the heavens, and the winds howled. The *Amore Islander* groaned as it labored in Typhoon Diana's violence. It mattered little that she was the size of a one-hundred story building and heavier than the combined weight of the automobiles stuck in a Cross Island Expressway traffic jam. The ship continued to be tossed about like a beach ball at a rock concert.

Old and tired, the *Amore Islander* was laden with nearly thirty percent more cargo than it had been designed to carry. The cargo had been carelessly stowed and shifted in the holds due to Strauss' greed and lack of conscience. Now, caught in the jaws of a typhoon and with no place to run, the ship and her crew were in dire straits.

Strauss quietly retired to his cabin like a cowardly fool. The fates of the ship and her crew had been carelessly cast before the merciful gods and unrelenting devils.

The dark and angry sea grew more confused and the winds howled like an ungodly beast. Lightening fractured the sky and thunder drove all hope from the men's hearts. Fast moving swells reached thirty feet in height and towered over the straining deck. Steeper and steeper the waves grew as the storm deepened. Violent winds tore off the wave tops and drove them horizontally against the hull with such force it could crush a man's skull like a melon.

The ship, like a person under duress, made guttural, raspy groans and quick, jerky movements. The *Amore Islander* moaned again as it labored under the tons of water crossing its decks and the heavy rolls generated forces that tore at the weakened hull.

Screeching mewls were heard by the crew, like Dante demons in *The Inferno*. The violent movement made it all but impossible for the crew to move. Only the bravest dared and their movements were slow, deliberate, and they cautiously held on each step of the way.

Normally, the crew gathered in common spaces to spend time together. Tonight the unnerving sounds and convulsive motion put an end to that. The crew inched their way to their rooms, crawled into their racks, and made peace with their God. Thousands of miles from safety and squarely in the jaws of a monster storm, no one aboard was unaffected.

The loud and confident became silent and withdrawn. The most timid of the crew were outwardly frightened and sobbing. The officers had long since retired to their staterooms, concerned with their own affairs and Strauss had not been seen in twelve hours.

With laborious effort, Ian entered the bridge with a sandwich in one hand and a quart of milk in the other. He set the milk in the refrigerator inside the door to the left and walked into the chart room where he saw Dieter. His face had a greenish-yellow cast and he hugged a bucket to his chest. Ian took a step back when Dieter started gagging and thought, *Whoa! Never seen him seasick before! We're west of Hawaii by a thousand miles or so and there are no ships, islands or anything to hit. I'll fix our position for him as soon as I finish my sandwich,* Ian thought. He never guessed Dieter hadn't updated the chart in over four hours.

Ian swallowed the last bit of crust and went to check on his friend, Carlos, in the wheelhouse. It took him a while, the ship careened like nothing he had ever seen before. Stumbling and swaying worse than after a week-long bender, Ian held on to the rails. He squinted to see through the heavy rain. The ship rolled deeply and he found himself looking down into the sea. Seconds later the ocean was replaced by the stormy sky.

Christ, this is worse than I thought! He was about to change course to reduce the battering the ship and her men were taking when he glanced into the corner. Carlos was huddled there, clinging to the rail as if his life depended on it.

"Carlos, I need you at the helm. We'll change course." It was hard to see forward. The rain pelted against the windows. Carlos' face was grey and his bulging eyes were blinking at an erratic pace. Ian feared he may be catatonic.

Outside the winds drove the water across the deck and the mountainous swells crashed over the bow, rolling down the deck. Some came as far back as the house seven-hundred feet away. Then all hell broke loose and Carlos screamed, Ian looked over at him and then forward in time to see a sixty foot wall stand before the bow and engulf the forward third of the ship. The *Amore Islander* stopped in its tracks and pitched forward. The house shook violently and then, a terrible noise stopped their hearts. Steel groaned, twisted, and snapped. The deck cracked open near hold five and the bow twisted to the right and severed from the rest of the ship. Now unstable, the aft portion of the ship rolled to the left. Ian, still holding on, stood there helplessly. The *Amore Islander's* back was broken.

Chapter Eleven
Final Moments

Strauss locked himself in his office with the one joy in life that never disappointed him – Scotch whiskey. The six empty bottles that rolled around on the office floor were testimonial to their one-sided love affair. They moved back and forth thrown around by the sea's motion. The bottles clanked as they somersaulted along the deck and were proof the ship was no longer under command. The only other person qualified to assume command had been ruthlessly murdered two weeks before.

The captain sobbed like a child as he sat in his chair. His hands shook, his clothes stained with sweat, tears, and urine as he drowned in cowardliness, greed, manipulation, and criminal disregard. The guilt he felt for Neil's murder and the horrible peril the ship faced drove him bat-shit crazy.

Like all weak men, he wouldn't accept responsibility for the mess he made, preferring to play the victim in his twisted mind. Everything seemed to close in around Strauss and he slowly suffocated in the shrinking room. He drank deeply and directly from his last bottle of Scotch. With the bottle in one hand, he slouched, leaning forward to brace against the violent motion of the ship. He lowered his face down near the sticky and stained surface. His greasy and balding head was only inches from desk lamp, duct taped to the metal surface. In a nightmare of movement, filth, misery and hopelessness, he struggled to pull a pleasant memory from the recesses of his mind. Tears running down his cheeks and knees trembling, he thought back to his youth.

He closed his eyes and could smell the North Sea. The sounds and the familiar odors of his hometown, Rostock, Germany fueled his feeble mind. He saw his father sitting in an easy chair, the consummate educator. He was a slight man with thick glasses perched on his large nose. Strauss remembered his father as a quiet man who would avoid confrontation at all cost, preferring to put his nose in a book barricaded in his study.

Strauss thought about the hours he and his father spent fishing in the harbor with a simple pole and pieces of sardines for bait. They watched the ships in the harbor and the shipyards busy building Hitler's navy. His father had told stories about faraway places only accessible by ship and fascinated with ships and the adventures that lay over the horizon, Strauss dreamed of being a seafarer.

The *Amore Islander* dove into a sea and shook violently. Strauss grabbed the desk and whimpered and thought of his mother, Anna. She was a good Christian woman content with running a proper German home, in the Neinpreen district where she raised three children under both hers and God's guiding hands. Helmut remembered the color of her hair and the sound of her soothing voice as she called him out of a pleasant slumber each morning.

Strauss cringed as he remembered wartime Germany. It didn't go well for the Nazis or for the hundreds of thousands of families in Europe like the Strauss family. Helmut's safe and secure childhood was shattered as the war went from bad to worse. The sites, the hunger and pain changed him forever. He began to cry.

DRAWN TO THE SEA
(First Revision)

He took a deep pull from the bottle, and not knowing why, threw it against the bulkhead. It shattered into a thousand pieces and the alcohol dripped slowly down the wall. Strauss, so far gone, opened memories he'd suppressed for years.

Any hope of climbing out of his depression ended as he relived his father's murder at knife point by a retreating SS officer over a piece of stale bread, and the nightmare of helplessly watching his mother and two sisters repeatedly raped by the Soviet hordes as they drove on Berlin.

When the soldiers were finished, the women were murdered and their bodies cast aside like garbage. Just as in nineteen forty-five, the man's soul was void and he was alone and scared. He sobbed and trembled, a broken man.

At that moment, the killer wave boarded the ship, the end was upon them. The unbearable sound of the hull tearing itself in half startled him back to consciousness. The ship rolled to port and the blood curdling sounds of men screaming as they drowned were the last things he heard and felt.

The captain grabbed his pistol and took the easy way out.

Chapter Twelve
Two Minutes

Carlos was frozen as the aft section of the ship rolled over to the left. He began to pray through his tears. There was no time for the general alarm, call the captain, or even alert the poor souls in the engine room. The storm raged and the bow section began to sink. The bow rose to the sky in defiance, the seas swirled around it and in an instant the whole bow section dropped below the boiling surface.

A large bubble of air escaped as if to temporarily mark the location and the sea momentarily opened up, then violently closed behind the bow as it dove quickly to the ocean bottom. Carlos and Ian were the only witnesses.

The stern section of the stricken vessel continued its roll over. Carlos and Ian looked at each other in panic, not a word between them. The ship was in one slow death roll and soon lay on its side. The winds and sea continued to pound the ship without sympathy. Cold water rushed through the bridge port door and the windows around the wheelhouse began to break. The ocean came in from all sides.

There was no use trying to get to the life boats and they were either flooded or inaccessible. The two men stared at each other and neither could speak. The other forty-one souls aboard dealt with their own destiny and there was nothing anyone could do to change it.

It may be best to die in the sinking ship than brave the extreme weather only to drown later. Only Carlos and Ian had the option, the others would drown in their bunks without a chance for survival.

The broken ship sank from the front first and in a moment it was vertical, the now stationary propeller was poised in the air. Carlos and Ian were about eighty feet above the churning sea facing straight down into the cauldron of death. The ship held still for what seemed like an eternity.

There were a series of loud explosions from inside the hull as the bulkheads began to collapse and water rushed into the holds, engine room, and the house where men's screams were being suffocated with gallons of water. Ian's eyes filled with tears. *We're done for. I'm sorry mother, I'm sorry Susan.*

Another tormented sound of steel letting go drove his stomach to his knees. The ship began her final plunge to the bottom. Ian looked at Carlos, his old friend. They whispered, "Good bye," to one another.

The last of the *Amore Islander* dove into the boiling sea. The frigid water stole Ian's breath as it came rushing into the wheelhouse for the second time. Deeper the ship sped to the bottom and Ian could do nothing to resist. The frigid water grew darker and darker and the pressure crushed the remaining air from his lungs. Numb and nearly unconscious, he saw a bright light shining.

He reached out with his left hand and held onto Susan's memory and it seemed dream-like. *I love you Susan, forgive me.* Her image burned in his heart and soul. Then he reached out with his right hand to the image of his mother. *I love you mother. I am sorry I failed you and the family. Please forgive me.*

Somewhere in his subconscious, or the dream that carried Ian to his death, he focused on Susan. Her eyes burned into his soul, her hair reflected the light of the bright summer sunshine. She had always been the woman of Ian's dreams on the Rio de Janeiro beach. She was the one.

She had been there for him all along and it wasn't until death it was so clear to him. She was his soul mate and he'd been given an opportunity only to squander it.

Ian's final thought in this life … *Together we could have had a good life, raised a family and grown old together. There were so many things I should have told you, so many promises I should have kept, and so much life we should have experienced together.* As Ian left his body, he prayed she would somehow understand what he had discovered in death.

At that moment thousands of miles away, Susan thought about Ian and she started to sob. She wondered, *What if …* and felt a cold chill pass through her. For some unknown reason, she knew she'd never see him again. Ian looked down at Susan and attempted to embrace and console her. *Alas,* he softly kissed her cheek and walked into the bright light. Ian van der Waterlaan was now only a memory.

Susan stood at the window with tears streaming down her rouged cheeks. Her young daughter clung to her waist. "Mommy, what's wrong?"

"I'm not sure, baby," Susan said, stroking the little one's hair. "There's just something not right."

Thousands of miles East in Amsterdam, a mother received news of the ship's disappearance. That same day a letter arrived from her son, postmarked from San

DRAWN TO THE SEA
(First Revision)

Metalous, Peru. She wouldn't open the letter until she knew whether her son Ian van der Waterlaan was alive or dead.

The End

***

About the Author

The author was raised in the rolling hills of Marin County, not far from the Golden Gate Bridge. He grew up on and around the San Francisco Bay and it was there he developed a keen passion for sailing, merchant ships and the foreign ports they frequent. He pursued a career in the maritime industry where he spent 27 years between afloat and ashore assignments including 4 years sailing as a deck officer on Liberian flag bulk carriers.

Most of the story is the product of his imagination. Others were influenced by his personal experiences. Readers, decide for yourselves which is which.

Today the author is semi-retired and living in New England where he spends time with his wife exploring the New England coastline, its harbors and inlets aboard their boat.

Rex Inverness

Readers,

    If you enjoyed *Drawn to the Sea*, please look for my other books available soon.

    Torn Between Destiny and Desire / The Gentleman Pirate / Two Warriors Collide / Bonnie Mae / The Cursed Seven / Lobsta / Leviathan and Death of a Liberian Seaman.

Contact me at: rex.inverness@gmail.com

Check out: www.rex-inverness.com

Maritime Fiction Novels
Bristol, Rhode Island
02809
www.rex-inverness.com